Geneva's Promise

Geneva's Promise

Tammy D. Thompson

Pen & Publish
Saint Louis, Missouri

Published by Pen & Publish, LLC, USA

www.PenandPublish.com
info@PenandPublish.com

Saint Louis, Missouri
(314) 827-6567

Print ISBN: 978-1-956897-20-3
e-book ISBN: 978-1-956897-21-0
Library of Congress Control Number: 2022917146

Cover design by Randi Gammons.

Author photo by Donna Jackson.

Printed on acid-free paper.

DEDICATION

Geneva's Promise, the second book in the Geneva Series, is dedicated to Geneva Nettles, my inspiration for the series in the first place. I am forever grateful for the influence she has had in my life. I would also like to dedicate this book and series, to the spiritual leaders I've come across, even if only for a brief time. Brother Wallace and Todd Hervey, as pastors of mine from when I was younger as well as now, you have helped me to walk the right path. There were times I took the wrong turn a time or two, but, at the end of the day, when I hear the powerful words God gives you to speak, I am put back on course. Thank you, Geneva, Brother Wallace, and Brother Todd. Each of you have played a role in my daily walk as well as those who planted a Godly seed, which I know has grown each day. If not for you, this book, this series, this spiritual idea to touch lives, could have never come to life. Things happen for a reason, and I know this Geneva series will touch people because of what I've learned from you all . . . Thank you and God Bless!

CHAPTER ONE

"**M**y gracious," Geneva hollered from one end of the porch to the other. "Elijah, what are you a doin'? We gotta get this here front porch painted. It's been a lookin' neglected for a long time now. Just think how pretty it'll be."

"I'm workin' fast as I can," Elijah said, shaking his head from her bossiness echoing in his direction. "We'll get it done dear."

"We better," she replied in a snappy tone. "You know when I get my head set on somethin', I want it done, and this here paint's been crackin' and a chippin' for years. I want it to shine like a new penny. You know how I like shiny things."

Though hard to believe, it had been over nine months since Geneva's little disappearing adventure and since then, things changed for the better. Elijah always did what he could, jumping through hoops for her, unlike how he was before the incident, and everyone started visiting more. They had company over almost every other day. Sometimes, folks just dropped by for a quick social call, other times, like Caleb and Ella, it was for supper. Geneva loved to cook, which made her Caleb's favorite person. She always made sure she cooked more than enough to send home with them when they came.

The heat the Summer carried with it, had no mercy on anyone. Even the breeze blowing by, made it feel like you were in a sauna, not comforting at all, but the view was still beautiful. As they did their work on the porch, one at each end, making their way to the center, Geneva commenced to singing all those songs she loved so much. Heat or not, nothing ever kept her from singing. It was funny because when she'd start belting out those melodies, the birds would gather closer to her and join in.

"See that Elijah?" Geneva laughed, pointed to the porch railing. "Them there birds are helpin' me sing. God musta sent them to be a part of my little choir."

"I thought you were supposed to be paintin'?" Elijah aggravated, slightly grinning and then turning to get back to his own work.

Geneva dropped one fist on her hip, gave a devious look, then dipped her brush in the paint bucket slowly. She trimmed off the excess and held it up in the air, looking in Elijah's direction. "You say I need to be paintin'?"

"That's what I said," Elijah answered, his back to her.

With no warning, she took off, scurrying fast as she could toward Elijah who had just acquired more paint himself. She took her brush and ran it down his back to his bottom. "Now that's painting," Geneva said, laughing so loud, her neighbors across the way could probably hear her. "It's a good color on you honey, don't ya think?"

Elijah turned slowly, still holding his paint brush tightly in his right hand. "You think so? Well, I think it's a good color for you too, honey."

Before Geneva could take off, Elijah painted a streak down the front of her, like a line in the middle of the road, and he couldn't help but laugh. It didn't take long before paint was flying everywhere, and they both looked like human canvasses. Their laughter rang out and they ended up in one long embrace, paint, and all.

"We're too dad blame old to be actin' like this Elijah," Geneva said, trying to wipe away some of what he smeared on her. "Besides, if anybody came up right now, they'd think we done lost our durn minds."

"Too old?" Elijah replied, giving a look of disbelieve she would use that phrase. "Woman, you've always told me you're only as old as you feel. So how old do you feel?"

"I feel good, but I'm no spring chicken. I'd feel better if I could get this here porch finished before dark," she said, giving Elijah a quick kiss, then heading back to her station. "Enough horseplayin', let's get this here done. The kids are comin' by tomorrow and I don't wanna have to work on it then. So, shake your tail feathers honey."

After a while, the heat had its way with them and taking a break was needed. Geneva's loose curls were stuck together from perspiration and beads of sweat sparkled on her forehead like tiny diamonds, the sun's rays spotlighting every single one. Elijah took off the full coveralls he had on, leaving his regular clothes beneath, and went inside to get them some sweet tea. One thing Geneva loved, was good ole southern style sweet tea. Geneva cleaned off a spot for them to sit and he came back out carrying two glasses. A few paint splatters still lingered on their faces from playing around, but it wasn't anything that couldn't be washed off.

"Good grief," Geneva said, breathing heavy and drinking her tea. "God must be cookin' and I swear his ovens on the highest setting Elijah. I'll be glad when it starts coolin' down. You know how I love a cool night and that there fireplace with ragin' flames. There's nothin' like it."

Elijah shook his head then put his paint covered hand over hers, "Well honey, it's going to be a while, so I guess we best learn to like it."

Probably fixing to say something profound, Geneva could see the swirls of dust that only came from company approaching. I guess you could say it was their country alarm system. Sure enough, company it was. A truck pulled right up by the flowerbed on the right side of the house.

"Eli," Terry Larey said. "Sherry and I thought we might swing by to make sure you hadn't lost this young lady again."

Sherry, Terry's wife, soft spoken with a sweet nature about her, came around the truck laughing at Terry's comment.

"Don't let Terry bother you Elijah," Sherry said. "You know if he didn't like you, he wouldn't aggravate at all."

Elijah stood and walked toward the front steps as they came up, "Then he must love me. Anyway, Terry don't bother me a bit. In fact, I owe him the world."

Swatting at the air like he was shewing a fly, Terry said, "You don't owe me nothin' brother. But I will take some of them homemade biscuits one morning, that beautiful lady over there is an expert at making. Ohhh Weee, those things would make you want to slap your mama."

"Not my mama," Geneva chimed in immediately. "If you slapped her, there would be a heap a whoopin' comin' right back at ya."

"By the way," Terry asked, looking around the porch and then back to Elijah and Geneva. "I thought ya'll were supposed to be painting the porch, not each other."

"You see, what happened was…" Geneva started.

"You two just started playing in paint. I understand. So, Sherry and I decided it would take you two a while to get this whole thing done by yourselves, so we brought some paintin' clothes to help you get it finished today," Terry said, glancing to Sherry as she made her way to the truck to get their working duds.

"We couldn't ask you to…" Elijah started.

"You didn't ask, we offered," Terry interrupted. "So, let's get this done. Watcha think Geneva?"

"I'll take it as a blessing," she said, giving an energetic nod. "I think we can do it."

After changing clothes, Terry and Sherry jumped in with both feet, painting the porch, the rails, then trimming it all in to make it look absolutely perfect. When it was all said and done, they painted themselves into the house. The sun finally got tired of hanging around and slowly started to lay down for the night. The four of them got cleaned up and met back into the living room. Geneva cranked up the air conditioning and they all found a comfortable spot on the couches.

"You were a sight Eli," Terry laughed. "And Geneva, you were too. Both of you covered in paint. Sounds like me and Sherry. I tell you somethin', there's nothin' like living each day and having fun."

"Amen to that," Geneva said robustly. "If I can't have fun, God might as well take me right here where I sit. Life ain't for work, work, work, with nothin' else to do. I'm glad Elijah figured it out. I'll be honest, I couldn't believe he did."

"Eli's always been a good guy. He just needed some direction. Anyway, that's all behind us now. We put our heads together and found you. I knew we would all along," Terry said.

"You did?" Elijah said. "I remember a few times I could hear doubt in your voice, but you kept trying to keep me believing. I've known you long enough to know when you're hoodwinking me. But I also knew why you did it, and I appreciate that."

Sherry, sitting quiet for a moment, broke in, "Geneva," she asked timidly. "Were you scared?"

"When that fella hit me and knocked me out?" Geneva replied. "I don't remember much a that to be honest, but I was scared when I knew I had family somewhere but didn't remember enough to find 'em."

"When Terry came home one day and said he was going to find you, I thought he was crazy. I figured you didn't want to be found if you took off like that. We didn't know the terrible thing that happened to you. I'm so sorry I thought that," Sherry said, sincerity showing across her face.

"No sorry needed honey. Everything happened like it was supposed to. That fella was supposed to hit me," Geneva said, everyone staring at her for more explanation.

"No, he wasn't Geneva," Elijah replied quickly. "It never should've happened. I should've taken you to town like you asked."

"And if you had, would you have found Jesus?" she asked calmly.

"Well…I…maybe," Elijah stuttered.

"You woulda just kept on with your rude talk, not listenin' to me and doin' your own thing. That's not who God meant for you to be, so he took control," Geneva continued. "You hear me talk about God's plan all the time Elijah, but this was the perfect example of it. You see honey, if you hadn't gone to find me, you'd a never found yourself. I'd be sittin' here with the same ole man who didn't want to mutter the word God, but instead, you're a new man. So, in a way, I thank that there guy for hittin' me. He didn't know it, but he did me a favor," Geneva finished.

Geneva covered herself in enjoyable conversation with friends, then hopped up suddenly. It's like she got a boost of energy from out of the blue. "How 'bout we go grab somethin' to eat in town. I'll be honest, I don't much feel like cookin' tonight. I think that there heat done took it out a me," she said.

Elijah looked at Terry and without a doubt, her idea, was a no brainer. Since Elijah wasn't much of a cook, if she wasn't cooking, they had to eat something. It wasn't often she didn't feel like whipping up an incredible home cooked meal, but for the first time in a while, work did her in.

"Where you thinking you want to go," Terry asked, holding Sherry's hand sweetly.

"I don't know. What sounds good to yall?" Geneva answered, showing her usual look of thinking.

"I'm guessing you want country cookin' right Geneva?" Elijah laughed.

"Country cookin's the only kind a cookin'," laughing right back at him. "How about that there Dixie Diner restaurant off interstate thirty. Boy, I'll tell you one thing, they make the best potato soup and them there rolls just melt in your mouth."

Terry gave a long sigh, "They melt in my gut too, but I can't say no."

"It's settled then," Geneva said, hopping up and grabbing her purse. "What ya'll waitin' on? This old woman's hungry. Paintin' works up an appetite ya know."

Not making her wait another moment, they got up and went to the door, looking to make sure the paint was dry enough to walk across. Terry offered to drive and there was no objection from Geneva or Elijah, and they carefully treaded across the porch and down the steps to his truck.

Even though the sun was bedding down for the night, the warmth in the air welled around them. Since living in the south meant dealing with humidity, at times, it was unbearable. It didn't matter though, it's where they grew up and how they learned to live. One thing Geneva wasn't afraid of, was work, in the heat or the cold. Something was bred in her when she was a youngster to work for what she got, and she carried that with her every minute of every day.

Terry cranked up some good ole country tunes on the radio and they all started singing along like they were on a big stage somewhere performing. Even though Sherry was always a little quiet, she belted those lyrics out just as loud as the rest, without a doubt, enjoying their time together.

After about ten or fifteen minutes, they pulled off the interstate toward the restaurant and on the side of the road was a stray dog, wandering around by the edge of the trees on the right side of the road. Geneva's eyes focused in on that dog and her happiness, turned to distress in a moment.

"Ah, Elijah," Geneva said, giving him a pitiful look. "What a poor baby."

"No more dogs Geneva. I swear, we done took in half the dogs in the county because they acted like they didn't have a home," Elijah said, knowing what she was asking. "Beside's we're fixin' to eat."

"I'll get extry so I can give that little'un somethin' to eat when we come out," she replied, nodding her head, like her mind was already made up. "I just can't stand the thought of a little doggie goin' hungry. It's a durn shame."

Terry started laughing, "That's our Geneva Eli. That's our Geneva."

Elijah added, "If it was up to Geneva, we'd have another house next to ours to keep all the orphan dogs that come our way. Thank goodness the ones we have, are outside dogs."

Geneva turned her head toward Elijah and shot him a look he knew all too well. It's like she was telling him to hush his mouth without saying a single word. With that look, he did just that. Not another word came out of his mouth. Sherry got tickled at the way they communicated and bickered without really bickering.

"I need to learn how to do that Geneva," Sherry said, grinning.

"Do what honey?" Geneva asked. "You mean make sure this man right here knows when he's done gone too far? Well, I'll tell ya somethin'. All you gotta do honey, is get your bluff in from the get-go and that's it."

"Don't be getting my wife in trouble," Terry said, glancing back at Geneva. "You're gonna turn this sweet lady into…"

"Me?" Geneva cackled loudly. "There ain't nothin' wrong with that now, is there?"

All Elijah could do, was shake his head and smile at that feisty woman who had his heart completely. Terry and Sherry, being used to Geneva's ways and attitude, were entertained by her colorful language and her spirit that was always young at heart. Then, Terry pulled into a parking spot right in front of the door.

Since it wasn't long before the placed closed for the night, they hopped out and scurried inside to find a table. Most folks were finishing up their meals and only a few other couples wandered in after them. Geneva knew the lady behind the counter well. Her name was Sharon. Anytime Geneva needed donations to help a family or for a fundraiser, she always accommodated with no questions asked. Her friendly smile and kind disposition radiated all around her, putting off a positive feeling to everyone she came across.

"Miss Geneva," Sharon said, going around the counter to give her a hug. "Hadn't seen you in a bit. Where you been hiding?"

"You know I can't hide nowhere," Geneva said. "If I did, somebody'd find me."

"Very funny dear," Elijah said, putting his arm around her and resting his hand on her waist.

"Well," Geneva continued. "To be honest, we been a paintin' that there front porch of ours and I didn't have enough get up and go in me to whip up nothin' tonight. Besides, yall have the best food in these here parts, almost as good as mine."

"It's good to see you," Sharon said. "And you just let me know the next time you need my help with anything."

"You betcha," Geneva said, noticing another lady walking up to show them to a booth.

They followed her and took a seat. Geneva skimmed over the entire menu as did the others. So much to choose from, it was hard to decide. Then she looked around the place and saw someone she hadn't seen in a very long time, got up and went their direction.

CHAPTER TWO

"Who do we have here?" the man said, standing as she approached. "You are definitely a sight for sore eyes."

"Right back at'ya Paul," Geneva said, giving him a big hug. "So, you still a preachin'?"

"I wouldn't want to do anything else Geneva," he smiled. "What have you been up to? I heard through the grapevine, you got lost or something like that."

"Well, I'll tell ya," she laughed. "I didn't get lost. Some ole fella musta thought I had two dimes to rub together and knocked me over the head. Elijah over there, went lookin' for me and, well, here I am."

They stood there for a few minutes talking, and Geneva couldn't help but think about all the times Paul helped people and always did everything he could to make a difference in someone's life. Maybe that's why they got along so well. In fact, any time he had a grand idea for a new adventure, he'd call Geneva to join in on it, and she was always game. His wife, Ramona, sat there quiet as always. To say they made a great couple, would've been an understatement, and their family was tight knit.

"You still got the same number?" Geneva asked. "'Cause I might holler at ya one a these days and we'll meet at the Cracker Barrel. You know that's where we always met for lunch back when."

"I remember well," he smiled back. "And you always tried to pay for the food."

"If I'm gonna eat it, I'm gonna pay for it," she said, squeezing his hand before she walked off. His smile lit up the room and he carried himself in a very Godly manner.

Geneva sauntered back over to her table where Elijah and the others waited for her to stop visiting. She couldn't help but look around the room. From old pictures to license plates from everywhere you could think of, the décor was unique and always caught her attention. It gave the place a feeling of home, surrounding them with history, but treating them like family at the same time.

"I thought you were hungry," Elijah said, downing a hot buttered roll.

"I am, but you remember Paul don't ya Elijah? I swear, I always said I was gonna go listen to him preach sometime, but it's just hard not goin' to my own church."

"Are you guys ready to order," the waitress said in a peppy voice.

Before anyone could say a word, Geneva chimed in, "Yeah honey, I'll have that there pan-fried sirloin with potato soup and fried okra. And don't forget some more a those hot rolls. I think my husband here done ate all you brought."

Elijah just looked at Geneva, shaking his head at her remark and the waitress wrote the order and took the rest as well, then rushed off to the kitchen. Since only a few people were left in the restaurant, they were probably trying to get everyone gone so they could go home themselves. It didn't take long for the food to come out. When the waitress sat down the basket of fresh, out-of-the-oven rolls, Geneva buttered them things up and inhaled several before she knew it.

"So, Geneva," Terry said, with an inquisitive look in his eye. "What are you planning on doing now? I know you and Eli aren't gonna just sit around the house all day every day and do nothing."

"To be honest, I hadn't give it any thought. I guess my idea of livin' is takin' it one day at a time. Today I wanted to get the porch painted, and we did," she replied honestly. "I suppose, if the good Lord decides he wants me to wake up in the mornin', I'll figure out tomorrow when it gets here."

"I was just wondering," Terry continued. "We're trying to open up a place for at-risk teens or just a place kids and families can come when they need help. Some might be homeless or have a bad home life. I just thought you might be interested in helping. And I'm sure these folks will need some guidance and I thought you'd be a good one to do just that."

Geneva's eyes lit up and then started getting teary, "You betcha I would," she replied. "I'd love to help. It's God's work, and I'm all about doin' God's work. Where you plan on havin' it?"

"We found a building in the downtown area and are just about finished fixing it up. We should be up and running in a week or so," Terry said. "We're going to find some food businesses who might sponsor us so we can provide meals too."

"Oh, honey," Geneva said, wearing her emotions on her sleeve. "I love that idea. I swear, there's so many kids, and adults for that matter, who need direction Terry."

Terry nodded, getting a look across his face that showed empathy for everyone who needed his help. "I know and I figure if I make a difference in just one person's life, it was worth it."

"Sounds like Geneva's your girl," Elijah said. "And… uh…count me in too."

"Eli," Terry smiled big. "I would say I'm surprised, but God does perform miracles and he sure did on you. thank you, sir."

"Just let us know what we can do to help. At least it'll get me out of 'around the house' chores," Elijah replied, glancing at Geneva as he said it.

Geneva shot a look at him, "You won't be gettin' outa nothing Elijah James. We can fix up that there house and help Terry."

"Yes dear," he responded respectfully.

They finished their meal and noticed most of the tables already had chairs turned upside down on them and the staff patiently waiting on them. They all got up, leaving a hefty tip because of such great service, and made their way to the register.

"How was it, Geneva?" Sharon asked, smiling as always. "Hope you got full."

"Oh, honey, I'm full as a tick. If I'd a ate anymore these three would be rollin' me to the truck," Geneva replied comically, laughing as she talked. "Good to see ya."

Terry stepped in front of everyone and laid a one-hundred-dollar bill on the counter. Elijah tried to squabble with him about paying for a minute, but it was obvious, there was no stopping Terry when he wanted to do for someone. Finally, Elijah gave in and escorted the ladies to the truck while Terry got his change.

"Wait a minute," Geneva hollered out, running back inside, and talking to Sharon. It wasn't long and she came right back out.

"What in the world?" Elijah asked. "What was that about?"

"I told Sharon there was this stray dog that looked hungry, and she said she'd put a mess a leftovers outside for it. I sure hope it finds the food," Geneva explained. "Sure would hate for that poor pitiful thing to go hungry Elijah."

"I know it Geneva," he replied, pacifying her.

When they finally got back home, Elijah and Geneva got out of the truck. The crickets were playing their unique song as they did every night and fireflies were everywhere. The sky was crystal clear, and the moon shone big and bold in all its glory. It almost looked like you could reach out and touch it. The night sky was the perfect canvas for the stars.

"Boy, would you look at that," Geneva said, admiring God's work. "I betcha he was proud after he put them stars up there."

Terry leaned his head out of the window and looked up. "It's amazing alright Geneva. Most folks don't even take the time to notice these days, but they should."

"You durn right they should," Geneva replied in her usual peppy tone. "I notice 'em every night."

"You two have a good night," Terry said. "We enjoyed it."

Elijah waved him down before they could drive off, "Next time it's on me."

"Right," Terry said, smiling as to say *no it's not.*

The sounds of nature surrounded them as they made their way to the porch, and the flowers framing the place put off a smell of sweetness like none other. From the red and white roses to the marigolds Geneva loved so much, the array of colors compelled visually as well. Like the first time they ever saw the house, it was home.

"After you Mrs. James," Elijah said, taking Geneva's hand and leading her up the front steps.

"Oh my," Geneva said, her mouth wide open and eyes the same. "Don't this here porch look beautiful. Shinin' like a new penny I tell ya. Shinin' like a new penny."

"Couldn't have done it without them. They're good people and he's a great friend," Elijah said, opening the front door.

"Folks like him are few and far between," Geneva said, setting her purse down on the table in the entryway. "We're lucky."

Without hesitation, Elijah pulled her close. "I'm lucky in a lot of ways Geneva. You're a blessing to me."

"Why, Elijah James," she giggled. "It does my heart good to hear ya say you're blessed. You used to snub at talk like that."

He took her hand and led her into the living room, then sitting on the couch. "Geneva, I can't tell you how much I have treasured every minute with you since we got you back. I just regret…"

"No regrets Elijah," Geneva said, interrupting him quickly. "I don't regret nothin'. Like I said earlier. If that there guy hadn't done what he done, things wouldn't be the way they are. Like the good book says in Romans 8:28, *And we know that all things work together for good to them that love God, to them who are called according to his purpose.* See honey, God orchestrated all of it whether you know it or not."

"You're an amazing woman," Elijah said, lifting her hand and kissing it.

"Oh, shoot," Geneva laughed. "I'm me and I guess I'll stay that way…nothin' special, just me."

"You're special alright," Elijah said. "Now, are we ready to hit the hay. It's been a tiring day. I think that porched kicked my tail."

"Kicked mine too," she chuckled. "One a these days I'll realize I'm not a young'un anymore and start slowin' down."

They both knew that would never happen and as soon as she said it, they both laughed out loud, falling into each other for a sweet embrace to end a perfect day. The house was quiet as a mouse, but the dogs outside were barking here and there. It wasn't enough to disturb anything, just being dogs, and they went upstairs to retire for the night.

Geneva readied for bed, brushing her teeth, combing her hair, and putting on a comfy, but cool, cotton gown. She folded the covers back, running her hand over the quilt on top. Her thoughts roamed throughout a time when she made it, remembering every square, every moment it represented, and every time she smiled as she added another piece to something so extraordinary. She could see Ella as a little girl, all smiles, as happiness exuded from her. And just those thoughts brought a smile to her face in the moment. Those memories remained etched in her mind like treasures being stored safely in the center of her heart, recollections of times gone, but never forgotten.

"You look like you're in another world," Elijah said, raising his hand up and yawning. "Care to share?"

"Just a thinkin' 'bout this here quilt. Every time I look at it, I see my life, our life," Geneva said still peering at it.

Elijah laughed a little, "Yep when you were gone and I didn't know if I'd ever see you again, I spent lots of nights thinking back on when you made that thing. I didn't think much about it when you were piecing it together, but when I didn't have you, it's all I had left of you."

"I'm not going anywhere now," Geneva said, wearing that joyful smile Elijah loved so much.

The crickets outside were so loud, it's like they were in the room with them, and it was a sound amazing to hear. Although the heat wasn't something either of them loved, the other aspects of summer brought back memories from years ago, making it all too familiar in a reminiscent manner. They found themselves snuggled up as many times before. Geneva laid there quietly which was unusual for her, but Elijah could tell she was in deep thought. He reached over and turned off the lamp on the table next to the bed and found his place once more next to her.

"Goodnight honey," Geneva said, sweetly kissing him on the cheek.

Without a word, he communicated with her by only pulling her close to him. It was a moment he dreamed of when he didn't know where she was, and it created another memory he wanted to store in his heart forever.

They both fell into deep slumber by the tune nature continued playing outside, and Elijah's arm stayed draped around her. Geneva laid there, said her nightly prayer and her mind started to wander. That time, months ago, when she didn't know if she'd ever see her family again, came to the forefront of her thoughts, and the experience came back to her. Somehow, the things her mind blocked for so long, came rushing in like a tidal wave, filling every ounce of her recollections of the past, and putting the puzzle pieces into place.

CHAPTER THREE

Her dreams placed her in a time she never wanted to relive, in a hospital bed with unfamiliar faces surrounding her.

"Where am I?" Geneva asked, noticing a bandage around her head. "What happened?"

"Ma'am, someone hit you," the nurse said, steadily straightening her blanket and covering her. "And you were knocked out for a while."

"Hit me?" Geneva hollered out, very dismayed by what the lady said.

"Ma'am, what's your name?" the nurse asked sweetly, still caring for her.

"It's…a…my name is…uh," Geneva said, stuttering, trying to remember. "Dad blame it, my name is…"

"It's okay," the nurse continued. "I'm gonna take good care of you. My name is Gloria."

"Gloria…I, uh, I," Geneva said, trying to grasp the magnitude of the situation. Nothing came to mind. Everything in her mind was a clean slate, like someone had wiped the blackboard of her life.

"How are you feeling today?" a man said, walking in. He had on a white coat and wore a stethoscope around his neck. "I'm Dr. Mayes. It's good to see you awake."

"Doc, I don't know how I got here," Geneva said. "How'd I get here?"

"The important thing is, we're going to take great care of you. We need to get you all healed up and if you start remembering anything, let us know. In the meantime, get some rest," he said, placing his hand on hers briefly, then walking out.

Gloria was still standing by her bed making sure Geneva had all she needed. The room held a bland quality at best and those ice blue eyes of Geneva's roamed around the space trying to find some hint of remembrance, something to jar her mind. The more she tried to remember her name or anything else for that matter, the more her head hurt. After a while, she just stopped trying.

"Miss…" Gloria said, trying to figure out what to call her.

"Miss is fine," Geneva answered, not knowing what they should call her. What should be the simplest thing to do for anyone, was the absolute hardest to her. Telling someone her name was something she couldn't do because she didn't know it herself.

"How about Missy? I'll call you Missy for now," the nurse said, a smile painted clean across her face.

"I suppose," Geneva replied, confusion taking over every ounce of her. "Maybe one day I'll tell ya what it really is."

"You will," Gloria said. "Now, if I can do anything for you, push this little button here, and I'll come a runnin'."

Without responding verbally, Geneva only nodded her head, thinking the entire time, she must be dreaming. There was no way something like that could really happen to someone. Then she closed her eyes, hoping she'd wake up somewhere else, anywhere but there.

"Geneva," she heard a voice say.

"That's it. That's my name," Geneva hollered out, sitting straight up in the bed, only to find Elijah standing there. "Elijah."

"What in the world?" Elijah said, sitting next to her.

"I had the most horrible dream," she said. "I dreamed I was at that there hospital and I didn't know who I was. They didn't know what to call me and I didn't know nothin'. It was terrible Elijah, just terrible."

Elijah just put his arms around her, knowing sooner or later, that time would come back to her. He kissed her forehead, then her lips. A hint of a few tears looked like they tried to form in her beautiful blue eyes but hit a roadblock from her wiping them away as they fell. He felt so bad for her, knowing how difficult it was to deal with something happening so uncontrollable, but at the same time, she was safe at home.

"It was just a dream," Elijah whispered. "Let me fix you some breakfast."

Geneva shook off the short-lived flash from the past and swung her legs around and plopped her feet on the floor, "You'll do no such thing," she replied. "B'sides, you don't know how to make biscuits."

"Pillsbury," Elijah laughed.

"I'll have no such thing," she said, putting on her house shoes and heading downstairs. "You can help if ya like."

Glad he could pull her out of the momentary funk her dream put her in, he also knew what it was like to wake up and be completely oblivious to what's going on. Although it was different, in a way, it was the same.

"You a comin'?" Geneva hollered out from the kitchen as Elijah made his way down the stairs.

"On my way," he answered.

About the time he made it to her, Elijah's phone started ringing. He had laid it on the table in the entryway, and he ran to grab it before it stopped.

"Hello," Elijah answered.

"Who in tarnation is a callin' this early in the morning," Geneva said, starting breakfast at the same time.

Elijah covered the phone, "Shhh, it's Terry." Then put it back up to his ear once more. "Yes sir…I imagine we can. Uh huh, yep. See you then."

Geneva was standing there in her apron she had for more years than she could remember, covered in flower, and pounding the dough like it needed a beating. Her eyes never left Elijah the entire time.

"Well, you gonna tell me what he wanted?" she asked, continuing her duties as she talked.

"Oh," Elijah said. "He said they were going down to the center in a few hours to check on the progress and asked if we wanted to meet them."

"You told 'em yes didn't ya?" Geneva said, finally placing the round pieces of dough on a baking sheet.

"I did. I figured you'd want to see what he was talking about last night. Anyway, we can make a grocery run to make sure we have enough food for when the kids come by tonight," he continued.

Geneva nodded her head in agreement and began frying bacon, grease flying everywhere. The smell took over the entire house. There was always something about the smell of bacon frying that got them both going. Geneva always said she had to start the day with a good breakfast, or it wasn't going to be a good day. Her way of putting together such a meal was like art to her. From the biscuits and gravy to the scrambled eggs and bacon, she had it down to a science. No matter what, it was like everything got ready at the same time, never having to wait on anything.

After she fixed their plates, they sat down at the table. Elijah picked up his fork and started to tear into his food, but he was stopped.

"Say grace Elijah," Geneva said. "The good Lord didn't give us this kinda food to eat for us not to say Grace before we start a eatin'."

Elijah grasped her hand and they both bowed their heads. *"Dear Lord, I want to thank you for this meal we're about to eat. Thank you for the many blessings you bestow on us each and every day. And Lord, thank you for my Geneva. Please watch out for us and our entire family God and help us to always do what you would have us do to honor you. In Jesus name…* AMEN."

"Amen," Geneva muttered. "I swear Elijah, you're gettin' better at prayin' than I am. Of course, we all pray different, but I'm just happy you're prayin'. Like I said, it does me good to see it."

It wasn't long and their plates that were jam full moments earlier, were cleaned. There was nothing left but a few crumbs from the biscuits. Elijah sat there wiping his mouth and still savoring the deliciousness his wife had prepared. She got up, washed the few plates, and put them away. The morning rays shone through the kitchen window, brightening up the place. No lights were needed. God provided all the light they needed that morning and Elijah treaded upstairs to shower before she had a chance to beat him to it.

It was still comfortable outside, so she grabbed her bible and went on the porch to do her morning routine of giving God her time. She couldn't help but think about her dream and how her subconscious remembered something she didn't. All the while, wondering how she could recollect it at all. Then she turned to the book of Mark chapter four, verse twenty-two and read out loud, *For nothing is hidden, except to be revealed; nor has anything been secret, but that it would come to light.* She thought on that scripture for a few moments, and a smile appeared, taking the place of any doubt she might have had.

"You're just showin' me what happened, right Lord?" Geneva whispered, looking to the sky. "I just hope you don't let me get lost again."

Lastly, she turned to one of her favorite scriptures of all, one that got her through many times of fear and anger. It was in the book of Joshua, chapter one, verse nine. Once again, she read it aloud.

"Have I not commanded you? Be strong and courageous. Do not be frightened, and do not be dismayed, for the Lord your God is with you wherever you go," Geneva finished. "I guess I need to listen to ya, huh God?"

Still sitting on the porch swing outside, she got to thinking about the many times she feared something or when her doubts tried to take over. She would just open that sacred book and it always gave her the answers she needed to keep moving forward. Somehow, it never failed her. There were people who failed her, family, and friends alike, but God never did. Even when she didn't know who she was for that short period of time, he knew.

"Geneva James," Elijah yelled out from inside the house.

"Out here honey," she answered, bellowing out just the same. "Just gettin' my quiet time in. I'll come get ready."

She placed the tassel back where it was in her bible, and went inside, putting it back in its usual spot on the entry table. Elijah was standing at the top of the stairs with pajama bottoms on and a towel draped around his shoulders, his hair going in ten different directions.

"That a new hairstyle honey?" Geneva laughed, making her way to him. "I'd wear it that way if I was you."

"You trying to be funny?" he said, beginning to tickle her once she made it to the top of the stairway.

They wrestled around for a minute until Geneva broke away and made it to the bathroom, slamming the door shut and locking it before he had a chance to come in. She was laughing so hard, she had to hold her belly while she finally caught her breath from running.

"We'll continue this later," Elijah said through the door.

"Promise?" Geneva laughed, all the while running her water so she could soak in a hot tub. She always said there was nothing better than soaking aching bones in a hot tub of water.

Geneva did just that, laying there until the water was trying to cool off, then she got out and hurried to get ready. She knew Elijah was waiting, but there was one thing he was good at, waiting on her. She put on a little make up, enough to make her feel more youthful and fixed her hair. It didn't take long to finish getting dressed, and she trotted down to meet Elijah. He didn't say anything about how long it took her to make herself all pretty, he was just glad she was there, and they headed to town.

He turned left on the main road and the sun overhead, was beating down. It was a sure thing it would be as hot as the day before, maybe even hotter, but their focus wasn't the heat. After Terry told them what he was doing, Elijah and Geneva both wanted to be a part of something so charitable, helping those who needed it the most. There was something about helping others that gave Elijah a satisfied feeling deep down and Geneva always told him the same.

"Boy, I can't wait to get to that there place and see what they got goin' on. I know we can help honey. I know we can," Geneva said, her energy speeding up the more she talked. "I swear, if I was to win that there lottery, I'd be broke in a week."

"A week?" Elijah asked, knowing what was coming next.

"Yeppers," she replied. "I'd give it all away."

He looked her direction and reached over and put his hand on hers, "That's what I love about you Geneva. I want to be just like you."

Geneva swatted the air, "Oh, get outa here," she grinned, giving a short cackle afterward. "We're the same honey. We didn't used to be, but we are now."

Elijah turned under the bridge and was only a few blocks away from the address Terry gave him. When they pulled in, there sat a large building with double doors and an awning in the center of the building. A few benches sat on either side of the door and a few picnic tables were randomly placed in front as well. It was nothing fancy to say the very least, but it was a big enough place to accommodate. He parked just to the left of the door. Before they could get out, their eyes focused in on something they saw by the building…something that pulled their heart strings.

CHAPTER FOUR

On the far corner of the building, was a lady with two children. They were sitting on the ground with a couple of backpacks next to them. The kids couldn't have been any more than four to six years old. Geneva got out but instead of going inside, she slowly went in their direction. Each step she took, she kept thinking what to say to them, but she knew God would give her direction when it was time.

"Geneva," Elijah called out to her.

She turned to him and smiled and held up one finger as if to say, *hold on a minute.* The closer she got, the more curious she became as to why someone so young with kids would be on the streets. And when she reached them, she felt a heaviness in the pit of her stomach. The woman was dressed in faded denim shorts, a threadbare t-shirt and flip flops that looked like they were in their last days. It was obvious she hadn't bathed in sometime, and the same with the children.

"I'm Geneva," she said, extending her hand. "Me and my husband are here to help get this here place up and goin'."

The woman lowered her head and reached out to shake Geneva's hand. "Emily," the woman said. "This is Katy and Joshua. I…"

"Nice to meet you," Geneva smiled, not giving her a chance to explain. The way she saw it, she wasn't one to judge, only one to help. "Katy, that's a beautiful name, and Joshua, that's from the bible. Did you know that Joshua?"

"No ma'am," the little boy said, holding tight to a little figurine.

"What'chu got there?" Geneva asked, trying her best to get them talking.

"My daddy gave it to me," Joshua said, holding it up briefly for her to see. "It's the last thing he gave me before he…"

"I'm sorry to take your time," Emily said, getting up and gathering the few things they had. "We should be going. Come on kids."

"Wait," Geneva said. "Where are you going?"

"Somewhere to get in from the heat," she answered, taking hold of each of the kid's hands.

"Why don't ya come inside with us? Terry won't mind. That's what this place is for…to help people," Geneva replied, hoping to keep them there. "Terry's a good guy and it'll get you out of the heat. This blame summer is about to get to me too."

"We're fine," Emily said. "We'll just stay here. This tree is some shade anyway."

Geneva heard a truck pull up and realized it was Terry and Sherry. They went to the front door and unlocked it, waving Geneva over. Elijah was already standing with them giving her a sympathetic look. She knew he knew her heart was hurting just seeing someone live that way and they communicated from afar.

"I'll be back," Geneva said. "Wait here, okay?"

The woman gave no response, just a look, and Geneva went to join the others. She was sure if Terry knew about them, he would do all he could to help, but not knowing what the facility looked like, she didn't know what he could do until it was finished.

"Come on in," Terry said, waving them inside. "Well, this is it."

Geneva and Elijah walked in first and admired the first room they entered. It was sort of a great room, large enough for all kinds of things. Then there were probably a dozen rooms to the side and a large kitchen in the back of the place with a huge freezer to store plenty of food for anyone they needed to feed. It had a bland look about it, but that was an easy fix and Geneva's mind started turning, thinking about things to do to make it more inviting and homey feeling.

"What do yall think?" Sherry said, walking around in the larger area, pushing chairs up to the tables and straightening as she went along.

"This is somethin' else," Geneva said, her mind still creating ideas by the second. "You could do a lot with this here place."

"I knew you'd see it Geneva," Terry said. "We need a little décor, a few beds and things to make it feel more like home and we're in business."

"We could do so much," Geneva said, picturing the place in her mind when it was all finished.

"I like you using the word we," Terry said. "Now we need to make it welcoming. Any ideas?"

"I have a few, but first, did you see that lady outside with the two little ones?" Geneva said, trying not to take away from his grand tour, but knowing they were in need.

"I didn't Geneva," Terry answered.

"The woman's name is Emily, and her kids are Katy and Joshua. Terry I'm pretty positive their homeless. You know I can't stand nothin' like that. Makes me feel guilty of havin' a place to sleep myself," Geneva continued, showing a look of heartache on her face. "It's just not right."

"Where are they?" Terry asked, heading to the door.

Without hesitation, Geneva scurried in front of him, "Over here."

She walked as fast as her little legs would go and Terry followed close behind. Elijah and Sherry waited for them at the entrance. But when Geneva turned the corner where they had been sitting, they were gone. All that she saw, was a little pink ribbon that appeared to have fallen out of Katy's hair. At that moment, Geneva's heart sank. Every scenario ran through her thoughts, thinking the worst and wanting to know where they were. She didn't even know them, but knew they were in trouble. She knew they needed help, but for the moment, it was in God's hands.

"They were here?" Terry asked, looking around to see if he could see them anywhere.

"They were," Geneva said, her emotions grabbing ahold of her. "I don't think they have anywhere to go."

"Did they say that Geneva?" Terry asked sincerely.

"No, but…"

"Maybe they were just out for a walk. Maybe they just sat down to rest," Terry said, trying to think as positive as he could, knowing he would worry just as much as Geneva.

"I don't think so Terry. By golly, I shouldn't a left'em. Why did I leave'em?" Geneva said, guilt overtaking her.

"It's okay Geneva. I'll find them. If they're from around here, I'll see them again and I know you'll be around a lot. We just need to pray for them if they are in trouble," Terry said, resting his hand on her shoulder. "Let's pray."

Geneva bowed her head, closed her eyes and started talking to God, *"Dear God, I know you already know why I'm a reachin' out to you about. You know some of your children are in need and I don't know what to do. Lord, them little ones looked so pitiful and I'm just praying you keep them safe. I know you promise this in your word and I'm asking please God if I'm meant to guide them, tell me what to do. If Terry is here to help them find their way, give him the tools he needs to do so. We are here to serve you Lord and helping others is one way. I ask this in Jesus' name…AMEN"*

Terry gave Geneva a hug to comfort her and they went back to the center. Sherry and Elijah sensed what happened by the expression on Geneva's face. It showed a multitude of emotions. From sadness to regret, the lines in her face were like a roadmap to her soul.

They went back inside and sat down, planning on what to do next and how to finish fixing up such a dreary space. From how to arrange the tables and chairs, to brainstorming about how to fix the side rooms up for people who needed a place to sleep, they mapped it all out. The more Geneva talked, the more ideas floated around them, to make such a venture, a successful one. But still, that woman and her kid's faces were etched in Geneva's mind. It's like she couldn't get the image out of her head, especially the little boy holding the small toy. What happened to their daddy? Did he run off or did something tragic happen to him? Nonetheless, whatever it was, it left that sweet little family in dire straits.

After writing down everything they needed to do, Geneva jumped up, "Come on Elijah. We're a goin' shoppin. And I know just the place to go. We'll check out that there salvation army and see if they got anything to fix some a these rooms up with beds and such and if they have any decorations, I'll grab them too."

Terry pulled out his wallet and tried to hand her some money, but she took off toward the door, "Come on Elijah or Terry's gonna con you again. We said we was gonna help and by golly, that's what we plan on doin'. We'll be back," Geneva said, rushing out the door, dodging Terry's attempts to finance her ideas.

Elijah minded Geneva and met her at the truck. She already had her seatbelt on and was ready to go. Still, she caught herself looking all around to see if she could catch a glimpse of her newfound friends, praying the entire time they were okay. He could tell she knew exactly what she was looking for and there was no stopping her.

They made their first stop at the salvation army store and found some things that suited the place well. From a few basic bedroom sets and some cots to small furniture pieces to match, they both knew it would fill the place nicely. Geneva called Terry to let him know what they had bought, and they all decided to meet up around lunch to talk about things more. She even found a bunch of matching tablecloths to go on the rectangle tables they already had in the large area, to bring in a hint of color.

"We knocked a dent in it anyway," Geneva said, glancing back at some of the things they picked up, still needing to go back and get the big items. "I think Terry's gonna love it."

"He will," Elijah said. "It felt good Geneva…you know doing for others."

"It always does honey," she said, positivity glowing from her. "Besides, we got all we need, and you know what the good book says about that don't ya?"

Elijah smiled back at her, "Tell me."

"Well," she continued. "In Proverbs 19:17 it says *Those who are gracious to the poor lend to the Lord, and the Lord will fully repay them.*"

"You amaze me sometimes," Elijah said, one hand on the steering wheel and the other holding her hand. "I don't know how you remember all that."

"Ya read the word enough, it kinda gets stuck in your head. And if it gets stuck in your head, you learn to live by it," Geneva said. "Some folks don't read the bible enough to know any of it and that's the problem."

"I learn more from you every day, Geneva," Elijah said, parking in front of a local diner.

They both looked around to see if Terry's truck was there yet and it wasn't, but they went inside to grab a table and to order their drinks. Geneva always said shopping made her thirsty. From behind the counter, sat a familiar face. It was Carol who took the restaurant over after her mom passed away. Sue and Carols was always a popular place in Texarkana and the home-cookin' food was unmistakable. It was only a minute and Carol made her way over.

"I haven't seen you two in quite a while," she said, placing two menus in front of them.

Geneva laughed and looked over at Elijah, "We been a fixin' stuff up around the place. Elijah loves doin' stuff around the house, you know."

"Love it," Elijah muttered in response.

Carol and Geneva got a good laugh out of his, not so energetic banter and made small talk for a few minutes. Carol's mom Sue was one of Geneva's good friends for years when she was growing up. Sue always loved cooking and opened that place with the hopes that mama's style cookin' would be just what people wanted, and she was right. The same people made their way to that little place every single day, like a meeting point to sit and catch up from the day before. On any given day, like clockwork, you always knew who you'd see when stepping inside. To be honest, they made a great business off regulars if no one else ever came.

In the corner, left of the door was a big round table. As usual, there were six older gentlemen gabbing, laughing, and telling stories over coffee and homestyle breakfast. One of the guys was someone Geneva knew from way back when. His name was Ken. He always tried to aggravate by bringing his ticket over and dropping it off like he was making her pay for it. It was just a game he played every time they saw each other there. Of course, it was just his way of communicating and saying hi. Everyone has different ways about them and that's something Geneva learned through the years.

They didn't want to order before Terry and Sherry arrived, so she and Elijah made small talk, looked around the room to see if there was anyone they hadn't seen in a while, and skimmed over the menu to decide on what they were hungry for. The first thing Elijah always had a taste for their chicken fried steak with white cream gravy. It always covered half the plate, but he didn't have a problem putting it away.

After a few minutes, they noticed Terry pulling up right at the front door. He got out and instead of going around to open Sherry's door, he opened the back door to his truck instead. Geneva's eyes lit up at what she saw next.

CHAPTER FIVE

Amidst the crowd of people enjoying their lunch and their conversations floating all around, laughter filling the place, for some reason, Geneva's focus was on Terry and the surprise he had for her. Sherry walked in first and Terry followed with three special people she didn't expect to see. Her eyes began to tear up, but she wiped them away before anyone could see. There was something about getting emotional that Geneva couldn't help. It's like her heart ruled who she was, in turn making her the woman she had become.

"Who do we have here?" Geneva said, reaching and sweetly holding the little boy's hand. "You're name's Joshua, right?"

The little boy didn't answer, only nodded, squeezing her hand right back. Geneva lifted him and placed him on her knee, bouncing him like she used to do Ella when she was a little girl. Though his clothes were dirty, and he looked a mess, the smile he wore overshadowed such a minuscule thing that could be taken care of with no problem. Terry grabbed another table and pulled it together with the one they were at, to make more room. Everyone found a place to sit, and Emily, the kid's mom, Geneva met earlier in the day, held her head down as before. She scooted a chair close to her so her little girl, Katy, could sit, wrapping her arm around her.

"Me and Sherry saw them walkin' down the road over near the overpass toward the library and figured they might want to join us for some lunch," Terry said, his energy overflowing and smile, contagious. "Heck, who wouldn't want a Sue and Carols chicken fried steak with all the fixins?"

"I was just thinkin' about getting that Terry," Elijah joined in, trying to get the conversation going. "It's the best in town."

Geneva continued loving on the little one in her lap and looked up to see Emily acting so out of place. It was obvious she thought everyone was staring at her.

"Where you from honey?" Geneva asked in her own friendly, peppy way.

"I'm…f…from the Dallas area, but," she started to say when Geneva jumped in.

"Oh, my goodness, I love that there Dallas. I used to spend all day just a shoppin' and come back with a car load a stuff I didn't need," she said, laughing as she spoke.

"Well," Emily continued. "My folks were from there, but they passed away in a car wreck several years ago."

'Oh, honey I'm so sorry," Geneva replied sympathetically. "I bet that was hard."

"Yes ma'am," she answered.

"Good golly don't call me ma'am. That makes me feel like my old grandmother and I ain't old yet," Geneva spoke out, then smiling after. "But I do appreciate the respectfulness. You can call me Mama G, you kids too."

"Mama G?" Joshua said, still sitting in her lap.

She gave out her usual cackle and said, "I'm everybody's mama honey. I didn't have a hundred kids, but I sure feel like I do. I was blessed with lots a family other than my own."

"Mama G," Joshua muttered, then looked up at her with eyes that showed happiness in the moment.

The waitress came over with her pad and pencil and went around the table taking orders. When it got to Terry, he ordered and said, "Give me the ticket."

"Now see here Terry," Elijah started, until he saw that look Terry was beaming his direction. After that, he let it go, knowing there was no way he was going to win that argument.

Emily and the kids looked on and seemed to be getting a little more comfortable with them. When the food came out, Emily and the kids ate like they hadn't eaten that good in years. There wasn't a crumb remaining when they were done, but there were smiles on their faces.

"Ya'll save room for pie," the waitress said. "We got coconut pie, chocolate pie and pineapple pie."

Most everyone shook their heads as to say no, but the kids and Emily, had a different expression. Their eyes got big as saucers, but then when everyone else said no, they looked back down.

"Whatever these young'uns want," Terry said.

"We couldn't," Emily muttered, showing she felt embarrassed to ask for more.

"Yes, you can. Tell the lady what you want. I insist. All their pies are the best, so you can't go wrong with anything," Terry said kindly.

They ordered several pieces of pie, the two kids sharing one and the mom thoroughly enjoying the other. Geneva and Sherry made sure Katy and Joshua got their fill as the men watched, smiling at such a scene. When everyone was full to the brim, people were starting to leave since they closed at two o'clock.

"That was delicious," Emily said, wiping her mouth and leaning over to do the same for the children.

"You're a good mom," Sherry said, making clear eye contact and putting off a positive vibe at the same time. "I can tell you are."

"Sometimes I wonder," Emily replied, half-grinning.

All of a sudden, Geneva hopped up out of her chair, "Hey, I feel like a goin' shoppin'. How 'bout ya'll?"

Of course, the guys were shaking their heads no, right away, but Sherry was one hundred percent agreeable, knowing what Geneva was up to.

"Emily," Geneva said. "Why don't you and your little'uns come along? We'll have a good time. I promise."

"You can't help but have a good time around Geneva. That's what everyone says around here," Sherry agreed.

"I…I…" Emily stuttered.

"Oh, come on sugar. We might find something to get you dressed up all perty, and for the kids too," Geneva said. "It's settled then. You guys go pick up that there furniture we done paid for and take it to the center. The rest of us are going shopping."

Terry paid the bill and Elijah followed him to his truck. Of course, they knew what Geneva was up to, but they wanted to play it off, so Emily didn't feel like a charity case. Like Geneva always said, nobody wants to be treated like a charity case. After they drove off, Geneva and Sherry got their guests all settled in the back seat and headed to town. Geneva didn't know where they were going, but she knew before the day was over, that woman and her kids would have something to wear and would be spotless clean.

It took a few minutes, but Emily spoke up as they drove down the road. "Thank you for everything. I really didn't know what we were going to do."

"Honey," Geneva said. "I don't know what you're a goin' through, but God does and that's who told us to help you. The way I see it, God's helpin' you through us. And that's the way I like it."

"You are something else," Emily said, one corner of her mouth tilting to show a smile trying to get peek out.

Geneva laughed, "That's what Elijah tells me all the time and I'll tell ya somethin'. I ain't nothin' special. I'm just me."

"I like you," Joshua, the little boy, chimed in surprisingly.

You could tell Sherry's emotions started getting the best of her. She turned her head away from them and looked out the window, wiping the few stray tears trying to trickle down. Just the purity and sincerity in that little man's voice, spoke volumes. He only met Geneva twice and for some reason, she left an imprint on his heart.

Obvious Geneva got a little choked up herself, she didn't miss a beat. "Well honey, I like you pretty good too. Whatcha think about that?"

The small laugh he let out from her country twang and spirited tone, was entertaining to him and it showed. It didn't take long, and they pulled up in front of a store Sherry and Geneva went to often. They had everything from home goods, clothes to shoes, anything a body would need. After parking, Geneva got out and opened the back door, lifting the little fella out. He immediately wrapped his arms around her when he did, who she was, made her give him one of her famous hugs everyone loved.

"What a great hugger you are," Geneva said, putting him down and taking his hand.

"My daddy gave good hugs too," Joshua said sweetly, grasping tightly to her hand as they walked.

There were no words to say after such a comment, especially considering she knew nothing about what they were going through or why they were on the streets. So, Geneva just smiled back at the little boy holding his hand, acknowledging his dad by saying nothing at all.

Emily paused just before going into the store, "People will stare," she said, trying to fix her hair a little so she didn't look so ragged.

Before she could say another word, or anyone else for that matter, Geneva spoke up. "And I'll tell you something sweetie, if they do, I'll put a knot on their head. Ain't nobody got the right to judge other folks. Don't ever forget that."

That's all it took to pull a smile out of Emily in a hurry. It's like being with Geneva and Sherry, gave her a little security. They all gathered together and walked in. Sherry held onto Katy's hand while Geneva clung to Joshua's. Emily started going up and down a few aisles of clothes and shoes, and it was obvious she saw plenty she liked. At the same time, you could tell she didn't want to ask for anything.

"That there top would look precious on you," Geneva said, lifting it up in the air. "And with those shorts, you'd look like a model I tell ya."

"Oh Miss Geneva, you're just saying that." Emily replied in the shyest manner. "You're very sweet."

Again, Geneva started her cackling laugh, "I bet Elijah would say different honey. Now grab that shirt and shorts and keep a lookin'. I'm takin' this fella here over to find him some new duds and some shoes."

Joshua didn't say anything, but his smile was worth more than a thousand words. The stars in his eyes lit up with everything she picked up to see if he liked it. All he could do, was nod his head and she would fling it into the buggy. After a while of looking through every rack in the place, she met up with Sherry and Emily in the center of the store.

"We found some pretty things for Katy," Sherry said, looking down at the little girl clinging to her. "Didn't we Katy?"

"Yes ma'am," she answered, holding onto a soft cuddly pink and purple blanket with white stars on it. "Miss Sherry said I could have this blanket mommy. Can I?"

Emily noticed the smile on Sherry's face, seeing the joy it was giving them to be able to help. "Sure, you can sweetie. It's your favorite colors."

"It'll be warm when it starts to get cold too, mommy," the little girl continued.

Sherry and Geneva immediately looked at one another, their hearts communicating without a word being spoken. It was an unspoken conversation, but they knew what they had to do.

"I tell ya what," Geneva said, stooping down to be eye level with the children. "How about you guys come stay with me and Elijah for a few days. I got a big place and…"

"We couldn't impose," Emily cut in. "You're doing too much already."

"And you're more than welcome to stay with Terry and I. It would be fun," Sherry jumped in, trying to show them they didn't have to be homeless.

Both kids started jumping up and down, never losing sight of their mama, "Can we? Please."

Before she could answer them, something caught Emily's eye. It was a picture that had writing on it. For some reason, it drew her in. She stepped toward it and picked it up. It was a scripture in plain black writing on a white backing, but there was something special about it.

"What is it honey?" Geneva said, going to her.

"This reminds me of something I thought I forgot," she replied, emotions encasing her. "My mama used to say this to me whenever I was down."

Geneva focused on what Emily was holding, and read the words in front of her.

CHAPTER SIX

"It's Romans, Chapter five," Geneva said. "I know that one well."

"We had a tough time when I was growing up and mama used to read the bible to me. This one scripture always stuck out. I haven't seen it in a long time," Emily said.

"Read it for me," Geneva asked.

She paused only momentarily, but then she began to read, "*But not only that, we even take pride in our problems, because we know that trouble produces endurance, endurance produces character, and character produces hope. This hope doesn't put us to shame, because the love of God has been poured out in our hearts through the Holy Spirit, who has been given to us.*"

Sherry and the kids listened to those awe-inspiring words being spoken from Emily with so much feeling. When she lowered the framed piece of encouragement and put it back where she found it, she began to nod her head.

"Miss Geneva," Emily said, turning to her. "We'll stay with you for a few days if that's okay."

"Honey, it's more than okay," Geneva replied, overflowing with enthusiasm, then picked up what Emily had just put back. "And I think I want this here picture to hang in my hallway. I think it'd be just perfect. Don't ya think?"

They took the two buggies they had full to the brim with clothes, shoes, toys, this and that, and went to the register. When it was all rung up, there was no arguing who was paying. Sherry and Geneva split it right down the middle gladly, smiling all the while. Emily and the kids watched, still looking a little dazed. They were probably wondering why perfect strangers would go through so much trouble for someone they didn't even know. But just like that scripture she read, Geneva was a character and character produces hope. They were people trying to give them just that...hope.

"I guess that's it," Sherry said, taking a few bags and distributing the others to Emily and Geneva to tote out to the vehicle. The two little ones carried a bag as well and appeared happy to do so. Although they weren't cleaned up, they were still shining in the moment.

"You guys are gonna get to meet my daughter Ella and son-in-law Caleb, this evening. They're comin' for supper," Geneva said, filling the back end with everything they bought. "You'll like 'em? They're not crazy like me, but then again, there can't be two a me."

"You can say that again," Sherry said, aggravating and laughing at the same time. "I don't know what we'd do with two of you."

"You'd have double trouble, that's what you'd have sister," Geneva said, bantering the best she knew how, Emily and the kids looking quite entertained at their behavior.

Emily and the kids loaded up and they headed back to the center to meet the guys. It's like the entire feeling in the air was different than before. There were smiles and laughter, joking and aggravating, being playful to say it best. Geneva sat there driving and catching herself glancing back to see such a sweet family. She listened to the kids whispering about all the things they got, and it did her so much good. Then, talking silently to God, Geneva thanked him for giving her the opportunity to help someone who needed it most. Her heart was full of love for her newfound friends, and she wanted to do all she could to get them back on their feet.

Geneva and Sherry talked on the way, then turned the radio up when one of their favorite songs came on. She cranked up the sound and they all started to sing. The kids didn't know the song, but looking in the mirror, Geneva could see the kids swaying left and right and bobbing their heads up and down. Emily, on the other hand, knew the song, and although she was shy earlier in the day, something changed. She started belting out each line of that tune like she wrote it, with energy in her voice.

"Listen at you," Geneva said. "We got ourselves a singer. You betcha we do."

"Yes ma'am," Sherry replied, both glancing back at Emily, smiling and still singing with her.

It was more than obvious she was feeling more and more comfortable by the minute, and the kids acted the very same. When they pulled into the center, they all got out and headed inside. Terry's truck was parked right in front of the door, backed in, assuming so they could unload the furniture. And when they went inside, Terry and Elijah were working hard, putting everything where they thought it went. Of course, when Sherry and Geneva saw where things were, they automatically took over. Terry found a place to sit and watched them rearrange everything, and when they were done, they sat down as well.

"There," Sherry said. "That looks good, don't it Geneva?"

"It looks great if I do say so myself. You did good work guys…great work," Geneva answered and looked over at Elijah and Terry with a wink.

Both shook their heads, knowing it would do no good to say a word, they listened to the girls, including Emily, gab about what a good time they had shopping. Elijah knew they could talk about it forever and he broke in.

"We gotta get back home Geneva. The kids will be over in a few hours, and you have to cook supper," Elijah said, trying not to sound bossy, but trying to get his point across at the same time.

"You betcha honey," Geneva said, then going over to Emily and the kids. "By the way Elijah, we got ourselves a few house guests. And I bet these young'uns will love that there yard of ours. I might even get Ella and Caleb to stay over, and we might just go fishin' tomorrow."

Both kid's eyes opened wide and Joshua spoke up, "I never been fishing Mama G."

"Well then, we're gonna see what we can do about that. And I know where to find the best night crawlers around," Geneva said, getting the kids more excited by the minute. "Heck, I remember me and Elijah went fishin' when we first met. I think that's when he got bit by the love bug."

"Love bug?" Katy asked, eyes squinted like she was trying to figure out what that kind of bug looked like.

Everyone laughed at her reaction, and Geneva kneeled and hugged that little girl just for putting joy in her heart. Katy didn't know why they were laughing, but she laughed right along with them as kids do. Emily stood there not saying a word but saying a million words at the same time. The expression on her face, was one of satisfaction of seeing her kids happy and content. The gleam in her eyes was thank you enough for Geneva, a sign from God that she was doing what she was supposed to do.

As everyone said their goodbye's, shaking hands and hugging one another, Geneva sat back and admired the miracle of God at work. Her thoughts landed on a scripture that, for some reason came to the forefront of her mind. It was Matthew 11: 28-29 it said, *"Come to me, all you who are weary and burdened, and I will give you rest. Take my yoke upon you and learn from me, for I am gentle and humble in heart, and you will find rest for your souls."*

"Geneva," Elijah said loudly, snapping her out of her intense thought. "You ready woman?"

"Woman?" Geneva replied, knowing he was playing around. "You just wait Elijah James…I'll whoop you if you don't watch it."

Immediately after she said such a thing, her contagious laugh echoed. Emily and the kids made their way to the vehicle and climbed in. Elijah got behind the wheel and started to back out, when he heard the little girl say something.

"Mr. …uh," Katy said, not remembering Elijah's name.

"You can call me Eli," Elijah said in a very kind tone. "What's wrong Katy?"

"If you don't have enough room, I can sleep on the floor. I don't mind, as long as mama and my little brother can have the bed."

Before Elijah could even think about answering, Geneva inserted herself into the conversation. "Honey, I'll tell ya what. How about your mama have her own room and you and Joshua share a room…a bed for everyone? And anything you need is yours."

"Really?" Katy said, excitement showing in her sweet voice, then turning to her brother. "We get to share a bed Josh."

Geneva turned back facing the front asking God to please help her control her emotions. A part of her wanted to bellow out, crying for answers as to why these kids had to live the way they were, but another part, knew his plan was in the works already. Deep down, she knew he was using her as his tool to make a difference in some kind of way, although she wasn't quite sure what tomorrow would bring. At the end of the day, no one really knows, so living in the moment, was all she could do.

After a few moments of driving, Elijah pulled down their dirt road, and a cloud of dust surrounded them since it had been dry for two or three weeks. One thing for sure, they were in desperate need of some rain, but there was no sign of it in sight. Every day was hotter than the day before and that bright sun showed its face proudly. It was a job just to keep the flowers where they weren't parched, but as much as Geneva loved them, they were always well taken care of.

"You live here?" Joshua said, like he was in awe of the sight. "Wow."

"It's just a house young'un, but we make it a home. Now, let's get your things out and get inside. I might let ya'll help me with supper too if ya want to," Geneva said, her smile showing sincerely.

Emily got all she could carry and handed a sack to each of the kids. Elijah and Geneva got the rest and they started toward the house. The kids walked slowly, looking around, then out to the hills in the distance where a multitude of colors from the flowers and trees, were showing themselves proudly. Geneva felt like she was looking at a miracle right in front of her, those two little ones admiring God's gift of nature and the beauty it held.

"Kids," Emily said sweetly. "Don't make Miss Geneva wait on you, let's get inside. Mr. James is holding the door open for us."

"Oh honey," Geneva said. "He don't mind a waitin'. He's been waitin' on me for years and I suppose he's used to it… besides, I think these young'uns like the view."

"It is beautiful," Emily said, glancing out in the same direction as her kids. "And so peaceful."

"Yeppers," Geneva replied, going over and putting her hand on Emily's shoulder. "There's enough craziness in this ole world, this is what I look forward to every day, seeing what God created."

They guided the children to the porch and up to where Elijah was standing with the door wide open. The smile he wore was something to behold. The old Elijah wouldn't have given a second thought to anyone living on the streets, but the new Elijah found a heart that was always there, caring, and gentle.

"Come on kids," he said, taking their sacks from them as they came in.

Once more, Emily and the kids took a mental note of everything around them. They didn't say a word, but Geneva could tell they were glad to be there.

"Now, let's get you settled in and then I'll start supper. Ella and Caleb should be here in a bit," Geneva said, grabbing a few bags from their shopping trip and striding up the steps. "Come on and I'll draw a bath and you kids can get all cleaned up for supper."

"Can we wear some of our new clothes Mama G?" Katy asked.

When they got to the kids' room, Geneva leaned down to her, "You betcha you can sweetie. And I can't wait to see you in them there new duds."

After getting them set in their rooms, and got their new clothes put away, Geneva came back down and started preparing a special dinner. It looked like she pulled everything out of the cabinet before it was over, and the kitchen started looking like a storm struck it. But standing there in her apron, Geneva looked like a happy soul. She sliced and diced, peeled, and mashed, all in perfect motion. One thing she always did, was make sure everything was ready at the same time. Elijah always said she was OCD about such things, but it's how she was from the time she was old enough to learn to cook.

The last thing she needed to do, was finish the homemade biscuits she loved to make and when she placed them in the oven, lights pulled up in front of the house. Geneva knew who it was, and a smile immediately appeared. She untied her apron and hung it on the hook in the pantry.

"Elijah James," Geneva hollered out. "Ella's here."

Elijah came from the living room and went straight to the front door to greet them. He opened the door, and they were just walking up the front steps.

"Paint your porch Pop?" Caleb asked, that grin of his, a sight to see.

"Yeah," Elijah said. "If it wasn't for Terry and his wife, it'd still be half done. They came over yesterday and chipped in. Thank God for good friends."

"Hey dad," Ella said, coming around Caleb and hugging Elijah. "Sorry, we haven't been by in the last week or two."

Elijah, walking in the house, "It's not a problem. Me and your mama just been doing stuff around here and Terry's got a new project we're helping with too. I'm sure your mama will tell you all about it."

Caleb followed Elijah in the living room and Ella joined her mama in the kitchen. Geneva was waiting on the timer on the oven to buzz off so she could take the biscuits out to finish dinner up. Ella gave her a big hug and was a sight for sore eyes. It hadn't been too terribly long since they had come around, but since she was their only baby, she was always missed when she wasn't there.

"What's cookin' mama?" Ella said. "Smells delicious."

"Let's see what we got here," Geneva said, uncovering everything like she was revealing a masterpiece. "We got these here fried pork chops, fried taters, buttered squash, homemade gravy and the biscuits are about done."

"You sure did make a lot mama," Ella said, finding a place at the table after fixing a glass of sweet tea.

"About that," Geneva said, sitting down as well. "We have visitors upstairs."

"Visitors?"

Geneva was just about to fill Ella in on the situation when she heard footsteps coming in their direction.

CHAPTER SEVEN

Katy eased around the corner grinning from ear to ear. Her strawberry blonde hair was flowing beautifully on her shoulders and her emerald-green eyes brightened the space. She was no longer dirty and looking ashamed, but instead, she was shining, a little princess walking toward her new friend, Geneva.

"Do you like it Mama G?" Katy said, lifting the ends of the bottom of her skirt and giving a sweet curtsy.

"You betcha I do sweetie," Geneva said, motioning for her to come closer. "I want you to meet somebody. Katy, this is Ella, my daughter."

"Nice to meet you," Katy said, nodding, then looking back at Geneva, a shyness showing like the first time they met by the center.

"It's nice to meet you Katy," Ella said.

Before she had a chance to ask the little girl any questions like how they knew each other or anything else, Geneva told Katy to run get her mama and brother for dinner. She didn't want Katy to feel out of place, or have to face the reality of the situation at that time. Ella just looked at her mama until Katy was out of sight, waiting for her to fill in the blanks. As soon as she was gone, Geneva started talking fast, telling Ella about how she found them and how she wanted to help them. Even though no one really knew what happened to them, it didn't matter. At the end of the day, making sure they had a roof over their head and food to eat, was most important. The rest would come.

After Ella let Caleb in on what was going on, he and Elijah fixed them a spot to eat in the living room in front of the television. It's probably where they wanted to be anyway, and the girls added a few chairs to the table in the kitchen. About the time Geneva pulled the steaming hot homemade biscuits out of the oven, Emily and the kids walked in looking nice in their new clothes and shoes. Joshua stood there straightening his shirt and pants, then putting one hand in his pocket like a GQ model or something.

"Would you looky there?" Geneva said, her enthusiasm discharging. "Who is that there handsome fella?"

"It's Josh Mama G," he said, his dimples highlighted as he smiled back at her. "You know it's me."

"Well by golly. It is you, Joshua. Don't you look shiny as a new penny?" Geneva said, going to pay him lots of attention. "I'll tell ya somethin'…them little girls better look out."

"Yuck," he said, making everyone laugh.

All the while, Ella and Emily were talking. It was obvious they had become fast friends, and together, they gathered the plates and silverware for everyone. Geneva poured the sweet tea, and they sat down. Josh was about to take a bite when he was stopped.

"Let's say grace first honey," Geneva said, then calling out for Caleb and Elijah to join in. "We gotta thank God for this here food."

"But you cooked it didn't you?" he replied in the most innocent manner. "Shouldn't we thank you?"

She laughed a bit and responded kindly, "You betcha I did, but we have to thank God for everything we have, even the littlest things."

Joshua lowered his head and didn't say anything else, and Geneva felt bad, knowing she had phrased that entirely the wrong way. He was probably thinking he didn't have anything, and she just made things worse. Elijah stood at the entrance of the kitchen and said grace. Everyone's heads were bowed and the air in the room, was one of love. When *amen* was spoken, there was no holding anyone back from digging in. Caleb made it back to his seat in the living room before anyone else could even take a bite. Geneva, Ella, and Emily carried on a nice conversation, but mostly small talk, while the kids didn't look up from their plates until nothing was left. Katy grabbed an extra biscuit and Geneva buttered it all up for her, and happy to do so. Joshua, on the other hand, looked like he was full as a tick as he sat back after taking the last bite.

"Honey, you want some more?" Geneva asked, knowing there was no way he could stuff another bite in that little body of his.

"No ma'am," he said, resting his hands on his stomach. "I'm stuffed."

The look on his face, was priceless. His belly wasn't the only thing full. As he spoke, he blew his cheeks out at the same time, then let the air out. The biggest grin grew on Emily's face the more she watched her little man. Then she turned to Geneva, breaking the silence a little about how she felt at the moment.

"Miss Geneva," she said. "I don't know how to thank you for everything. You didn't have to…"

"Honey, I have to do what I'm told," she replied.

Emily looked at Geneva, doing her best to figure out this woman who inserted herself in their life and immediately started to make a difference in them. You could tell she felt lucky to have run into her in the first place.

"Who told you what to do?" Emily asked, pretty sure what her answer would be.

Beaming rays of sincerity, Geneva started picking up their plates and then stopped and turned around. "Have you ever read in the book of Isaiah?"

"Uh…well," Emily started to say. "I've not read much in the bible, I hate to say."

Geneva put down the dishes and found her place next to Emily, then rested her hand on hers, "The book of Isaiah talks a lot about God being with us no matter what and sometimes he uses us to help others out, to keep them safe. I like to think he uses me as his tool to point folks the right way."

"I don't know Miss Geneva," she replied, shaking her head, obvious doubts were looming over her.

"How about this?" Geneva continued. "In Isaiah 43:2, it says *When you pass through the waters, I will be with you; and when you pass through the rivers, they will not sweep over you. When you walk through the fire, you will not be burned; the flames will not set you ablaze.*"

If anyone ever had a look of truly concentrating on something, Emily did right then and there. She had no words and Geneva didn't expect any. Sometimes people have to figure things out on their own, but it is the responsibility of God's people to plant the seed.

Surprised, Katy asked, "Is God here right now?"

"He sure is honey," Geneva answered. "He's always with you. You're never alone."

"We've been alone since daddy left," Joshua added, resting his hands in his lap, his expression magnifying a deep sadness he felt. "He's been gone a long time."

"Honey," Emily said, changing the subject. "Why don't you two go and visit with Eli and our new friend Caleb?"

They did what she said, and Emily started to break down as soon as they were out of sight. It's like the wall she created trying to be strong, suddenly came crashing down before their eyes. A flood of emotion came rushing in giving her the chance to lean on someone else instead of being the one to lean on.

"Let's go outside and sit in the swing," Geneva said, taking her hand and sneaking out where the kids didn't see.

They did just that. Geneva and Emily sat in the swing and Ella took a seat in the wicker chair against the house. For a few moments, nothing was spoken. The silence had a healing presence they all knew. It was in the slightly cool breeze blowing by and in the scent of the flowers gracing the air around them. With no words, so much was being spoken.

"He was a good man," Emily said. "He really tried. We both did."

Geneva felt it best not to respond. For some reason, God was telling her to listen. Ella did the same, giving Emily their undivided attention. In a way, it showed her she could trust them and could tell them anything. Before it was all said and done, she began to open up even more.

"See, when I met Chris, I was in a bad place," Emily said. "My mom and dad were killed in a car wreck not long before that and I turned to drugs and alcohol. I didn't know what else to do. I felt alone, and that's when we met."

"Was he doing the same thing?" Geneva asked quietly, trying not to be too intrusive.

"He was, and the crowd of people we hung out with were not really desirable folks. To be honest, I didn't like any of them but Chris. It was just people to be around even if they were like that," Emily kept on. "Anyway, it's no excuse for doing the things I did. But after we fell in love, we both got straight and started a normal life. Then I found out I was pregnant with Katy."

"What did you do then?" Ella asked.

Emily's sadness somehow turned to a smile when Ella asked such a question. It's like the memory of that time was one she clung onto and kept close. After a short pause, she answered. "One evening when I got home after working my shift at the restaurant, I was dead tired. We lived in a loft apartment downtown and when I walked in, the place was dark. I knew Chris was already home because his truck was parked out front. When I turned the corner toward the kitchen, the entire area was lit with dozens of candles."

"Good Heaven's honey," Geneva said, sitting on the edge of her seat to hear the rest. "Sounds romantic."

"It was," Emily said, showing a giddiness like it was happening to her all over again. "And right in the middle of the kitchen, surrounded by candles, he was down on one knee, holding open a small box and the most beautiful ring."

Considering Ella and Geneva were two of the biggest romantics, they were hanging on every word. Ella had her head tilted slightly, waiting to hear what happened next. Geneva's feet were steadily tapping, something she did when she got nervous or anxious.

"You can't stop there honey," Geneva said. "You done got me seein' it all in my head."

"He told me I was the woman he was meant to be with, and our child was a gift, and put the ring on my finger," she finished.

"I'm a guessin' you said yes," Geneva laughed, lightening the mood from earlier.

"Of course, I did," Emily replied quickly, letting her smile out once more. "I loved him more than anything."

"Loved?" Geneva said. "Sounds to me like you still got that there love. It's just a little misplaced right now honey."

"What happened after that Emily?" Ella asked, wanting to hear more.

Emily's fingers caressed the cross etched into the armrest of the swing, somehow becoming one with it, then stood up and walked to the railing around the porch. She stared out for a second, then turned around. "We had an intimate little ceremony, nothing fancy. And when Katy came along it seemed like life was perfect."

"Sounds pretty perfect to me," Geneva chimed in. "But what went wrong?"

Suddenly, a quiet took over like none other, Emily didn't want to continue the conversation, or it was too painful, either way, her silence said it all. With her arms crossed, looking at the most majestic painting God created for them in the sky, nothing else was asked. Somehow, getting Emily to even start to open her heart, was a step in the right direction. It was a start and Geneva knew that all too well. She could tell that young woman was reaching for help, but not yet comfortable enough to completely give in. That's when a scripture came to Geneva's mind. It was Roman 8:25 and it said, *"But if we hope for what we do not see, we wait for it with patience."*

If there was one thing Geneva had, it was patience. From all the verses the bible talked about in regard to that, she had probably read them all. She wanted to be someone Emily could talk to when she was ready, and Ella appeared compelled to get to know her as well. The expression on Ella's face when she was listening to Emily tell her story, was one of wonder and curiosity.

Geneva thought of something she wanted to share before they all turned in for the night, and after Emily found her seat back on the swing, she did.

"You know life's a journey and we all got different travels," Geneva started. "I read a poem one time that sure 'nuff stuck with me. I think you just might like it," trying to remember all of it for a moment, then started.

> *I may travel near, you may go afar*
> *It doesn't matter, for in the end,*
> *You are who you are.*
> *Our paths are pre-determined*
> *By the one and only up above.*
> *He knows our every moment*

Because he crafted it with love.
Things don't always go
The way we wished to be,
But the end's already written
He wants us to be free.
There will be happiness
Sadness, hurt and pain,
But if you keep believing
The sunshine will follow rain.
So, when you have moments of distress
Don't think it will forever last,
Because his plan is not to hurt us
We have to throw away the past.
It's when you look ahead of you
A light begins to show
And that's the very moment
Inside, you start to grow.

After Geneva recited such a profound poem, Ella and Emily looked at one another. Emily started to say something, then stopped.

"What is it honey?" Geneva asked.

"So, I shouldn't remember?" she replied. "I shouldn't remember the good times."

"Sure, you can darlin," Geneva answered sweetly. "It just means when you let the past hold you down, you can't move forward for what the good Lord's got in store for ya, that's all. You have to be open to what's a comin' next."

"I don't see anything coming Miss Geneva. We have nothing but each other," Emily said, leaning her head over and resting it on Geneva's shoulder.

"You know what? Sometimes havin' each other is like havin' a gold mine…a real treasure," Geneva said. "I remember when me and Elijah didn't have two pennies to rub together, but we had each other. Them were good times. And honey, you gotta change the way you think. Think positive and positive things'll happen."

"Mama," a little voice bellowed out loudly and Emily jumped up to see what was wrong.

CHAPTER EIGHT

They all rushed inside and stopped suddenly when they saw Caleb wrestling on the living room floor with Joshua. He was tickling him, and Joshua's laugh was the sweetest sound that house had in a while. A child's laughter always did something for Geneva, and as that little one filled the place with the most beautiful music, Emily and Ella went in and sat down. Emily wasn't saying anything, but just staring at them two crazy rascals playing around, having a great time.

Joshua got up and was huffing and puffing, doing his best to catch his breath after such horseplay, then went to his mama. He fell into her and rested his head on her shoulder, still breathing heavy. He gave her the tightest hug and sweet kiss on the cheek. The bond between the two, was evident and everyone could tell she was a wonderful mom just by the way her kids wanted to be near her.

"I like Caleb," he whispered to her. "He's fun like daddy used to be."

"Oh, baby," Emily replied, hugging him once more as to say everything would be okay. "He is pretty entertaining, isn't he?"

He may have whispered, but sitting next to Emily, Ella heard it loud and clear. She couldn't help but look at Caleb in a different way, one of more love than before. Of course, Caleb was a little winded too and fell back on the adjacent couch. With each breath, his belly went up and down, showing the incredible meal they had and that he probably had a tad too much.

While everyone was paying attention elsewhere, Katy was standing by the window staring out. She appeared overtaken by something. The sound of the crickets found its way inside like a symphony and the fireflies lighting up the darkness outside could mesmerize anyone. Her big green eyes stared ever so carefully as her fingers were laced together resting in front of her. Before Emily could, Geneva went and sat in the high back chair next to where Katy was. At first, she didn't say anything to her. Then Katy turned to Geneva and smiled. A million words couldn't have said as much as that one smile from such a little angel, then she climbed in Geneva's lap.

"Whatcha lookin' at young'un'?" Geneva asked, sweetly caressing her arm and cradling her in a sense.

"Just everything," she said, still peering out. "I like it here. I feel safe."

"You betcha you're safe honey. I can promise you that," Geneva said, giving her a little short squeeze. "Now, how about we surprise everyone with some homemade cookies. You ever made any?"

Her eyes opened wide, "No ma'am."

"Then come on while everybody's busy with their shenanigans," Geneva continued, taking Katy's hand, and leading her to the kitchen, tippy toeing like no one could see them.

Conversation in the living room never ceased. From Caleb telling everyone about his new children's book coming out to trying to find something agreeable to watch on television, everything was as it should be. But in the other room, Geneva and Katy had every ingredient they needed, all over the counter. From flower to eggs, chocolate chips, nuts and more, they were a sight. When everything was put into the bowl, Geneva handed Katy something to stir it up and she did. It looked like she was trying to row a boat and she put all her efforts into that little confection of theirs. When she was done, it needed a tad more mixing, so Geneva finished it right up.

"Now," Geneva said, bringing over one of her biggest flat baking pans. "Just use this here spoon and dip some out and put it on that there pan, and we'll have cookies real soon."

"How much?" she asked, not knowing exactly what she was doing.

Geneva did her little cackle, "Honey, however big you want your cookies to be. I'm leavin' it up to you. You're the chef."

That little girl couldn't stop smiling. She made some big and some small and a few in between. It didn't matter though because she was having a good time. Whatever negative things creeping in her mind earlier, were dead and gone while she focused on making the most perfect cookies for the very first time. And after she plopped down the last little bit of dough, she lifted the pan to Geneva.

"Oh, would you looky there?" Geneva said. "Good Heavens, that's whatchu call cookies. You told me a story young'un. You've done this before because this is perfect."

The glow Katy put out from the tiniest of a compliment was amazing to see. She needed to be fed attention more than anyone realized, maybe even her mama. The magnitude of their situation and what happened to them until that point, was still unknown, but Geneva wanted to know more. It was the only way she or anyone else could help them. And as she placed the pan in the oven and set a timer, Geneva and Katy sat at the table and waited. Katy watched that timer as each second ticked off, waiting anxiously for it to finish so she could get a hold of one of those cookies she made almost all on her own.

"I smell cookies," Caleb hollered out from the other room, and it was no surprise. It wasn't but a few minutes until everyone joined them just as she was taking them out of the oven.

"Wait a minute," Geneva said, then looking down at Katy. "Katy gets the first one and any one she wants. You know, she did make these here cookies, so it's only fair."

The most authentic grin graced her adorable face as she went over and mulled over which one she wanted. A few were very big and, without waiting another minute, she pointed at one of them. As she requested, Geneva took the spatula and lifted it, putting it on a saucer so it would cool.

"Josh can have the other big one Mama G," Katy said with a nod. "That's why I made two big ones."

Josh took a deep breath in excitement and didn't argue, and he went over to get a little piece of Heaven. Geneva poured a glass of milk for everyone, and it didn't take long before every last cookie was history. The kids didn't have to say they enjoyed them, the noises they made after each bite, was communication enough. Ella and Emily talked and laughed like two old friends and Caleb and Elijah continued their funny banter that was common upon every visit.

Geneva sat there watching the moving scene in front of her and had no words, but her heart was utterly full. Just the thought of never being asked to help Terry, never going to the center, and never meeting this little family, Geneva knew God put her where she was supposed to be at the perfect time. There was no other way to explain them meeting when they did and Terry intervening to find them again. Somehow, she knew everything was going to be fine.

Emily glanced toward the clock. It was a little after nine, but it had been a long day for everyone, especially Emily. There was no doubt she was ready to get a good night's sleep, so she gathered the kids and put their dishes away. Elijah and Caleb continued talking, laughing, and aggravating one another, and Ella washed the few plates and glasses in the sink.

"Tomorrow's Sunday," Geneva said, looking toward Ella. "Why don't you and Caleb stay, and we'll all go to church tomorrow? I bet these little ones would like that too."

"You cookin' breakfast Geneva?" Caleb asked, sharing his perfect smile.

"You know I am Caleb. And I'll make extra bacon just for you," she replied.

"Sounds good to me. How about you honey?" Caleb said, reaching over and grabbing Ella's hand, his personality always taking over every time he was around.

"I guess we're stayin'," Ella replied, going over and hugging Geneva. "I wouldn't miss a chance to spend more time with you guys, all of you."

Emily told everyone goodnight and headed upstairs with the kids. Since they already had their baths, they put on the pajamas and climbed into bed. Emily kissed each one sweetly on the forehead and went to her room after, taking one final glance at them before she shut the door completely. The admiration she had for those two-little people, showed without a hint of doubt. Then, feeling at peace for the first time in a long time, she found her place, snuggled in a comfortable bed.

The others were still mulling around downstairs and tried their best not to disturb Emily and the kids. They all knew they needed rest more than anyone and they wanted to be respectful of that. It didn't matter because Geneva and Elijah loved their time with Ella and Caleb, especially Elijah, ever since they were with him through the ordeal when Geneva was gone. That time created a bond he knew would never be broken. Even though Elijah always loved Ella, something happened to their relationship in a magical sense. For the first time, they understood one another. And when Geneva came back, the puzzle was complete, and their family bond was unbreakable.

After a bit of catching up, Geneva got up and quietly started toward the stairs. "I think I'm a gonna peek in on them kids to make sure they're okay."

"Now don't you go waking them little ones up Geneva," Elijah said. "You know they have to be tired."

"I know it honey," she answered. "I just wanna look at'em. They're such angels. I swear, I feel like I've known them my whole life. God works that way, ya know."

Without any other comments from anyone, knowing if they did, it wouldn't keep her from looking in on them. So, step by step, up the stairs she made her way and reached their room. First, she put her ear to the door to see if she could hear anything, but it was quiet as a mouse. Then, she couldn't help herself, and turned the nob slowly, cracking open the door where, with one eye she tried to see them. There was a small night light in the far corner of the room, and it gave just enough light to see they were both moving around.

Geneva opened the door just enough to slip inside to see why they were still awake. Katy was lying there, eyes wide open facing the window where the moonlight shone in vibrantly, and very focused on something. Joshua just laid on his back, looking up at Geneva with the tenderest look. Maybe it was because they were in a strange place, but regardless, they were restless.

"Kids," Geneva whispered. "Why ain't you a sleepin'? I figured you'd already have sugar plumbs dancin' in your pretty little heads by now."

Katy turned facing Geneva and answered, "We miss our daddy Mama G. Mama does too, but she acts like she doesn't."

Geneva sat there listening to that child, all the while trying her best to say the perfect thing to give them some peace. Then a story in the bible came to mind. Not sure if they would understand it, but she was going to try.

"Have you ever heard the story about the lost sheep in the bible?" Geneva asked, hoping to get their attention.

They only shook their heads as to say *no,* and she continued. "You see, in the bible it talks about one hundred sheep and a sheep herder. If one of his sheep gets lost, the herder goes and finds him. Even if he has ninety-nine other sheep, that one lost sheep is special and important."

"What does that mean?" Katy asked, not even blinking, paying very close attention to every word Geneva was speaking.

"Honey, it just means, wherever your daddy is, he's lost, but that doesn't mean he's not special. It means that God is watching over him," Geneva continued. "Do you want to pray for him?

"We don't know how," Katy answered.

"How about this?" Geneva said, reaching and holding each of their hands. "How about I show you? What do you want me to ask God for?"

"I hope daddy is okay," Katy simply said, sincerity showing without a doubt.

"Okay," Geneva said. "Now, close your eyes and think real hard. Focus on God and concentrate. We're gonna talk to him, okay."

Again, giving a nod in agreement, she started to pray. Geneva was unaware that Emily was standing at the doorway, listening. The door was barely cracked, but enough to be able to hear everything. And this is what she heard.

"Heavenly father, I know you see these two beautiful kids and they miss their daddy so much. God, I don't know what happened or where he is, but you do Lord. I pray, just like in the story

of the lost sheep, if he is one lost sheep, you help him find his way back to these precious ones with me right now. I also pray for their mama, Emily. Lord you know what struggles she has and how she's hurting inside. I ask that you lay your hand on her and heal that hurt with peace and love. I pray you give them the hope they need for the days ahead and help them to stop dwelling on the pain from the past. Lord, give us what we need to help this beautiful family find their way. They have been a blessing to us in such a short time and I know you are proud of them. Thank you Lord for your many blessings, for my family, for this family and for all the lessons you teach us through your word. I ask all of this in Jesus' name…AMEN.

When Geneva finished praying, Joshua had the most bewildering expression. "Do you think he heard you?"

"Honey he hears us no matter where we are," she replied honestly. "Any time you want to talk to God, just talk. I promise he hears every word."

Just as Geneva started to get up, she heard the sweetest thing coming from Joshua. *"God, tell my daddy I love him."*

Still standing outside the door, Emily heard her precious son speak words to God that spoke to her at the same time. It reached to the very core of her heart, piercing the very part Chris held from the first time they met. Somehow the insecurities she was feeling before, started to dissipate, an incredible moment. There was something spiritual about it in the strangest way, considering she was never that way before. Then she saw Geneva get up. Emily turned and scurried back to her room and shut her door about the time Geneva came back into the hallway. She found her place in bed and laid her head back on the pillow, all the while thinking of the courage and trust her son had to talk to God.

Maybe I should try it, Emily said to herself. *He probably wouldn't hear me if I did,* she continued. Then a tapping came at her window, or at least that's what it sounded like. It came from a few little branches caressing the glass which made it sound like morse code. Deep inside, something told her it was a sign he would hear her, so she took a chance.

"God, it's Emily. I don't know if you remember me or not. I've been pretty messed up for a while now. I know Chris is really messed up. I just need to know if he's okay. I know me and the kids will be fine thanks to these incredible people who are helping us, but I miss my husband and my friend. Anyway God, thank you for listening to me. I know I'm a lost cause, but to hear my friend Geneva, you can find me if I am. Thank you for everything and we'll be talking again soon…AMEN," Emily said, lifting her head after saying that prayer to God.

Somehow, the tapping on the window, started to lull her to sleep. It was like it provided her with reassurance and a rhythm of nature leading her into the next day. Lying in that cozy bed with soft covers over her and a pillow giving her head a soothing place to land, it was a huge blessing. It was a far cry from going place to place, never knowing where you were going to be from day to day. Somehow, in a day's time they went from wandering the streets to finding a kindness in strangers they had never seen before. It didn't take long for her to find peace enough to rest. Never moving once she slipped into a state of slumber, a calmness consumed her, one that was well needed.

The following morning came all too soon, and everyone could hear Geneva holler out to everyone from downstairs. *"Breakfast,"* Of course, Elijah, Ella and Caleb were used to it, but Emily and the kids were tucked comfortably in their beds they didn't want to climb out of. Ella went to help her finish cooking, setting the plates and so forth, when the two kids slowly came dragging up. Still in their pajamas, Katy's hair was going in every direction as was Joshua's, a beautiful sight to see and they sat at the table, doing their best trying to wake up so they could enjoy whatever it was Geneva planned on giving them for breakfast.

"Goodmornin'," Geneva greeted them, wearing that smile God gave her. "You two sleep good?"

"Yes," they both said in unison.

Ella looked at Geneva and couldn't help but get joy out of their response and went over to straighten up the mess on their heads. It wasn't long until Emily came in as well. With arms stretched up in the air, giving a long yawn as she stepped in, she looked rested.

"Smells wonderful," Emily said, putting her arms around the kids.

"Why thank you," Geneva said, steadily stirring her homemade gravy, making sure it didn't burn, and keeping an eye on the biscuits at the same time. "It's about done."

"Mmmmmm Mmmmm," Caleb sounded off, finding his way next to Geneva at the stove. "I sure love coming to visit, Geneva."

"I betcha you do," Geneva said, elbowing him in the side at the same time. "Now get your plate. I'm pullin' these here biscuits out. I know how you like it all hot son-in-law."

"I always tell Ella you're the greatest," Caleb continued, buttering her up best he could. "And make sure you save me an extra biscuit. You know how I love your biscuits."

"Don't you always get plenty?" Geneva asked, pulling the pan from the oven and sitting it down. "And you always get as many as you like."

Emily and the kids sat back and watched them go back and forth, smiling at the show the entire time. Ella was on the other side of Katy and felt like she had to explain about their relationship.

"They always act like this. Mama always knows what Caleb likes and gives it to him, and Caleb tells her what he likes every time. I guess it's a little game they play. One thing's for sure, they love each other," Ella said.

"It's obvious," Emily replied. "It's good to see. We're happy to be here."

Everyone was there except for Elijah, and he had yet to come downstairs. They had fixed everyone's plates already and had one waiting for him. Caleb was over half finished as well as Ella, and Geneva kept glancing up the stairs.

CHAPTER NINE

"**E**lijah James," Geneva yelled out. "You best get down here before Caleb eats all the biscuits."

Even after her calling out to him, Elijah still didn't answer, so she went upstairs to see what was keeping him. At first, she got concerned, but when she opened their bedroom door, she let out a breath of relief when she heard water running in the bathroom. She did her best to sneak up on him, trying not to step on the part of the floor that always creaked. And when she started opening the bathroom door, a fragrance floated toward her. It was an intriguing manly smell of her favorite cologne on him. She had bought it for him months back, but he always said it was overpowering and it might draw too much attention.

She opened the door all the way to find him standing in front of the mirror making that face all men do when shaving, then he ran the razor over the water, tapping it afterward. That's when he noticed Geneva in the mirror, admiring his grooming skills. Her one-of-a-kind smile sparkled when she got closer.

"Didn't you hear me calling you?" she asked, but not in an angry way. "Breakfast is ready. And by the way, you sure do smell good."

Elijah finished, then wiped his face clean and putting on his shirt, "I wanted to go ahead and get dressed so everyone would have a bathroom to use before church. I wanted to make sure the kids got to enjoy a good long bath."

Geneva showed a look of admiration, then went over to the love of her life. She put her hands gently on his face and just stared at him for a moment. "How did I deserve such a sweet man?" she said.

"Wasn't always sweet," he laughed. "But I do try now."

"You don't have to try honey. God changed you and it shows. It was a good thing I had that accident last year. It was in his plan," Geneva said.

"What's the plan for Emily and those kids? I kept waking up last night thinking about what's going to happen to them," Elijah said, showing his sensitive side.

"I don't know sugar. I guess God's the only one who knows and all we can do, is let him use us. And right now, I think that's what he's a doin'. So, let's just take it day by day. Today, they are happy, and for me, it's a win."

They took advantage of such a sweet moment, and Elijah gave Geneva the sweetest kiss then pulled her close, letting an embrace say everything he felt in his heart. Then, footsteps came closer, and Caleb popped his head in. Instead of leaving like most folks would, he had to comment.

"You two up here making out?" Caleb laughed. "We thought something was wrong, so they sent me up here. But I see everything is okay."

"Caleb, don't you ever knock?" Elijah asked, his arms still wrapped around Geneva.

"Door was open," Caleb said. "Just wanted to tell you Ella is heating your breakfast. I know you don't like cold food Pop."

"We'll be right down. And everyone can start getting ready for church. I just wanted to get a head start since so many need to use a bathroom," Elijah said.

Caleb nodded and left with Elijah and Geneva right behind him. When they reached the kitchen, everyone was finished and there was one plate sitting at the table with a cup of coffee. Emily and the kids greeted him with a smile and went upstairs to get ready. He sat down and enjoyed the tasty breakfast Geneva had made. With every bite, he made the same noises as Caleb did, like moaning, but showing how good it was. Geneva had perfected her homemade biscuits and gravy over the years. She always said she watched her mama when she was young and her grandma later on, but she used her own style with a pinch of this and that, a recipe only she could master.

While everyone was getting dressed, Elijah went into the living room and turned the television on one of those evangelistic channels and watched a preacher he had never seen before. With his arms swinging in the air and his voice rising and falling, he got his point across all too well and left Elijah ready to go to their church for a little more Godly learning.

It wasn't long and Caleb came parading down the steps and found his normal spot in the corner of the couch facing Elijah. He was dressed in dark khakis and a starched striped shirt. Around his neck, hung a long silver necklace with a unique cross pendant. It's what stood out the most.

"I don't think I ever saw that necklace Caleb," Elijah commented. "I've never been one to wear jewelry, but I like that."

Caleb lifted the cross and looked at it, "Yes sir, Ella gave it to me. She is so sweet."

"She gets it from me," Elijah laughed.

Another set of steps were heard, and Joshua came around the corner. He went over and plopped down next to Caleb with a grin on his face. He didn't say a word, but he didn't have to. He was simply saying he was glad to be there without making a sound and that was a great feeling for Elijah, knowing he was helping someone.

"Mama G said you might take us fishing," Joshua said to Caleb, his innocent eyes basically asking if he would.

"Well, there is a nice little fishing hole not far from here," Caleb replied. "It's on this property. We can walk there. How about we go after church?"

"Really? You'll take me?" Joshua said, his voice full of excitement.

"I may just go along too," Elijah added. "It's been a piece since I've gone fishing. Sounds like fun. And I betcha one thing for sure, Geneva's going to want to dig up the worms. For some reason she likes them squirming things."

They all found that comical, and were laughing when Geneva walked in. Joshua looked up at her and giggled once more. For some reason, you could tell he had a hard time believing a lady her age would like playing with worms, but she did.

"What are you fellas talkin' 'bout? You talkin' 'bout me?" Geneva asked, noticing them all gazing at her.

"You like worms Mama G?" Joshua snickered.

"You betcha I do," she replied confidently. "Why, we goin' fishin' today? I wouldn't mind cookin' up a mess a fish this evenin'."

"It'd be a shame to catch the fish and not enjoy eating, but me and Ella have to get back home afterwhile. But I'll sure help catch all we can until then," Caleb said, reaching over and tickling Joshua like he did the night before. And as before, that little boys laugh was music to hear, the sound of happiness. Joshua squirmed around like he had ants in his pants and the smile he wore was more beautiful than the most valuable painting because it was truly priceless.

It was almost ten o'clock, and, as usual, Geneva's voice rang through the entire house, summoning everyone to shake their tail feathers. Elijah found her amusing as always, her distinctive personality demonstrating the core of who she was and always would be. Something about her tone and use of unusual country slang, made everyone love her.

It's something Elijah fell in love with from the start and continued to grow year after year.

It didn't take long after Geneva made her announcement for everyone to hurry up, the rest came down looking spiffy. Emily knew they were going to a cowboy church, so she put on a pair of jeans Geneva picked out just for her, along with a beautiful white top with lace trim. Her reddish blonde hair was pulled up with little bits curled and hanging down. Coming down the steps, she looked like a totally different person, one who held confidence.

"Oh, my Heavens," Geneva said. "Don't you look prettier than a newborn calf."

Emily looked at her wondering if that was a compliment, but figured it was considering who was saying it. She was still getting used to such a unique individual. And when she reached the last step, Geneva took her hands and held them out like she was showcasing how nice she looked. Emily started to blush, not being used to anyone saying such kind things to her, then Katy going to her side, hugged her affectionately.

"You look beautiful mama," she said, looking up at her, flashing her long eye lashes.

"Thank you, sweetie," Emily smiled. "And I think you look like an angel."

"Oh mama," Katy said, blushing just like Emily.

"Like mama like daughter," Geneva shook her head, enjoying the sight.

Ella was bringing up the rear and Elijah stood at the front door waiting. One by one, everyone went out single file. The kids wanted to ride with Ella and Caleb and Emily climbed in the back of the car with Elijah and Geneva. When they were all set, Elijah led the way. For some reason, it wasn't as hot as it had been and the breeze blowing that day, made it comfortable outside. As much as Geneva talked about the heat, he was sure she was happy about the way nature changed its mind for the day. And since they were going fishing, it was a welcomed thing.

Geneva started messing with the radio, trying to find what they always listened to on the way to church. Finally, she landed on 103.9 KPGG radio, who always played nothing but country gospel music on Sunday mornings. They played everything from the Statler Brothers to Hank Williams and everything in between, all giving glory to God, and somehow it got them in the right mindset before entering the church. Geneva sat there and sang along with energy, eyes closed and focusing on the message it was giving. Elijah, not much of a singer, just watched, doing nothing but smiling at her.

"I love this station," Emily said. "I guess I've never listened to it on Sundays."

"Oh man, I tell ya honey, it gets me geared up to hear that there Sermon brother Todd has for me. There's somethin' about listenin' to songs of worship," Geneva said, stopping her singing for a moment. "If I'm ever in a bad place, I can listen to this here music and it just fixes everything. Don't get me wrong, things still aren't perfect, but it does give me peace. That crazy music you can't even understand what they're a sayin' does nothin' for me. But give me a song about Jesus…well, there's nothin' like it honey."

"I understand," Emily replied. "It is making me feel better."

"That's God speakin' to ya honey. The thing is, when he speaks to ya, you gotta listen. Some folks don't ever listen. And don't nobody know when God decides to stop talkin' to ya."

Emily glanced back to the car behind them where Joshua and Katy were riding. She could see Caleb and Emma's mouths moving like they were singing. If they were, she knew the kids loved that. The next few minutes, she just enjoyed the ride, as her thoughts wandered here and there, but landing back to the moment at hand. A week earlier, she never would've pictured herself sitting where she was, and she didn't know what tomorrow had to bring. All she knew is her kids were happy and safe.

Elijah turned, exiting off the loop, and up ahead, she saw a huge arena, and when he started down the church drive, she was compelled by the place. It was unlike most churches she had seen. It was a plain metal building with wood columns holding up the roof over the porch. A few picnic tables were sitting around it and people were congregating in groups, talking. Men and ladies alike, had on jeans and boots, topped off with an array of cowboy hats. There was a pasture off to the side with a few horses walking around and Elijah pulled in on the far side of the church close to the fence.

Since they were in somewhat of a drought, the dirt lot, was dry as a bone. Elijah got out and offered a gentleman-like gesture, by opening Emily's door, then ran around to do the same for Geneva. He took Geneva's hand and they both held their bibles in the other. They waited for the others to get there, and when Caleb pulled up and parked, the kids jumped out before they knew it. They ran up to their mama like a ray of sunshine, blinding in the most wonderful way.

"Mama, we sang all the way here," Katy said, bouncing up and down. "And Caleb is funny."

"I could've told you that young'un'" Geneva laughed. "He's always a comedian child, but he's a good egg."

"Thank you, Geneva," Caleb said, walking up about the time she spoke. "You're a pretty good egg yourself."

She gave him a playful nudge and started for the front door. Emily had Joshua on one side of her and Katy on the other, holding their hands. As they made it to the porch, Denny, one of the elders, was standing out front shaking hands with everyone who passed by. The way he greeted people, represented the church in the most perfect way. No matter who it was, he offered the same smile and same positive message. Somehow, everyone could tell it made Emily feel welcome.

Miss Geneva's name was being called out from every direction. Everyone greeted her with hugs. In a sense, it was like she was a celebrity, but the reality was, she had just touched everyone in one way or another. The love in the place was more than obvious, and it was hard not to feel at home. The laid-back atmosphere covered everyone and the music from the church played as everyone entered. Then Katy's attention was shifted almost immediately when she looked to the left after walking in.

"Donuts," Katy said. "Can I have one?"

"Well," Emily started, then Caleb jumped in.

"Come on you two," Caleb nodded, taking their hands. "I think I'll take one too."

Emily couldn't help but shake her head watching her two little ones truly enjoying such attention. Everyone around the table kept telling Joshua how handsome he was and Katy, how beautiful she was. Oddly enough, they didn't shy away, but welcomed such compliments, appearing to enjoy every minute of it.

"Honey, they act like they've been here a hundred times," Geneva said, linking their arms together. "They sure do look happy."

"They do, don't they Miss Geneva? I have to say, it's good to see. I worry about how they feel and what they think about me," Emily said, glancing to Geneva then back to the kids.

"They love you. I can surely tell that honey. Besides, kids are more resilient than you think, sometimes even more than us," Geneva said. "I can't tell you how many times Ella would hurt herself and I'd go crazy. In just a minute, she'd be runnin' and a playin' all over again."

"I sure hope so Geneva because I want my kids to be proud of me," Emily continued. "Right now, I'm not giving them anything to be proud of."

"We're at this here church, aren't we?"

"Yes ma'am," she answered.

"That's somethin' to be proud of honey. You coulda said you didn't want to go and I wouldn't a made you come, but you chose to bring them because you knew they needed it. Deep down, I think you knew you did too," Geneva finished.

All Emily could do, was let out a long sigh in agreement to what Geneva just said and they both looked on as Caleb acted just as much like a kid as the two little ones with him. They all had a mini box of chocolate Yoo-Hoo in one hand, and donut in the other. Their mouths were smack full. With such a small thing, Caleb brightened their day a little bit more.

A friend of Geneva's, Debbie Laster, walked up. Her hair was pinned up and her joyful attitude showed as always. The first thing she did was hug Geneva as everyone else, but then the look in her eye, showed she had a surprise for Geneva.

"Brother Todd isn't here today," she said. "Guess who's preaching?"

Geneva cocked her head sideways, "Well, I guess brother Tony. You know he does one heck of a job too."

"Brother Wallace," Debbie said.

"Good Heaven's, he hadn't done a preachin' here in ages, it seems like. I sure do love Brother Todd, but I love Brother Wallace too. I guess long as we get the word, that's all that matters," Geneva replied.

"Yes ma'am," Debbie said, squeezing her hand and heading back to her seat.

"Who's brother Wallace?" Emily asked.

"Well," Geneva started. "Our pastor Todd learned under brother Wallace. Sometimes it's undeniable 'cause a them phrases he uses. You can tell they came from brother Wallace and kinda got stuck in Todd's head. No matter, they're both Godly men and sure do throw it at ya where ya need it."

Elijah and Ella had already gone to get their seats, a few rows back from the front, and Caleb walked up with the kids. It was picture perfect. Joshua, Katy, and Caleb all had a hint of chocolate lingering around their mouths. Geneva and Emily couldn't help but laugh.

"What?" Caleb asked, looking around to see if they were laughing at someone else.

"Son," Geneva continued laughing, then pointed at his mouth. "In case you get hungry durin' the service, you still got a bit a that there chocolate you can munch on till lunch."

He ran his hand over his mouth then licked it right off, "No sense in wasting good chocolate, huh kids."

Before Emily could grab a napkin, her little ones did the same thing Caleb did, cleaning off every last bit of chocolate left over by licking it off. It was a priceless sight to see. If there ever was any shyness in those two, for whatever reason, it dissipated. Geneva knew they could go to class with the other kids, but for the first visit, she thought it best to let them sit and listen to the sermon.

Geneva looked at her watch and noticed it was about time for church to get started and they all joined Elijah and Ella up front. Elijah was sitting there with his eyes focused steadfastly on the huge wooden cross on the wall behind the stage. He told her one time he was mesmerized by it from the first time he saw it. Geneva always got the feeling he was in his own little spiritual world as he peered at such an incredible sight. And the glowing light behind it, made a statement.

They all got in their seats, but something seemed wrong with Emily. She kept glancing back to where they entered the building with an odd look on her face.

"What is it honey?" Geneva whispered. "What's wrong?"

CHAPTER TEN

Emily started to answer, but then the band started playing. Geneva had already told her about them having a recording artist at their church. Emily was excited to hear him.

"That there is Marlon Sharp," Geneva whispered once more. "I could listen to him sing all day long."

She nodded, acknowledging what Geneva said, and paid close attention to the words in the song they playing. You could tell the upbeat, old-school, country-style music, wasn't what Emily expected to hear, but her feet got to tapping and her hands got to clapping before she knew it. Soon after, the kids joined in. They looked up at her like they were following her lead, and a good lead it was. The song he sang, was *The Lord beat the devil out of me,* and the words cut straight to the point. After that, the congregation joined in on some old hymns done in a southern style, and everyone stood. The words were on a big screen on each side of the stage, so she did her best to keep up. The kids just hummed along, holding her hand the entire time.

When the last song was over, walking up the steps on the right side of the stage, was a tall, slender, older gentleman carrying a bible you could tell he had for quite a few years. His gray hair was perfectly fixed and beautiful, if a man's hair can be beautiful, and there was something about his presence. Emily didn't even know him, but something about him was different. Before he even spoke a word, she felt a peace come over her. Then he started to speak with words more powerful than Emily had ever heard before.

Brother Wallace said, "If there's any one question that I am being asked today," brother Wallace said. "Are we living in the days just before Jesus comes. Are we living in the last days? I don't know, but I can tell you this…that what we're going through with all the turmoil and all the confusion and all of the heartache today, does not mean that the Lord is about to come. Doesn't mean that at all. For some of us, he may come before the sun goes down this evening…see. Jesus says in Matthew twenty-four *Heaven and earth shall pass away, but my word shall never leave you. For no man knoweth the hour, know not not the angel of Heaven, but my father only. For in the days that were before the flood, there were eating and drinking and marrying and giving in marriage until the Lord came and took them all away.* "You see, he could come for you before the sun goes down. So, it's incumbent on each of us to make sure we know the Lord. So, if you get ready and stay ready, then it doesn't matter when God gets ready."

Emily listened attentively, clinging to every word this preacher said, doing her best to take it all in, knowing she didn't end up at that church by accident. She knew this family wasn't taking care of them by accident. A sense of being grateful came over her as she continued to listen to this sermon placed before her. Then, not realizing she was listening to a comedian preacher, he told a story.

"Heard about a boy one time," brother Wallace said. "And he came running into the kitchen and said *mother, mother, mother, is it true we came from dust, and we go back to dust?* She said *that's true son.* He said, *well mama there's either someone coming or someone going under my bed.*"

She sat there letting a grin grace her pretty face and listened on as he talked about when he was watching his little boy one time. He talked about how his son got in trouble and at the dinner table he told him to pray. The boy bowed his head and said "Jesus, help me…to be good. Not real good, just good enough I don't get a whippin'."

Brother Wallace explained further, "You know most of us are like that, aren't we? We don't want to be real good, just good enough to get to Heaven. So, I want to help you do that. If you're not saved, you need to be saved. And if you are saved, you need to live that way."

Those words resonated in Emily's heart and soul. Somehow, it was like he was talking to her. He was directing everything right at her, like an arrow being shot in her direction. Then he asked everyone to turn to James chapter one. Emily didn't have a bible, but Geneva leaned over, sharing hers. They stood together as the preacher asked and he read the scripture. It was so new to Emily, and some of what she was hearing was hard to understand, but at the same time, it made sense. The talk of having new behavior when someone gets saved, living a new life. She found herself swimming in every scripture he read and in every explanation of it. The one thing she realized, was that she didn't have to be perfect.

Every few minutes, Geneva would pat her hand or even give a little wink. And the more talk of new beginnings and living for God, started to work on her. Emily knew her past and the things she had done wrong, but just like the preacher said, those things are in the past. Joshua and Katy sat still next to her not making a sound. Their eyes stayed fixed on the man walking back and forth on the stage in front of them. And when they heard the soft, welcoming music being played toward the end of the service, brother Wallace sent an invitation to everyone there.

Brother Wallace said, "I don't know if you're saved or not. The only person I know is saved, is me. I hope you are. Once you're born again, you know it. God will give you the greatest gift in Jesus. You will never be the same again. Let us pray, *Lord I don't' know who is saved or lost, who wants to be or doesn't want to be. I don't know if those who are here because they were made to come or someone invited them to come…I don't know all of that, but I do know that your will is that everyone be saved. But I pray today, if there is a man a woman, a boy or girl and they don't know if they're saved but they want to be. God, I trust today that your sweet holy spirit will give such a sweet assurance in their hearts, that when we leave here today their life will be changed by asking you to come into their hearts and make them new. I ask you give peace to those who need it and wrap your loving arms around each and every person here. I ask this is Jesus' name…Amen*

When the last *amen* was said, and the band started playing one last song, Emily was greeted by most who passed by, some with a handshake, and some with a surprising embrace from the friendly folks welcoming her. Geneva watched and saw a glimpse of change in her. Brother Wallace walked by, and Emily reached out, tapping him on the shoulder to get his attention.

"Well, hey young lady," brother Wallace said, answering with a smile.

"I…uh, I just want to say I enjoyed the sermon sir," Emily said. "Thank you for…I just wanted to say thank you."

Brother Wallace clung to his old beat-up bible with one hand and extended his other to her, "I can tell you're going through some struggles, but remember to lean on God. They won't seem quite as bad when you do. God bless ya."

Emily nodded after he expressed such a thought to her and watched him walk away in a majestic sort of manner. Still, she could feel what he put out to everyone in the room, a holiness in a sense. His confidence in the word of God spilled over and landed on Emily in a most profound way, something she didn't bargain for, nor expect before they came. The more he talked about being lost and finding your way through Jesus, the more she listened, and it all found its way to her very core. Geneva, with her unique cackle that echoed all around, took the hand of each of the kids and started trotting out, then turning to Emily, motioning her head to *come on.*

Of course, the first thing the kids did, was rush to the table where the donuts were at before church, but it was all gone. Their excitement turned to disappointment instantaneously, but that's when Geneva got down on her knees and looked them right in the eye.

"How 'bout we go grab somethin' to eat?" she said to them, pinching each of their cheeks at the same time. "Then, remember the fishin' thing. Ella and Caleb's gonna stay a bit so we can go fishin'. What do you two think a that?"

That's all it took for them to cheer up in a hurry, and then they scurried outside where there were other children their age running about. Emily stood just staring at Geneva in awe of how she could turn one desperate moment into a moment of excitement. It was impressive and inspiring to watch. Just like brother Wallace, Geneva overflowed with something unique and powerful as well. She had a gift to lift people up.

They went out on the wrap-around porch and sat down at one of the picnic tables right outside the door. The kids were running and playing, and Emily looked down momentarily. Nothing rarely got passed Geneva and her intuition said something was wrong.

"What was it you was lookin' at in the church? You looked bothered by somethin'," Geneva asked.

"Nothing really," Emily said, giving a short pause, not wanting to sound like a crazy person. "I just felt like I was being watched. I know it sounds silly. A few times I felt that way this past week or so, but especially the last two days since I met you folks."

"Well honey, I don't know what to say, but I can promise you somethin'," Geneva replied kindly. "Ain't nothin' gonna happen to you. Long as you're with us, we'll protect you. Better than that, in Deuteronomy, God says to be strong and of good courage. He says don't be afraid for the Lord your God, he is the one who goes with you. It says he will not leave you or forsake you. So, you see Emily, you got all the protection you need."

"Thank you miss Geneva," Emily smiled, nudging her slightly, then seeing how much fun her kids were having.

Ella, Caleb, and Elijah were standing by the door still chatting with church friends, then headed over to where they were sitting. Geneva knew exactly what was going to come out of Caleb's mouth before he ever said a word and she was exactly right. The look in his eyes said it all.

"Are we going to grab lunch somewhere before we go fishing? I don't want you to have to cook Geneva," Caleb said, then turned to Elijah. "You know I can't fish on an empty stomach."

Already getting to know them in only a short time, Emily got tickled from Caleb just being who he was. The kids heard her laughing and ran over, covering their mama with love from every direction. There were hugs and kisses flying all around them and Geneva got a playful look about her. She stood and started at them young'uns tickling them and they took off running. Her age sure didn't show when she was chasing after Joshua and Katy around and around that lot until they were all too tired to take another step.

"Come on," Geneva said, doing her best to catch her breath and wrapping her arms around her two new best little buddies, "Let's go get some vittles. There's that there restaurant on Kings highway that sure 'nuff makes some good home cookin' food. I think it's called Texas Chuckwagon. Anyway, Caleb's right. I ain't cookin' till tonight...fish."

"Amen," Caleb said. "Come on kids. You riding with us again?"

Both kids looked at Emily and without them asking the question, she answered them with a smile and a nod. It didn't take them but a minute to get in the back seat of Ella and Caleb's car and get strapped in. They acted like they were on vacation, enjoying every second, every moment of being around this family. In a way, they looked as though they felt they were family, getting very comfortable.

Elijah, Geneva, and Emily were climbing into the van, and something caught Emily's eye, making her stop and look. The feeling she had earlier, came back full force. Something told her someone was watching. She didn't necessarily have a terrible uneasy feeling as much as a curiosity building a web of confusion in her mind, intertwining the many thoughts being wrangled inside her head.

"You gettin' in?" Geneva said, waiting for Emily, then giving a short chuckle. "You know Caleb don't like waitin' for his vittles."

"Yes ma'am," Emily said, finding her place.

"Oh shucks, don't call me ma'am. Makes me feel like an old woman," Geneva bantered.

Elijah couldn't help but take a glimpse in her direction when she said that, but he didn't dare comment. Geneva was a Godly woman, but she had a mean streak a mile wide, and he wouldn't dare get her riled up. In the meantime, Emily kept looking in the direction of where she would swear, someone was looking her way. With so many people coming and going, it was hard to know if it was her imagination or if it was really someone there.

Elijah followed Caleb and Ella and pulled onto the loop. It wasn't that far away, and when they pulled into the restaurant, one unique thing about it, was the wagon lifted way up in the air in front of the place, by the road. It was an attention getter to say the very least. Caleb whipped into the first parking place he came too and got out, opening the door for the kids, taking their hands on the way inside. For it to be right after church, the crowd of folks hadn't made it in yet, probably since they let out a few minutes earlier than normal.

They went inside and found Ella, Caleb, and the kids sitting at a round table in the left corner. Caleb was already aggravating the kids and their laughter was like the sweetest sound rumbling throughout the place. After looking at the menu for a few minutes, a young lady walked up, pad in hand. Her pretty, blonde hair was pulled up and her friendly nature was more than obvious. Geneva noticed a big sparkly diamond ring on her left hand. In the light, it was almost blinding, kind of like that young lady's smile.

"Looky there," Geneva said, gently touching the waitress's hand with the ring on it, shining in all its glory. "Somebody sure does love you honey."

The gleam in her eyes was prominent, and the waitress lifted it up where the light could show every single bit of glitter that ring displayed. "Yes ma'am, I sure hope so. I just got married a few weeks ago. My name is Amber."

"Hang on to 'im honey. This sweet man I got right here is good to me, but he ain't never liked pickin' out jewelry. He does lots of other things though. It don't matter anyways. Always remember honey, it's love that's important. All that other stuff is just extry," Geneva replied. "What's good today?"

Amber rattled off the specials of the day along with the vegetables and desserts like a pro, and everyone could tell Caleb's mouth was watering just from listening to such talk. After everyone made their choices and she went off to put the order in, it was like half the town started coming in, quickly filling the place. There were only two waitresses working, but they were on their toes, taking and bringing out orders quick as you please.

While waiting on their food, their conversation went from the church service to fishing and everything in between. The kids were ready to grab them a pole and head to the pond. There was a twinkle dancing around in both their eyes just talking about it. Still, Emily looked a little distant. It was obvious her mind was in another place. All Geneva knew, was that she would have to wait until the kids went off with Caleb before they could really sit down and talk.

"Now that was good," Caleb said after taking the last bit on his plate, then leaning back and putting his hands on his stomach. "I bet I won't be hungry for a week."

Without any hesitation, everyone there found his words comical, knowing that was far from the truth. When they were all finished, Elijah paid the bill and left a hefty tip. Before they walked out, Amber stopped to thank them for coming in. Her kind disposition was very rare and so welcomed.

"Remember what I told you honey," Geneva said, squeezing Amber's hand sweetly. "Don't lose the love. I promise that's the key."

Amber gave an appreciative grin and nodded as to answer, showing how much it meant that she took the time to give her such sweet advice. Before they reached the car, it's like a light went off in Geneva's head. She did as always when she would have an idea. She commenced to stuttering and stammering.

"Hey you guys, let's stop by that center downtown and see how it's a comin' along. I bet Terry and Sherry are there," Geneva said, looking giddy at the thought of just going by there.

With no objections, Elijah led the way. When they reached downtown, the decline in the buildings was noticeable, but many were being redone and turned into one thing or another. To look at it all, most buildings were being occupied by event places, clubs and so forth. It was a little scary to think that the place families used to go to spend time together and shop, would end up a place to party and drink, but then again, times had changed.

When they pulled up in front of the building, Terry and another guy were unloading something from the back of his truck. Sherry was holding the door open and waved when she saw them park. From the back, you could tell the guy helping Terry was a mess. His clothes were dirty and he was a mite skinny. He didn't look like he had strength enough to lift anything, but he was trying.

Emily looked up and noticed the man as well and instantly started getting upset. Her breaths got faster and faster and she started to cry. "It can't be," she said.

CHAPTER ELEVEN

For a moment, Emily acted like she'd seen a ghost, trembling and shaking, along with tears finding their way down her cheeks.

"What in Heaven's sake is wrong darlin'?" Geneva said, turning and reaching back to console her.

"I think that's Chris," Emily said, her words somewhat muffled from crying. "I can't go in. I don't want the kids to go in. I don't know what to say to him."

"But..." Geneva started.

Before they knew it, Caleb had already gotten the kids out and were walking into the building. Emily wiped her tears and jumped out of the car and followed behind Caleb. Of course, Elijah wasn't such a fast mover, but Geneva's get up and go, was still there, and she was inside before she knew it. Terry and the guy helping were already inside placing, what appeared to be the last piece of furniture that would fit in the room. The man's back was still to them, and Emily held tight to Joshua and Katy, still flustered and confused. When he turned facing them, she let out a sigh of relief.

The man standing before them, had on long shorts covered in wrinkles and a black pocket t-shirt graced with a few holes here and there. He wore an old cap that was tattered to where it was frayed on the edges of the rim. The scruff on his face, almost reaching the description of a beard, was misshapen, but there was something about his eyes that showed sincerity and kindness. Geneva couldn't stop looking into his eyes. They were identical to hers in a way, clear as a summer sky, but holding sadness amid them.

The man came closer as Terry followed behind, clapping, and rubbing his hands together to knock off whatever dirt remained. "I'm Jackson Duke," he said, tipping his cap as he addressed everyone. "But most folks just call me Jax."

"Yep," Terry jumped in. "This boy here is a worker. He's gonna be a great addition over here at Branches of Hope Community Center."

"You picked a name? Terry, oh my goodness, I don't think you coulda come up with a better name if you'd a tried," Geneva said, surprise and delight oozing from every ounce of her.

Terry looked at Jax, then leaned over and whispered something. Soon after, Jax went to the back wall and brought back something rolled up. From the way it looked, it was big and when he unrolled it, there lay a brand spankin' new sign for such an amazing place. On each side of the beautiful vinyl sign was a picture of a tree with colorful branches. At the end of every branch was an inspirational word like hope, love, believe, faith, pray and more. At the bottom, below the name of the place, it read *A promise of hope for all who enter.*

Not a word was spoken as every eye focused on every detail of the sign and what it all meant to the community. Terry explained how the branches signified the people reaching out to those in need. Those same people are the ones who offer the hope, love, faith and even more.

"And that phrase at the bottom," Terry said, peering at it without ceasing. "Is about God's promise to us and how we're here to give people hope through the promises he gives in the word."

"Oh, good gracious, these here allergies done got my eyes a waterin' again," Geneva said, wiping her eyes, knowing all too well, her emotions got the best of her.

Terry was amused by Geneva and her ways, always a breath of fresh air anytime she was around. Then, he went and talked to Emily and the kids. They sat down at the closest table with chairs all the way around it. Terry must've been telling them jokes because those young'uns were laughing every time he spoke. Since there was enough room, they all went to join them.

"Come on Jax," Geneva said, motioning, but he didn't move a muscle.

"I better keep working," he said, lowering his head slightly.

"Nonsense," she replied quickly. "I'm a tellin' you to join us. You can ask Elijah here. When I say somethin', I mean it."

She didn't have to say another word. Jax followed her and they took up every chair around the large round table. There was a crisp white tablecloth covering it with a small candle in the middle to give it some decor.

"I've had help today," Terry said. "We had this other fella who walked in and just started helping. I didn't get his name, but he looked like he was in a bad situation, so I gave him a few bucks and he left a little bit later. I wish I knew where he went off to. I didn't get a chance to get his story. That's what we're here for. I feel like I fell down on the job."

"I'm so proud of you," Elijah said, patting Terry on the back. "I never could have come up with an idea like this, but I'm glad you did, and I'm sure that guy will come back if he's in as bad a shape as you say."

"Terry's a nice man," Jax chimed in. "He saw I needed help and, well he didn't hesitate to help me. Most folks wouldn't do that."

"That's just how Terry is," Eli responded. "Long as I've known him, he's been one of the best guys I've met."

Joshua kept fidgeting in his seat, squirming left to right and looking at everyone, but more toward Caleb. He acted like he had ants in his pants and finally, he spoke up.

"We going fishing Caleb?" he sounded off. "I bet I catch some."

"Little man," Caleb answered, getting up. "I'm ready whenever you are."

Joshua's anticipation showed in the expression on his face and body language, dancing around like he was standing on hot coals. Katy was looking forward to it as well, but she carried herself with a little more patience and never let go of her mama's hand.

"I guess we best be goin' so these young'uns here can learn how to bait a hook," Geneva said.

"Bait a hook?" Katy said, wearing a frightening expression. Her nose curled up and eyes squinched, it was obvious she didn't want any part in touching a squirming worm.

"Why sure," Geneva said. "If you're a gonna fish, you gotta learn to bait that there hook. I learned that when I was a little girl. Shoot, my daddy made me bait my hook every time. After a while, I didn't mind them ole' worms. You won't either."

Katy didn't lose that dreadful look even after hearing Geneva tell her little story. Terry and the rest got tickled from her reaction and Joshua was still running around, anxious to get going. Then, Terry heard something and look toward the door.

"Hey," Terry called out, noticing a man peek in, then disappear. "That was the guy from this mornin', I think."

Terry trotted quickly to the door, trying to catch up with him, but when he got outside, no one was there. He looked in every direction and for a minute, got to thinking maybe he just imagined it, then went back inside.

"I would have sworn that was him," Terry said, showing concern for a man he didn't know. "Did you see him Jax?"

"No sir," Jax replied.

"Well, I guess he'll find his way back one day. I hope," Terry said.

"Oh honey," Geneva jumped in. "He will. At least he's reachin' out. That's a start my friend. I guess we're headed home to take these kids on a fishin' adventure."

Jax told everyone how much he enjoyed meeting them and walked them to their car along with Terry. Geneva stopped before she got in the car and looked Jax in the eye once more and silently said a prayer for him. She gave him a quick wink and a wave, and they were on their way. There was no question that Ella and Caleb were answering a thousand questions from the kids about fishing, and when they pulled up to the house, both kids jetted out of the car and ran to the door. They waited for Elijah to unlock it, then sprinted upstairs.

It was getting close to one-thirty which left them most of the afternoon to give the kids their first experience at the pond. Elijah offered Caleb some more suitable clothes to put on and he quickly went and changed. Geneva and Ella went to the shop and grabbed enough poles for everyone as well as the tackle box with dozens of colorful lures. For some reason, Elijah thought he was a fishing pro, and to watch him fish, he acted like it. The problem was, he never did catch too much.

"We're ready," the kids hollered, running out of the house behind Caleb.

They both had on shorts, a t-shirt and a pair of plain tennis shoes Geneva and Sherry had bought them. Katy had her hair pulled up in a ponytail, and she was cute as a button. It was only a minute until Emily came outside as well, stopping at the top of the steps and watching Caleb horseplaying around with the kids. If anyone had pulled up, they would've thought Caleb was crazy, flapping his arms, making faces, and doing anything he could to amuse the youngsters whirling around him.

About that time, they heard Elijah start up the side-by-side and reb the engine much as he could. Then he came rolling toward them. The pond on their property wasn't far off, but Elijah loved driving that thing.

"Who's riding with me?" he announced, coming to a stop right before he reached Caleb.

"Me…me…" the kids said in unison.

"How 'bout you fellas take the kids on down there and find a spot? I think me, Emily and Ella might just walk," Geneva said. "And don't be tellin' these little'uns stories about how many big fish you done caught. When they see you a fishin', they'll know they're just stories."

All Elijah and Caleb could do, was shake their heads. They loaded the fishing poles and tackle box and got the kids secured in their seats. Katy rode up front with Elijah and Joshua climbed in next to his buddy Caleb. From the minute those two met, they were like peas and carrots as it was said in a movie once. It's like they had known each other forever.

As they drove off and the dust spun around behind them, Geneva picked up a small pail and tool by the flower bed in case she found a good spot to dig up some worms. She knew it would give them some girl time to talk and it was well needed. It wasn't a long walk, but long enough to be able to get to know each other a little more. Emily, wearing a pair of faded Jeans she got on their shopping trip, looked like a real country girl with her hands in the front of her jeans pockets as they started on the walk to the pond.

"So," Ella started. "Tell us more of your story. You know you kind of left us on the edge."

"You sure did honey," Geneva agreed. "So, what happened to Chris?"

Emily looked up at the beautiful blue sky and then around at the remarkable scenery. "We were happy. Chris was a great dad and Katy was a 'daddy's girl'," she said. "When Joshua was born, I swear that man couldn't wipe the grin off his face for anything in the world. He was so proud. He kept telling me Josh was going to be a big football star or baseball player."

"Oh, honey, that's so special," Geneva said.

"It was Miss Geneva," Emily smiled, looking up at the sky once more. "I spent a lot of time just watching him with those two. Caleb reminds me of him. He played with the kids like he was a kid himself and that was fine with me. Hearing their laughter was the most wonderful sound in the world, but…"

Emily stopped talking for a minute. Ella and Geneva didn't push her to continue but were waiting to hear more. Then she kept going, but somehow her demeanor began to change, from remembering something wonderful to remembering something disheartening.

"Chris started a new job about six months back, and that's when he started to change a little at a time," Emily said, trying her best not to cry as she spoke.

"Change how?" Ella asked.

"He started coming home later. He would tell me he had a late client or that they had a meeting, but after a while, I knew he was lying," Emily resumed. "It had been a long time since either of us had messed with or even thought about pills and drugs, but I still remembered the signs. And I started seeing those signs in him."

"Like what honey?" Geneva inquired respectfully. "What was different?"

"To be honest," Emily said. "He wouldn't look me in the eye, and he started acting so erratic he was scaring the kids.

That wasn't like Chris. He never would've done anything to scare the kids. He loved them."

"Good gracious, I wonder what happened," Geneva said out loud, not necessarily directing it to anyone.

"Miss Geneva, he didn't start acting like that until he started that job. It makes me wonder if the people he worked with were pressuring him to do things he knew was wrong. That's the only thing I can think of to be honest. We both came so far from where we started and I was so angry at him," she kept on. "Then one day, everything blew up. He came home from work, and I knew he was really messed up. When the kids tried to run up to hug him, he pushed them away and Joshua fell."

"I'm so sorry baby," Geneva said, slowing down and putting her arm around Emily as she told them her story.

"I had to tell him to leave," Emily said, her emotions taking over. "I couldn't let the kids go through that. I didn't want to go through that. And I didn't know what we were going to do because we were already almost two months late on rent."

"So, he left?" Ella asked.

"He did," Emily said. "And the following morning there was a note on the floor by the front door."

"What'd it say honey?" Geneva asked.

Emily took in a deep breath and slowly blew it out, then stopped walking. She turned facing them and closed her eyes and recited that note like it was etched in her mind.

My sweet Emily,

I know I am a disappointment to you because I am a disappointment to myself. I can't allow myself to be around our beautiful kids and be like this. It's not right. It's not fair to you or my babies. So, for now, I need to get better. I will not bring you down with me. You deserve better than this and I won't come back until I can be who you deserve. Give the kids a kiss for me and tell them how much I love them. I love you and please forgive me.

LOVE,
CHRIS

Neither Geneva nor Ella had any words. Absorbing such an emotional note, one that changed the course of Emily's life instantly, was hard to swallow. The pain it inflicted on her, was easy to see and hard to watch as she relived it in front of them. Still, no one said anything, but Geneva just went and gave Emily a shoulder to cry on. She rested her head on Geneva and let out the aching she had been holding inside ever since the love of her life left.

"You have to forgive him honey," Geneva said.

"Forgive him for leaving me?"

"No Emily," Geneva answered in the most peaceful way. "Forgive him because that's what the bible says to do."

"What does it say Miss Geneva?" Emily asked, curious.

"Well honey, in Matthew Jesus explains how many times we oughta forgive folks. He says we don't need to forgive folks seven times but seventy times seven. In other words, always forgive. I know it's hard. Dad blame it honey, there's been times I wanted to kill Elijah, but God had to stop me."

In the oddest way, that last thing Geneva said, drew a smile out of Ella and Emily. A conversation that started as serious and awkward, ended up something different. Somehow, Geneva's way of talking found a ray of light in a dark storm. Then, without warning, Geneva got a new energy about her and took four or five steps ahead and got down on her knees with her pail and little shovel.

"Oh, by golly girls, there's gonna be some big ole night crawlers right here," she said, beginning to dig. "What'd I tell ya. Looky here at these fat ones. Good for fishin'."

Geneva lifted a huge worm that had to be at least four inches long. That thing was twisting and turning, but all it did, was put a smile on that woman's face. She shoveled a whole pail of worms and dirt and came back to her feet. She handed the pail to Ella while she wiped her hands off on her jeans, then took it back. Emily couldn't help but soak up the heavenly spirit floating around Geneva. Something about the way she handled situations was like magic. One-minute things could be grim, but the next, they seemed better.

"I hear them," Geneva said. "You girls here them up ahead? They're on the other side of this here hill past them bushes. I betcha them lures ain't doin' worth a flip, even though Elijah thinks they're better than worms. I swear girls, you can't tell that man nothin'. He's stubborn as an ole' goat."

Ella and Emily both paused and looked at Geneva in a peculiar way and started to laugh, trying to say silently that Geneva had a stubborn nature in her that wouldn't quit. She got the message and made that face as to say *just shut up* and keep moving forward. When they got through the last set of bushes before reaching the pond, at first it was giggling and talking they heard, but then Caleb yelled out. His voice screeched like they had never heard before.

CHAPTER TWELVE

Emily's motherly instincts felt threatened, and she shot through the bushes fast as she could, her heart racing in her chest. Geneva and Ella followed close behind and when they set eyes on Caleb and the kids, Joshua was holding tight to his pole. He had it lifted in the air and Caleb's arms were around him, yelling out to hold on. The uneasy feeling instantly vanished and was replaced by a beautiful sight. Her little boy was having a grand old time with his new friend.

A few more tugs on the pole, and up out of the water came a good size catfish. Elijah made sure to hold onto Katy while showing his enthusiasm for Joshua's first catch. Caleb grabbed the fish, showed Joshua how to take out the hook and put it in the bucket next to them. Joshua was so thrilled, he wrapped both arms around Caleb and hugged him with gusto.

"I got some big ole nightcrawlers, but it looks like you don't need'em?" Geneva said, her, Ella, and Emily walking to the pond.

"We dug up a few," Caleb said. "Me and Pop both know how you women like to talk and figured if we waited for you, it'd be a while."

Geneva turned her attention to Caleb trying to look angry, but it quickly turned to her contagious smile instead. Emily went over by Katy and found a spot to sit and watch. Geneva on the other hand, sat on the small dock that extended about ten feet into the pond, dangling her feet.

"You better hope no gators are roaming around Geneva," Elijah said, aggravating. "They'd eat you up for sure as sweet as you are honey."

She whipped her head around quick as you please and gave a look he knew was coming. One thing he loved to do, was aggravate that woman. Just her expressions were enough to amuse him, and the kids laughed at the way she looked back.

Emily had the bucket of worms and she sat down next to Katy by the water. She picked up the pole and reached to get a worm. A few times they both picked one up and would drop it right after, making the most dreadful faces. Since Ella was raised fishing and baiting her own hook since she was old enough to hold a pole, she went to help. Although she did her best to show them how, in the end, she baited the hook for them. It was obvious Katy was a true girly girl and wanted nothing to do with holding creepy crawly things, and apparently her mama was the same.

Geneva already had her line in the water and kept her eyes on that bobber like her life depended on it. The sun was beating down, but the gift of a nice breeze, made it bearable. It wasn't long and that red and white bobber went completely under, and she began moving left and right, lifting the line, but trying not to lose what was on the other end.

"You have one Mama G," Joshua squealed, leaning over, and watching attentively to see how big of a whale she was going to pull in.

"I know it honey," Geneva said, almost out of breath from fighting the line. "I think she's a big one."

Finally, after a few minutes of pull and tug, Geneva lifted out one of the smallest fish they had seen. Her mouth flew open in disbelief that something so tiny could have fought so hard. Again, Elijah got tickled by her and started to say something, but Geneva and her ESP felt it coming and stopped him in his tracks.

"God don't want me to catch all the good'uns. He's savin'em all for these here young'uns," Geneva said quickly.

One fish after another, filling up the bucket they had, was more than enough for a nice supper, and they got everything loaded up into the side-by-side. The kids loved riding in it, so they hopped in. Elijah and Caleb opted to let the girls take it to the house and they would walk. Geneva loved driving it, although she didn't do it much, and she jumped into the driver's seat as Ella and Emily each put a little one in their lap.

"See you at the house," Geneva said, waving as they drove off.

When they were out of sight, Elijah and Caleb headed in the direction of home. It wasn't far, but far enough considering it was going on ninety-five degrees, and they were both sweating like crazy.

"Them kids are something special," Caleb said. "I don't know how any man could just walk away from his family like that."

"Well son, we don't know what happened. Even if we did, it's not our place to judge anybody. God's the only one who can judge. I swear, from the minute Geneva came back to me after she was attacked, she has done her best to drill it into my head. It was somewhere in Matthew, I think, where it talks about you judge folks and you'll be judged. I'll be honest though, it's a tough one to master. It's hard not to give your opinion of what someone should or shouldn't do."

"I hear ya Pop," Caleb said. "I just don't get it."

"Maybe we're not supposed to," Elijah replied, his faith standing tall. "Maybe we're only supposed to be here to give Emily and her kids a place to land. That's what we've done, so I guess we've done our job."

Caleb couldn't help but stare at Elijah, remembering how he was back when they had no clue where Geneva was, or if she'd ever come back. He never would've said something like he just did. In fact, he would've been the most judgmental. It was amazing the change in him from the inside out.

"Pop, you're different, ya know?" Caleb said, patting Elijah on the back. "I'm proud of you. I used to be the one trying to get you to think right and now, well…now you're the one changing my thinking."

"All I know is, the more positive I think, the better things are," Elijah grinned. "And I want to help this family all I can. And Geneva, well, she was invested in them from the minute she saw them at the center."

They talked the rest of the way, which was only across the pasture, and the girls and Joshua, were on the front porch drinking some cold lemonade. Ella and Geneva were sitting in the swing with the kids and Emily was standing by the railing looking out at them. Her demeanor was so different from the first time they met. Somehow the uneasy feeling she showed, turned to more of a calmness and peace.

"What took you fellas so long?" Geneva asked.

"It's a little hot out here honey," Elijah said, making his way up the steps.

"Then I guess you guys want a glass of Lemonade," Emily said sweetly, handing them a glass.

With the first drink, the noises they made said it tasted great, especially on such a hot day. Caleb downed his in two gulps, but Elijah nursed his for a few minutes, savoring the sweet mixture one sip at a time. Geneva entertained the kids with her little stories and unique laugh after each one.

Elijah and Caleb went inside to get cleaned up. In the meantime, Geneva toted the bucket of fish out back and started cleaning them. The kids looked on with a disgusted expression on their faces. When she'd finish one and throw it in a clean bucket, she'd start on another. Ella didn't mind baiting a hook, but she never was one to do the cleaning even though Geneva tried many times to teach her. Emily stayed as far back as possible. The smell of the fish was less than desirable, but she could tell her kids were amazed by that woman who took them in, no questions asked. It seemed like everything she did or said, their attentions were on her.

"Woman," Elijah bellowed out as he opened the door to the back porch. "Why are you doin' that? You know I always clean the fish."

"You was takin' too long," Geneva said, whipping her head around, giving him a glaring look. "B'sides, I figured Ella and Caleb might want a little of what they helped catch, so I just went on and done it. Is that okay with you? It kept you from havin' to get your hands all nasty again…right?"

Elijah didn't have any words. By this time in their marriage, he figured one thing out…she was always right, and he better believe that, or she would let him have it. So, he just took the cleaned fish inside and started preparing them.

"I guess one more hour won't hurt anything. Right Ella?" Caleb said, picking up Joshua and scurrying inside.

"You two seem like ya'll are great together," Emily said. "I envy you."

"We have our good days and our bad days like most couples, but he's a good man. He's a Godly man and he sure does love your two angels. I swear if he could run off with them, he would. It's a shame we haven't had kids yet. He'd be a great dad," Ella replied showing how blessed she felt to have Caleb.

"It's not too late," Emily said. "And he would be a terrific dad and I think you would be an incredible mom. Don't give up. You can do anything you set your mind to. Isn't that what Miss Geneva would say?"

"Now that's the kind of talk I like to hear from you," Ella replied, then leaned over and gave Emily an encouraging hug. "Come on, let's go help them in the kitchen. I know how antsy Caleb gets when he's hungry."

Katy held her mama's hand going inside, but when they reached the living room, she jetted to join Caleb and Joshua on the couch. Caleb was reading a story and Katy climbed next to them and listened in, snuggling close as she could get.

"See kids, there was this Philistine champion fighter named Goliath. He was a big fella. He was over nine feet tall and wore a full armor. He came out every day, for forty days, challenging the Israelites to fight. No one wanted to take him on. He was constantly provoking the armies of Israel and none of the Hebrew soldiers wanted to face such a giant of a man. Then there was David," Caleb said.

"Who was David?" Joshua asked, his curiosity peeking out.

"Who was David? Well, I'll tell you who David was. He was just a teenager, but you see, that giant Goliath, really offended him. When it came to people talking bad about God and God's people, well, David wasn't having any of that."

"What happened?" Katy joined in.

Continuing the story, "David was so enthusiastic about defending the Lord's name, he went after him. All he had was a staff, a sling and a pouch full of stones, five I think it was, but there was something he had that was most important."

"What? What?" Joshua asked intensely.

"See kids, David had the power God gave him. He had so much faith, God empowered him with strength, and he went and killed that big ole Goliath. When he did, the Philistines scattered all over in fear. David proved his bravery and after that, he was called 'man after God's own heart'."

"Is that true Caleb?" Katy asked sincerely, peering at him with her brilliant green eyes. "What does it mean?"

Emily stood in the entryway and listened in, waiting to see what Caleb came up with, knowing it would probably help her path of thinking as well. It wasn't long before he picked up where he left off.

"Well, it pretty much means that it doesn't matter how little you are, you can overcome anything if you trust in God. He'll give you all the strength you need to fight a hundred Goliaths," Caleb said, putting his arms around both kids and bringing them in for a bear hug.

I can overcome anything, Emily muttered softly to herself, thinking of that story Caleb so sweetly took the time to tell her kids. He didn't know he was telling her a story as well, one that made her think.

Unexpectedly, the kids darted by her and headed straight into the kitchen. The smell of fish beginning to fry, was enough to draw their attention, leaving Caleb in the living room by himself. Emily went and joined him, sitting across from him in the wingback chair. She was quiet for a minute, but Caleb could tell she wanted to say something.

"I heard the story you told the kids," she started. "Quite a story."

"Yes, it was," Caleb responded strongly. "I just wanted to make sure they know they're stronger than they think. You're never too young to learn that."

"What about somebody older?" Emily asked, smiling right after.

"You're stronger than you think too," Caleb said. "I don't think you believe you can do better, but you can. Just like in the story I told the kids, it has lots of lessons we can learn."

"Like what?" Emily asked, grasping for answers to the many questions she had.

Caleb looked away and then back to her, "I think you underestimate yourself because maybe you're not sure what you believe in. See Emily, if you let your fear be stronger than your self-belief and faith, you're finished before you get started."

"I don't know what I believe," she replied sadly.

Caleb stood and went over to her, "When you figure that out, your life will start changing for the better. And you have plenty of folks here who care about you and the kids."

"Anybody ready for fish?" Geneva hollered out, her voice carrying, filling every inch of that house.

Caleb extended his hand to Emily, "Shall we go partake of some good ole home cooked fried fish?"

"We shall," Emily answered, grasped his hand and smiled inside and out, their conversation being something she truly needed.

When they stepped in the kitchen, the kids were already sitting at the table as Geneva put their plates in front of them. They started to grab a piece of fish and Geneva stopped them.

"You young'uns gotta wait until we say the blessing. Katy, would you like to say the blessing?" Geneva said.

"I will Miss Geneva," Emily spoke up, surprising everyone. "If it's okay."

"Honey, be my guest," Geneva said, then bowed her head as did everyone else.

Emily wasn't sure what she was going to say, but suddenly, the words came to her. *Thank you God, for this meal and thank you for these kind people who have been so giving to me and my kids. I don't know where we would be without them. And God, thank you for sending them. I know you sent them… AMEN.*

Although her prayer was short and sweet, Geneva began wiping a few tears finding a path down her cheeks, her blue eyes shining bright. Ella found her emotions overflowing as well, and Caleb, he just turned his face away trying to hide his reaction. Elijah just stood there with a smile on his face.

"Honey, I couldn't have said a better prayer if I'd a wanted to," Geneva said. "How 'bout we all dig in?"

That's all Geneva had to say and everyone else fixed their plate. Elijah and Caleb took theirs into the living room. Joshua had his fish and fries ate up before they knew it and Katy wasn't far behind him. It was obvious that Geneva was pleased by the way she watched them take each bite. She got so much joy doing for them, she almost didn't eat much herself.

After a while, everything they cooked up, was gone, every piece. The kids ate to their hearts desire and looked worn out. Geneva wasn't sure if it was from fishing or eating, or both. Ella looked up at the clock and then to Caleb.

"I guess we need to be going," Caleb said, going around and hugging everyone.

"Do you really have to go?" Joshua asked, looking down and pouting.

Caleb gave his contagious smile and stepped slowly, then tickling Joshua as he lifted him in the air, "I'll be back Joshua. I promise."

"But...what if you don't?" Katy asked.

Caleb kneeled where he could look them in the eye, put an arm around each one and gave them a wink. "You couldn't get rid of me if you tried."

Those two covered him up like a warm blanket, hugging him tightly. Somehow, in such a short time, Caleb and those two kids built a bond that was unbreakable. Somehow, Caleb knew they were supposed to meet this beautiful family for more than one reason.

"You ready to go?" Ella asked.

"We'll be back," he told the kids, giving them one more quick hug.

When they left, Joshua looked gloomy, unlike the way he looked earlier in the day, and there was nothing anyone could do. It was obvious he didn't want to see Caleb leave. Emily took the kids upstairs to get a bath and to wind down for the night while Geneva and Elijah cleaned the kitchen. As they finished the last few plates and put them away, Geneva wasn't talking at all. To say the very least, that was unusual, and Elijah knew something was on her mind. He didn't press, but he figured she'd open up when she was ready.

They went upstairs and got ready for bed. It had been a long day, and Geneva still wasn't saying much of anything. She went to tell Emily and the kids goodnight and came right back. They both climbed in bed and rested their heads on their comfy pillows. All he heard was her breathing, heavier than normal, letting out long sighs.

"Alright Geneva, what's wrong?" Elijah voiced. "I know something's wrong. You're never quiet."

She cut her eyes to him briefly then looked straight ahead. "My heart goes out to that little Joshua. I know he was thinkin' Caleb wasn't comin' back 'cause his daddy didn't."

"But there's nothing we can do about that," Elijah whispered quietly. "All we can do is be there for them. Isn't that what we're supposed to do?"

"I have to do more," Geneva said. "Somethin' tells me their daddy is around somewhere, we just don't see'im."

"I don't get your thinkin' sometimes. We're helping Emily and the kids. Isn't that enough?" Elijah continued.

"No, it's not enough," Geneva said, sounding aggravated because she couldn't figure out what to do. "Gettin' this family back together would be enough."

"Now how do you figure you'll do that?"

"I'm gonna pray about it. He'll show me the way," she said confidently.

He smiled, then pulled her over to him, "You're right again Geneva. He helped me find you. I suppose nothing is impossible."

"I can do all things through Christ who strengthens me…right honey?" she finished.

Elijah kissed her on the forehead, and they found rest from a full day of activities. They might not have acted like it did them in, but at the end of the day, their bodies sure spoke something different. In only a few moments, sleep swept them away, rejuvenating them for whatever the next day held.

Geneva began to toss and turn. Instead of landing in a place of peace, her subconscious dropped her off somewhere else.

CHAPTER THIRTEEN

She opened her eyes and appeared to be standing in a dark alley. In a small glimpse of light, stood Joshua and a shadow was in front of him.

"Daddy don't leave me. Please don't leave me," Joshua pleaded with urgency.

He was reaching out his hands, but the shadow of a person, never reached back and was suddenly gone. Joshua's cries were louder than the biggest clap of thunder and his tears cried a river that wouldn't stop.

"It's okay Joshua," Geneva kept saying, but he couldn't hear her. "It's okay Joshua, I'm here."

"Why did my daddy leave us?" Joshua cried out, his pain panning out and filling the entire space.

"Joshua…Joshua," Geneva cried out to him.

Abruptly, Geneva was awakened by Elijah leaning over her. It was still dark, not even morning yet, but the tears that filled her eyes were a release of her worry for that child. Every thought, every concern she was feeling when she closed her eyes, directed her to a nightmare of a child longing for his daddy.

"Geneva," Elijah said, shaking her. "Joshua's fine. He's asleep. What were you dreaming?"

"I…I don't want to talk about it Elijah. Just go back to sleep. I'm sorry I woke ya," she said, turning back over, trying her best not to find herself back in that same dark alley once more.

The following morning, Geneva prayed a long prayer, asking that God take away all the uncertainty and worry.

She prayed to find a peace inside so she could help Emily and the kids find the same. Afterward, she felt the uneasiness lift. Something she always did, was worry about everyone, but at the same time, she had to find a way to not worry, but ask how to remedy whatever the situation. The only way she knew how to do that, was talk to God. For a brief moment the night before, she found herself in a weak moment, long enough to let something dark wiggle it's way in, something she didn't want to let happen again.

Elijah came out from taking a shower and sat on the side of the bed. He didn't say anything, but just leaned down and kissed his beloved Geneva on the forehead. It was his little way of telling her he was there for her to talk to if she wanted. She smiled back at him and rested her hand on his, smiling in return of such a sweet gesture.

Downstairs, the telephone started to ring, and Elijah jumped up and scurried down to catch it before it stopped. Usually no one called them before nine or ten in the morning, so Elijah figured it must be important. He snatched up the receiver, "Hello."

"Eli," Terry said. "Rise and shine. I know you wasn't still sleeping lazy bones."

Elijah laughed, "Terry you know I'm an early riser. Now Geneva's still laid up, but I figure when them kids get up, that'll be it. She'll be running around here like a banty rooster whipping up a breakfast fit for a king. What's going on with you so early today?"

"Well, I was thinkin' Eli. I know Emily could use the money, and I could use the help at the Branches of Hope Center," Terry said, somewhat beating around the bush. "I thought maybe she might want to come work over here. Sherry said she'd be more than happy to watch Katy and Joshua."

"I guess that's up to Emily, but I'll have her give you a call when they get up," Elijah said.

He hung up the phone and looked up to see Geneva starting down the stairs, her arms up in the air, stretching out every ounce of her body that was still trying to sleep, then let out a big sigh.

"Good Heaven's," she said in a groggy voice. "This ole body feels worn out this mornin'. Guess I better start breakfast. How does pancakes and sausage sound?"

"Anything you cook sounds good to me," Elijah replied. "Besides, you know Emily and the kids aren't too picky."

"Well, wait til I get it 'bout done and let them know," she said, starting to the kitchen, but turned back. "Oh, who was on the phone?"

"It was Terry. He said he wants to hire Emily to help out at the center and that Sherry wants to watch the kids while she does," he answered.

"That'd be wonderful for her," Geneva said, a little liveliness showing in her tone. "I think it'd give her somethin' to hold onto, don't ya think?"

"I can't be thinkin' for her honey, but you're probably right. We'll talk to her when they get up," Elijah said.

Geneva cackled, "You betcha they'll be runnin' down these here stairs when they smell food cookin'. I swear that little Joshua can eat his own weight."

She went and started breakfast, one thing she loved to do. She always said breakfast was her favorite meal of the day. Her mama told her when she was little, if she didn't eat breakfast she wouldn't grow, so Geneva made sure she at it every single morning, even if it was something little. As she got older, learning how to make homemade biscuits, gravy and so much more, was a fun lesson. Considering Elijah was a morning person, it made them perfectly suited for each other from the start.

After fixing up a mess of pancakes, sausage and scrambled eggs, Geneva went up and started to knock on Emily's door, but it opened before she could.

"Good morning miss Geneva," Emily said, bed hair, sleepy eyes, and all. "I smell something good."

"You betcha," Geneva said. "I just came to tell you breakfast is ready. You think the kids are awake?"

"I guess we'll see," she replied, taking a few steps to the next door.

Emily carefully opened it and Joshua was by the window, staring out and the sun was shining through putting the most wonderful light on his precious face. Katy was still in her bed, stretching and moaning, then sat up.

"Mornin' glories," Geneva said, going over to Joshua like she was sneaking up on someone, kneeling down and stealing a quick *good morning*, hug.

"Miss Geneva has breakfast ready kids. Are ya'll ready to eat?" Emily asked.

Without another word, Joshua took off and Katy was right behind him, their footsteps clattering all the way downstairs. Geneva and Emily couldn't help but laugh at them. Their energy lined that house like nothing else could, and they joined the kids and Elijah in the kitchen. By the time they made it, Elijah already had their plates fixed, their glasses of orange juice poured, and they were going after it. Even though Joshua was the littlest one, he ate twice as fast and more than anyone. It was hard to figure where he put all that food, but it was good to watch him enjoy it.

In conversation, Elijah told Emily about Terry's phone call and gave her his number to call him back. Soon as she finished eating, she did just that and came back with the most gigantic smile on her face.

"I have a job," she said, excitement oozing. "He said I could start today and Sherry will be there to take the kids with her for the day. You think it's a good idea Geneva?"

"Honey, it's a great idea. Look at it this way, you'll be helpin' folks and that's what life's all about, helping folks. It says so in the good book. It says whoever is kind to the poor lends to the Lord."

She gave a short chuckle, "But I am poor."

"No baby, it just means if you give of yourself, you know, your time, you're doin' God's work. It's a good thing Emily," Geneva explained.

"Well, then," Emily added. "I guess I'll do it. Besides, it'll help to get my mind off other things."

"You know Geneva," Elijah said, looking out to the shop. "We got that little Honda we don't drive. It's old, but I start it once a week and it runs good."

"Why are you talkin' in riddles Elijah," Geneva said. "What's your point?"

"I figure it'll give Emily a way to get around," he answered, giving his unique little grin she loved so much.

"Oh, Elijah, that's a wonderful idea," Geneva exclaimed. "You do have a driver's license don't you."

"Yes ma'am," Emily answered. "But you don't have to…"

"We don't have to do anything honey, but we are and that's that," Geneva replied quickly.

Elijah got the keys to the car and went to make sure he didn't tell a story about how it ran good, while Emily and the kids got dressed. Geneva did as always, making everything spic and span after breakfast and then out to tend the flowerbed. One thing she loved, was her flowers, and as hot as it was, she sure wasn't going to let them get thirsty. Elijah got the car running and then pulled it out into the driveway. Geneva was steadily caring for her colorful blooms and glanced in that direction. Elijah had a rag and was wiping that car down best he could. It had been sitting for sometime and to say it wasn't clean, would be an understatement, but he was trying to make it look a little better.

"It does have gas don't it, Elijah? We wouldn't want them to get out on the road and get stuck somewhere," Geneva hollered out. "I'd feel terrible if that happened."

"Believe it or not, it's almost got a full tank. I'm gonna drive up and down the road a few times to make sure it's alright, but I think it is," Elijah said, getting in the car and taking it for a spin.

While he was gone, Emily and the kids made their way outside and found a comfy place on the swing, swaying back and forth. The sun was waking up for the day and the heat hadn't set in just yet. Katy was sitting on one end of the swing, and she was doing as everyone did. She ran her fingers over the etched cross and stared at it the entire time. Her compelling green eyes focused in on the cross like many questions were twirling in her young mind.

Then, the sound of the car coming down the road, rang loud and clear. As Elijah made his way back the house, gravel was slinging left and right until he pulled up and parked. It was red, Geneva's favorite color for a vehicle, but she didn't like sitting so low to the ground. That's why she got the van. The kids ran up to the car before Emily could.

"Is this ours?" Katy asked, running her hand up and down it even though it was a bit dirty.

"No honey," Emily answered swiftly. "They're just loaning it to us sweetie."

"I like it," Joshua said, his face lighting up completely.

"So do I Josh," Emily said, rubbing the top of his head. "Now, are we ready to go?"

"Yes," both kids said in unison, climbing in and buckling up.

Emily paused for a moment and turned to Geneva and Elijah, "Thank you for everything. I didn't know anyone could be so kind, and Terry…"

"Terry wants to help too," Elijah said. "Don't underestimate people. Just because someone was not so great to you in the past, doesn't mean there aren't people who care."

She hugged them both and left, heading to the center to meet Terry and his wife. As the cloud of dust came and went, Elijah put his arm around Geneva and had no words. In an odd way, neither did Geneva. Instead of talking, they listened. In such a moment, God was whispering to them about how proud he was that they obeyed him by way of helping this family. Through the cool breeze blowing by and the birds singing their morning songs, the message was clear. Then, Geneva went back to her flowers.

Elijah still had a few things he'd started in the shop, so he busied himself. They both knew Emily and the kids were in good hands, so they continued working on the few projects they still had left to finish at home. Geneva was determined to do every little thing she had on her list to repair or update at their house, and when she was determined to do anything, it got done.

She could hear Elijah making hammering and banging noises and she knew he loved all of the tasks he set for himself. They both had different things they liked to do, but at the end of the day, it was all to better their life and home.

He was only in the shop for a short while, then came out to where Geneva was sitting on the steps of the porch taking a rest. Elijah wiped his brow and sat down to join her.

"You think they'll be okay?" Geneva asked, wiping the dirt from her hands.

"They're with Terry and Sherry honey. What do you think?" Elijah answered with a smile.

"You're right. I wonder what they're doing right now?" Geneva said looking out into the field.

CHAPTER FOURTEEN

Emily made sure she was careful driving the car Elijah and Geneva so kindly loaned to her. The kids were buckled tightly in the back seat and there wasn't much traffic on the roads since it was mid-morning. The sun was shining bright, and she knew it wouldn't be long until the heat was revealed once more. When she made it to Broad street, she turned in the direction of the center. It was only a few blocks away.

Still driving slowly to be as cautious as she could, she noticed a few people walking along the side of the road. They weren't together, but they did have one thing in common. It was obvious the streets was their home. The old man on the left, was carrying a sack in each hand and looked like he was alone in the world. On the other side of the road, was a middle-aged woman with a big, ragged purse draped over her shoulder. Her hair was half pulled up and the other half had fallen. The melancholy appearance she demonstrated, said a lot about her. Like the old man, she was alone.

Emily remembered days like those. The only difference, was, she had her kids, so she wasn't really alone. Regardless, she felt their pain and knew what they were going through. Not knowing where you'll get your next meal or where you'll bed down for the night, was a hard pill to swallow, and a part of her wanted to reach out to each of them and help.

When she pulled up and parked in front of the center, she looked up and saw their new sign had been hung over the entrance. The name, *Branches of Hope Community Center,* was fitting considering the ones running it, were giving people. They extended help to her and the kids without knowing a single thing about them, and Emily was more than appreciative. She felt like they were guardian angels, just like Geneva and Elijah. Somehow their paths crossed at the perfect time.

Jax was standing outside the front door placing a few decorative planters, one on either side of the door. They were in two large heavy pots and really adorned the place. She and the kids got out and started toward the door.

As they reached the entrance, Emily could tell Terry had fixed Jax up with some new clothes. They weren't fancy, just work clothes, jeans, and a new t-shirt, but there wasn't a hole in sight. He was wearing a new pair of tennis shoes and there was a glow about him that morning. Even though the center was just opening, it was already making a difference in so many ways.

"Did you have fun fishin'? You catch any?" Jax asked kindly, directing his question to the kids, sweeping the front as he talked to them.

"I caught a big one," Joshua said, holding his arms way out, like those fish stories men usually tell.

Jax kneeled down in front of Joshua, "You did? I wish I could've seen that little man."

"And we cooked him up too," Katy joined in. "We cooked up all the fish."

About then, Terry came out to greet them. He had been right inside the doorway doing something and heard the entire conversation. "Did I hear you say you caught a whale Joshua?"

Joshua didn't verbally answer, but his head was bobbing up and down joyfully, as to say a huge *yes*. It immediately got a laugh, then Joshua and his sister ran inside when they saw Sherry coming across the front room. When the kids reached her, she gave them a gigantic hug. They acted like they had known them their entire lives, and that left a warm fuzzy feeling inside of Emily.

"I guess me and these two are going to town for a bit then to the house. I just might find some fun things to do," Sherry said, holding each of their hands.

Emily couldn't help but smile, "Be good for Miss Sherry, okay?"

"Yes ma'am," they said in unison, holding tightly to Sherry's hand.

"We'll have a good time," Sherry said kindly. "Don't let these fellas work you too hard, and don't worry about the kids. If anything, they'll get spoiled to death."

Emily took that moment to give Sherry a hug for giving her time to them, then they were on their way. When they drove off, she watched the car disappear, but one thing was strange. She didn't have a single concern. Something was whispering to her saying they would be perfectly fine. Even though she hadn't been away from them in a long time, a peace came over her, the kind she hadn't really felt before.

"I have you a little help in the back," Terry said. "Stacey's in the kitchen. She's trying to organize all the food we picked up and stuff for the freezer too. I ain't never been too good at organizing so I called Nancy and asked if her daughter might help for a while."

"Nancy?" Emily asked, not knowing who he was talking about.

"Oh, Nancy Talley. She's our sheriff here," Terry answered. "Stacey called and said she'd be glad to help. She is a sweetheart and I figured you two might get along."

Emily followed him to the back and around the corner into the kitchen. In front of a long wall of cupboards with most of the doors open, stood a lady with light brown hair and glasses. She was putting everything that was the same, together, and stacking them neatly on the shelves. When she turned, her deep brown eyes showed a kindness even before she spoke the first word, and her smile was friendly and inviting.

"Stacey, this is Emily," Terry said, introducing them. "I guess you two are the ones that'll help keep this place in order."

"Someone needs to," Stacey said, aggravating. Then she put down what she had in her hands. "Nice to meet you Emily. Terry's working my poor fingers to the bone."

"Don't listen to her," Terry laughed. "She's just practicin' so she can tell her mom I worked her too hard. She's not foolin' me."

"It's a pleasure to meet you too," Emily said, reaching and shaking her hand. "I'm not sure what I'm supposed to be doing, but I guess you'll point me in the right direction."

Stacey went back to where she was when they walked up and motioned for Emily to follow. There were dozens of canned vegetables, cream soups and more, in boxes all around her on the floor and on the countertop. It was literally a cluttered mess, but like in a grocery store, she had already filled one shelf three cans high of green beans and was starting on the next. It was obvious she had a particular way she wanted it done, so Emily followed her lead.

"You can start on that end," Stacey said, but not in a demanding way. "And I guess we'll meet in the middle. How does that sound?"

"Sounds good boss," Emily responded cleverly.

Stacey started to snicker at such a comment, "I'm no one's boss. I'm just here to help. Terry's a good guy with a great heart for people."

"I can tell," Emily replied, placing each can just so on the shelf. "And that miss Geneva…"

"Geneva James?" Stacey retorted quickly, immediately wearing a beautiful smile. "I love Geneva. That woman is a one of a kind. Me and mom were talking about her one day. She's got more energy than two people half her age. We don't see how she does it."

"Well," Emily added, lowering her head. "She kind of saved me and my kids. It's like she's my guardian angel in a way."

Stacey stopped stacking for a minute like she had something very profound to say. "That's Geneva. That's who she is and who she's always been. And as for her talk, I hear she's talked that way forever. She used to tell the story about her family sending her off to California to learn how to talk right. She told them then like she'll tell you today. She said *I yam what I yam.*"

Emily let a grin pop out after such a comment, then glanced out the window in the kitchen. The day started with the sun hanging high in the sky, and bright as a diamond, but she could hear the wind picking up outside. A few clouds were in the distance from what she could see but it didn't look like much to worry about.

"Hey ladies," Terry yelled out. "Me and Jax is goin' down to the lumber place. He said he's a pretty good carpenter and might build a few things for us. Anyway, we'll be back."

"Okay," Stacey hollered back.

Emily thought about how she could ask questions about her without sounding nosy, so she just started, "Are you married Stacey?"

"I am," she said, joy immediately showing on her pretty face. "His name is Keith, and I have two handsome boys Jacob and Jaxson. I told Jax that earlier today."

"What about you?" Stacey asked, never ceasing her work. "I thought I heard Terry say it was just you and your kids."

"It is, but it didn't used to be," Emily slowly answered. "My husband's name is Chris, but we haven't seen him in some time."

"It's none of my business. I'm sorry," Stacey apologized. "I didn't mean to…"

"It's okay. I think it's probably good for me to talk about it," Emily replied, then continued. "He walked out a while back and I still remember what he was wearing when he did. Isn't that a crazy thing to recall?"

"Everyone's different, I think. Sometimes stuff like that gives us something to hold onto," Stacey said with an upbeat tone in her voice. "So, what did he have on."

Emily let out a breath and looked up like she was staring at the ceiling, "Funny as it might sound, he had on a cap I gave him when we first met. It was a throwback Arkansas Razorback cap that was red and white with frayed edges. Of course, as long as he had it, it looked like it had been through the ringer."

"What else?" Stacey asked, almost finished neatly stacking another box of canned goods.

"His wedding ring," Emily muttered softly, in a reminiscent manner. "When we decided to get married, he said he didn't want anything fancy, so I bought him one of those black stainless-steel wedding bands with a silver streak in the middle. It didn't cost much, but he said it was priceless to him, or at least until that day."

"If you don't mind me asking, what was the problem?"

With a short pause, "I have to be honest. He was an addict. And if I'm really being honest, I was too at one time…I guess I still am, just not using. I think Chris just stopped fighting the urges. I don't really know."

"Is he here in town?" Stacey asked.

"I don't really know. I figured if he was, I would have seen him. We got kicked out of our loft apartment because he stopped paying rent, so the kids and I just made the best of it," Emily answered, opening up to her new acquaintance.

"I'm so sorry Emily. I know it has to be hard," Stacey said in a very sympathetic tone. "You aren't alone though. You know that by now, right?"

"I guess so, but you know what?" Emily said, looking up and her eyes turning sad in an instant. "I miss him so much. It's like the more I try to forget him, the more I remember all the things I loved about him."

"Maybe that's God putting those thoughts in your head. Maybe you're not supposed to forget. Maybe you're supposed to forgive him," she said, finishing up one more shelf.

Emily gave a short snicker, "Why do you sound just like miss Geneva?"

"Probably because I've known her for years. I don't know why, but somehow the more you're around that crazy woman, the more she rubs off...even if you don't want it to," Stacey replied comically.

Emily began to shake her head and smile, a funny thought running through her mind. "I catch myself using her country slang language without even thinking about it. A few times, the kids looked at me kind of funny."

The phone on the table started ringing and Stacey answered. "Hello. Yes sir...yes we do. Okay we'll go pick some up. Yes sir. Bye."

Emily had just about finished stacking three shelves full of cans neatly and closed the doors, "Terry?"

"He wants us to run to town to get a few things he just thought about. Here before long, we should be stocked up enough to be able to feed a slew of folks. Besides, we could take an early lunch," Stacey answered.

Emily agreed and put the empty box she was working on, in the back room out of sight. Stacey looked in every drawer, cabinet and even in the freezer unit, to see what else they needed to pick up while they were out. With notepad in hand, she quickly jotted down everything she thought they were missing. She folded the yellowish piece of paper and put in her pocket.

"I guess that's all," Stacey said out loud, not talking to anyone, just talking, then dug for her car keys in her purse and whipped them out quickly. "Where you want to eat. What sounds good?"

"I...um, well," Emily stuttered, knowing she didn't have any money.

"Listen," Stacey continued, pulling out a credit card with Terry's name on it. "He said anything we need just put it on this little card. I figure we need to eat, don't you?"

The feeling in the air, was, they were becoming fast friends. There was no judgement, just someone who listened to Emily's story and let her talk. Something about it, was special. It wasn't often you come across someone like that.

Stacey locked up the building and started toward a white GMC parked next to Emily's. The trees around appeared to be in nature's recital, its branches dancing around to the music of the wind. The breeze whipping by, was soothing to the skin, but the clouds appeared to be coming in more and more. In a sense, the beauty of the cluster of white clouds mimicking marshmallows in the sky, was a sight. A few were dark, carrying a gloomy presence, possibly carrying a storm inside. None-the-less, they went on their way.

A few cars were coming and going, but overall, few were traveling that road. She went in the direction of downtown. There was some mail Terry wanted dropped off at the post office on the way. Stacey turned on the radio and stopped it on an old country station. Those were the kinds of songs Geneva and Elijah always listened to as well as country gospel. Regardless, country, was the key word.

Only a block from where they were supposed to turn, something happened. Although not many cars were roaming the roads, one caught their eye, but a little bit too late.

On Emily's side, an old truck was heading straight for them, driving reckless. For a split second, Emily thought she was seeing things, thinking "*This can't be happening*", but then, it did.

CHAPTER FIFTEEN

Like it was happening in slow motion, the truck collided with them, striking only Emily's side. Time stood still like a long prayer for their safety was being lifted on their behalf. Only a few seconds felt like an eternity as Stacey's car was driven hard sideways, stopping just before reaching the tracks to their left. Smoke from the collision floated around them and, for a moment, no one moved.

Stacey's eyes popped open and slowly looked around, trying her best to see if anyone was hurt. It was too early to hear an ambulance or fire engine since it just happened, but when she turned in Emily's direction, all she could do was cry for help. Fear took over every core of her body, stopping to pray before she did anything else. Emily was still buckled in but wasn't responsive at all. Her head was limp, resting on her left shoulder and Stacey could see blood down the right side of her face and head. Panic began to take over with a racing heart and struggling breaths. She wanted to shake her, but at the same time, didn't want to do more damage than had already been done.

"Emily," Stacey said, her voice shaking with every syllable. "Please say something."

Stacey's door flung open abruptly and there stood a guy probably in his late twenties. His blondish hair was a mess and scruffy face somewhat told a story. "Are you okay?" he asked.

"But my friend Emily…" she started saying, then he ran around to the other side before she could finish her sentence.

Before she knew it, that man had reached inside, un-hooked her, and lifted her out. The strength he showed was immense even though he looked like he didn't have strength at all. He laid her on the ground next to the car and Stacey slowly made her way around to them. You could hear the sirens coming and the noises got louder and louder.

"Emily," the man said, wiping the blood from her face as he spoke. "Say something."

When the ambulance pulled up, the man got up and took off running. Stacey called out to him, but he never slowed down. In just a moment, he was out of sight. The paramedics put Emily on oxygen and then placed a neck collar to be safe, checking all of her vitals, then the police arrived. They looked around but didn't see the driver of the truck. In fact, the truck didn't even have a license plate on it. It appeared to have been torn off. The door of the truck was still open, and nothing was inside to tell who was driving during the accident.

Immediately after talking to the officers, Stacey called her husband, mom, and Terry. She knew she needed to call miss Geneva too, but was afraid how she would react. After talking to her mom, she decided it best someone go out to get them and give an escort to the hospital. Their biggest fear was Elijah and Geneva having a wreck trying to get there faster.

Finally, after a few minutes of working on Emily, her eyes eased open in an extremely weak manner. Her breathes were slow and the way her eyes were communicating spoke more than a thousand words could've. Stacey could see a few tears progressing down her cheeks. The paramedics lift-ed her and put her on the gurney and started to make their way to the ambulance.

"Wait," Stacey yelled out, stopping them from taking her, then going over. "You're gonna be fine. I promise you'll be just fine. Don't worry about the kids. I'll call Sherry and Geneva, and…"

With her left hand, Emily faintly reached for her. Stacey took her hand and squeezed it gently, trying to give a smile although she couldn't stop wiping the tears flooding out. Even though they had just met, they clicked right off the bat and Stacey knew she'd found a friend.

Another paramedic walked up, "Ma'am, we need to check you out. Are you hurt?" he asked.

"I'm fine, I just need to go with Emily," she responded quickly, watching them put her in the ambulance.

"Ma'am, please calm down," he said. "Let's get you looked out first, then you can check on her."

They had laid her back and looked left and right, high, and low, making sure she wasn't hurt, and the sheriff's car pulled up. Nancy got out and ran fast as she could to her. Her husband Keith wasn't far behind.

"What about Geneva?" Stacey asked, still wiping tears. "She needs to know."

"I sent Terry Roberts out to their place. I told him to bring them to the hospital so they wouldn't get in a hurry driving. He'll be tactful. You know Terry," Nancy said, looking over her daughter like she was a doctor. "How did Emily seem?"

All Stacey could do, was shake her head. "She squeezed my hand," she replied.

"Okay, we'll take that as a positive thing," Nancy said. "We always have to see the positive side, right?"

The paramedics said she had to ride to the hospital to check a few more things out and they left. Nancy and her husband followed the ambulance. The entire ride, all Stacey could think about was, if they had left a few minutes later or earlier, or if they hadn't left at all, she would be okay. The beeping of the machines hooked up to her, oddly enough, lulled her to sleep. Maybe the stress of the accident took over, but regardless, her body needed it. When they took her into the emergency room, she kept asking where Emily was, but no one would give her a straight answer.

They placed her in a room and relocated her into one of those uncomfortable beds, then covered her with a thin sheet. The nurse placed a small pillow under her head and left the room. Still, she had no idea where Emily was, or if she was even okay.

She tried her best to get comfortable, but it was next to impossible, then the doctor came in.

"Mrs. Jones is it?" the short, salt and pepper haired, heavy-set doctor muttered. "I see you were in an accident. Any pains? Back hurt? Headache? Muscle pain? Anything?"

He shot those questions out swiftly without giving her a chance to answer one. Then he mumbled a few things, taking his pen and jotting down some notes. For a second, it was like she wasn't even in the room, invisible to the one who was supposed to be paying attention to her.

"Doc," Stacey hollered out, getting his attention. "Where's my friend? Emily, she was in the car with me."

"Hmmm, I'll have to check on that Mrs. huh…"

"Jones," she said, raising her tone a bit. "Is there another doctor I can see?"

When she spurted out the last question, he wheeled around quickly and left the room. All she could hear were people bustling in the hallway and one in the room next to her, crying in pain. Then, came a sound very familiar. Nancy, her mom's voice rang clear as did her husbands. It sounded like they were moving people out of the way to get to her. An even louder voice came soon after.

"By golly," Geneva's voice echoed. "Somebody better tell me where Emily is right now."

It was only a moment until they all came barreling into her room. Everyone was talking at the same time in a hysterical manner. Then the nurse walked in holding her hands up, trying to get a word in. Of course, between Nancy and Geneva, it was a hard thing to accomplish.

"Honey, are you okay?" Geneva said, running to Stacey's bedside. "What happened?"

"This truck just came out of nowhere Geneva," Stacey answered, showing anxiety even more than before. "I looked at Emily and she was out. Then this guy came."

"What guy?" Geneva asked. "Was it the driver of the truck?"

"I didn't think so because he took off running when the police and ambulance came."

About then, another doctor walked in. He was dark skinned and came toward Stacey in a calming way. Everyone moved to give him room and he started checking her. His kindness and gentleness, was far different than the one who was there before, and when he was finished, he wrapped the stethoscope around his neck.

"You seem to be okay Mrs. Jones," the doctor said. "Just stay calm and take deep breaths. I think you just got the wind knocked out of you. There are a few officers outside who want to ask you a few questions if you're up to it."

"Where's Emily?" Geneva bellowed out

"Are you family?" he asked. "I can't give any information unless your family. I'm very sorry."

"She don't have no family," Geneva said, tears starting to surge. "See doctor, a friend of mine is keepin' her two kids and her husband…well, don't nobody know where he is. Please tell me."

Placing his hand on her shoulder to console her, "Let me go see what I can find out. Just stay right here."

When he walked out, two officers came in. One short, heavy set, older gentleman and a young man who looked like he couldn't have been on the force for too long. With their hands grasping their belts like you see in movies, they nodded as they slowly made their way to Stacey.

"Ma'am," the older officer said, slightly nodding. "Is there anything you can remember that would be of help. We had the truck that hit you, towed because no one came to claim it."

Stacey let out long breath, "Like I told the doctor, this truck came out of nowhere. I figure he was going pretty fast as hard as we were hit, but I didn't have time to get out of the way."

"Did you see the driver?" he continued.

"No sir. It happened too fast, but…"

"But what ma'am? Any information would be of help," he asked.

"There was this man who opened my car door and helped me and Emily," she said, forcing her mind to remember everything. "When he saw Emily, he ran to the other side and pulled her out. I was yelling out because I was afraid she wasn't supposed to be moved, but he didn't pay any attention," Stacey recalled.

"What then, ma'am?"

"I made my way to where he laid her on the ground, and he was trying to get her to open her eyes. He seemed truly concerned, but when he heard the police coming, he ran away," she continued.

"Do you remember anything about this man? He could be a witness," the younger officer asked.

"He had on a…" Stacey started to say, then stopped, as a perplexed look showed on her face. "I don't remember officer. I can't remember much about him. I'm sorry. I wish I could help more."

The officer closed the small notebook he had in his hand and placed it in his pocket. He smiled a very comforting smile, "You feel better, and we'll look into this further. I hope your friend is okay. We'll check on her as well."

In the corner of the room, Geneva's words rang loud and clear even though she wasn't talking too loudly.

Oh Dear Heavenly Father, I come to you asking for you to wrap your arms around Emily and hold her tight. God, I know she's probably so scared, but you are the ultimate healer Lord and I know you can help her through this. God, I don't know how bad she is, but you do, and I trust you will do whatever your will is, but I'm asking please help her. She's got these little ones who need her Lord. They need her so badly. They done lost their daddy and they can't lose their mama too. Lord I've lived a long time and if I could, take me instead. She's got so much to live for. I don't know if she's ready Lord. I don't know, but if you give her a little more time…please. Thank you for being such an all-powerful God who knows our strengths and weaknesses and helps us through. I'm asking please help us through this too. I ask in Jesus' name…AMEN.

Elijah's eyes were teared up as he was kneeling with Geneva as she prayed. His emotions were as high as hers as she pleaded to God to save Emily. Although no one knew how badly she was hurt, just the thought of the worst possible scenario, lingered all around them. Geneva couldn't stop crying and, in a way, it appeared she was still having a conversation with God, but just between her and him. Hearing the small whispers, she always made when praying, told everyone she wasn't finished yet.

Nancy got an odd expression and went to Stacey's bedside, "It sounded like you started to say something to the officers about what you remembered, but stopped. What was it?"

"Nothing mama. It was nothing. I just thought I remembered something," Stacey said. "I was confused."

"Are you sure? Every little bit of information helps find who did this Stacey. I was so scared when I got there. It was a blessing to see you were okay, but Emily…"

The hospital room door opened as Nancy was talking and she stopped. All eyes were on the doctor. He was holding a clipboard and Nancy glanced, noticing it had Emily's name on the top of the page as he got closer. His expression was hard to read, but all eyes were on him.

CHAPTER SIXTEEN

The doctor's expression was less than desirable, and he glanced at the pages in front of him once more, writing down a few things. "I'm afraid that Emily took the hardest hit in the accident. She's got multiple contusions on her face and arm. Her right arm is fractured and she has a concussion. She's been in and out of consciousness and the nurse told me she's been talking a little out of her head at times."

"Can I see her doc?" Geneva stepped forward, asking in a begging sort of way. "I want her to know I'm here."

"Maybe in a little bit when she's a little more stable. I'll let you know, I promise. In the meantime," he answered, then turned to Stacey. "It might take us a little bit, but we'll get your paperwork to get you released. Just take it easy. I'm sure you'll be sore for a few days from the impact of the wreck. Don't overdo it."

"I'll see to that," her husband Keith, chimed in. "No worries doc."

He gave a quick nod before leaving the room and left everyone in wonder of how Emily really was. The silence gave way to worry, then worry to anxious thoughts of the worst kind. Although nothing was being said, many conversations were going on all at one time, mostly everyone talking to God, praying for good news.

You could always tell Geneva was praying with no question. She always closed her eyes and would slightly rock as her head was moving side to side slowly. Her mouth whispered words of praise as she talked to God. You couldn't understand any of the whispers from her lips, but there was only one person who truly needed to understand them. After a few minutes of everyone reaching out to a higher power, Geneva broke the stillness in the room. She got a quizzical look about her and took a seat by Stacey's bed.

"When they was askin' you about the fella who helped you and Emily, you..." Geneva started until she was interrupted.

"I really don't remember Geneva, really," Stacey said in a defensive manner.

"It's just I think there's somethin' you ain't a sayin. Don't make me get your mama involved. You know she's tough," Geneva grinned.

Nancy and Stacey's husband were in the corner talking to Elijah and Stacey cut her eyes back to Geneva, taking in and letting out a long breath. "Well, when he first opened the door, I didn't notice because I was in shock of what just happened, but then I saw..."

"We have you ready to go, Mrs. Jones," the nurse said, walking in with a few things for Stacey to sign before she could leave.

It was all Geneva could do to keep from telling that nurse to come back later. Her intuition told her something was going on with Stacey and she always said her women's intuition was right on target. None-the-less, she had to wait to hear the rest of the story. The nurse showed Stacey where to sign and what she was signing, and after the last one, she headed to the door and turned back momentarily.

"If you start having any problems, please come back to get checked out," she said, flashing a friendly smile and leaving.

Elijah's phone started ringing and he swiftly answered it. From the conversation, it was obvious, it was Terry and Sherry. They decided to stay with the kids and keep them busy and wait to hear any updates. Elijah filled him in on what the doctor told everyone, and they would call him when there was more information.

"I wouldn't tell the kids yet," Elijah said to Terry, then an earnest goodbye.

"You ready Stacey?" Keith asked, gathering the few things she had. "We'll go home so you can rest."

"I can't rest until I know Emily is okay. There's no way," Stacey answered. "We started to really talk, getting to know each other, then this…"

"Well, honey," Geneva said. "Me and Elijah ain't goin' nowhere. Where gonna sit right here till we get answers and you're darn welcome to sit with us. We can take you home afterwhile."

"Is that okay?" Stacey said, glancing at her husband sadly, her deep brown eyes staring into his heart.

Without a word, he gave her a short nod, a hug and kiss followed by an agreeing smile. Nancy said goodbye as well, knowing she had to get back to work since Stacey was okay. Elijah went into the waiting room while Geneva and Stacey told the nurses where they would be so they would let them know when someone could see Emily.

The affects from such a traumatic event, still had Stacey very shaken, especially adding worry on top of it. Geneva could tell she was struggling with something and waited until they went to where Elijah was. She led her to a corner where they could sit and talk. Elijah didn't pay them any attention as he thumbed through magazines on the table in front of him.

"Honey," Geneva said, holding her hand. "What was you 'bout to say back there before that there nurse came in? Is there somethin' wrong?"

"Geneva, the guy who helped us," Stacey started. "Came out of nowhere it seemed. He saw I was okay but when I said Emily's name, he immediately left me and ran to her side."

"Well maybe he saw how badly she was hurt. There ain't nothin' odd about that," Geneva replied.

"Yes, there was," Stacey said, lowering her head. "It's what I saw."

Geneva sat there waiting for her to continue her story and tried her best not to push too hard. Frustration and confusion showed clearly in those dark eyes of hers, and the shakiness in her voice gave the conclusion.

"Mama told me about Emily. Terry filled her in on the situation and I've felt so sorry for her. Then, today, when we met and started talking, she opened up to me," Stacey added.

"What does this have to do with that there man honey?" Geneva asked.

"When he reached out his left hand to help me, he had on a unique ring. It was black with a silver streak in the center all the way around," Stacey said.

"I don't know what you're a tryin' to say."

"And he had on an old Razorback cap that looked like it was coming all the way apart," Stacey kept on. "And when I said Emily's name…"

"Do you think…" Geneva started to ask.

"Geneva," Stacey said. "Emily told me the story about her and Chris. She told me about the ring she bought him… black stainless steel with a silver streak in the middle. And she said he always wore an old beat-up razorback cap."

Geneva sat back and rested her head on the wall behind her. You could tell a million thoughts were racing in her mind, some worry, and some joy. For some reason, those two things were in constant conflict. If he came back to Emily and the kids and was clean, that would be something joyful, but if he came back to cause more pain, that was something Geneva wouldn't stand for.

"Oh, good gracious," Geneva muttered. "What in Heaven's name is he a doin'? Did he look like he was on somethin' Stacey?

"It happened so fast," Stacey answered. "I really couldn't tell. It's just when he saw Emily like that, he got superhuman strength and pulled her out of that car and carefully laid her down. He was begging her to talk to him, but she didn't open her eyes. I was wondering why a perfect stranger would be so emotional. Then, when the police were pulling up, he ran off."

"He didn't say anything before he took off?" Geneva asked, curiosity showing in her brilliant blue eyes.

"No ma'am, but he did look back several times and it looked like he was crying. Of course, with everything going on, I couldn't corral my thoughts well," Stacey answered. "Anyway, he disappeared behind one of those abandon buildings going toward the Texas side of Texarkana."

They sat together, both looking like they were in deep thought on what to do next. Geneva wrapped her arm around Stacey doing her best to keep her calm, and it wasn't but a half an hour or so until the doctor came out looking for them.

"You can go see her now, but only two at a time. She's very weak, so don't stay too long," the doctor said. "Follow me."

"We'll be back honey," Geneva called out to Elijah, then followed the doctor to Emily's room.

The sounds from every room they passed, reminded Geneva why she hated hospitals so much. There was something about knowing someone was in pain and it always pierced straight into her heart, wanting to help everyone. Of course, everyone knows you can't help everybody, but the kindness inside of Geneva, made her want to, more than anything.

"Here we are," the doctor said, stopping in front of Emily's door. "Now, she's still pretty in and out, but it'll do her good knowing you're here."

"Thank you, doctor," Geneva nodded, then opened the door.

Even though it wasn't as bad as it could've been, seeing her lying there looking broken, was terrible. There were, what appeared to be dozens of cuts bandaged up on her face, neck, and arm. The right side of her face showed colors of black and blue, bruises the wreck left behind, and it was swollen on top of that. Her right arm was in a sling showing similar bruising on her hand. Geneva's reaction was nothing short of worry for this young woman she had gotten to know so well in just a few days.

Each of them took a side of Emily's bed and pulled up a chair, not wanting to disturb her. She looked like she was in a peaceful sleep as her breaths were long and slow. Then, from down the hallway, something was going on and the noise woke Emily abruptly. The gasp she let out, showed fear without a doubt, and her eyes opened quickly.

"Joshua…Katy," Emily called out, looking around as if she was trying to find them.

"Honey, it's okay," Geneva said, putting her hand over Emily's. "The kids are fine. They're with Sherry, remember. Terry's with'em too. They're just fine. We just need to take care of you."

"Chris," Emily whispered, looking straight to the ceiling, and a tear slowly treading down her cheeks. "I heard Chris."

Stacey reached and touched her arm, "It's Stacey. I'm here too Emily. I was so scared you were…"

Emily gave a faint smile and glanced to Stacey, "When it was happening, I thought about something Geneva told me about God. She said God said something like, don't be afraid because I am with you. I was afraid, but I figured if he was wonderful enough to send such great people in my life, surely he wasn't gonna take me out this quick."

"You got that right, honey," Geneva agreed. "You're a gonna be okay real soon. And you know me and Elijah are gonna take good care a you."

"Yes ma'am, but what about Chris? I heard his voice. Has he been here?"

"Umm, no I don't believe so, but..." Geneva started, unsure how to tell her. "When do you think you heard his voice?"

"I don't think it was here," she replied in a groggy tone. "I think it was before I came here. I didn't see his face; I just heard his voice."

"Do you remember what he was saying, honey?" Geneva asked, trying to confirm what Stacey believed.

"He just kept saying open your eyes and wake up, please. It was for just a moment, then I saw Stacey just before they put me in the ambulance. That's all I remember really," Emily said, closing her eyes, drifting in and out after that.

"We're gonna let you rest okay?" Stacey said. "We'll be back afterwhile after you've gotten some sleep."

"That's right honey," Geneva said. "We'll be in the waitin' area. We won't be far."

Emily floated off to sleep as they left her room. They took the few turns that led them back to where Elijah was still sitting and reading. By that time, about a half a dozen more people were waiting to be seen, so they joined Elijah. He closed the magazine and set it aside.

"How's she doin?" he asked sincerely.

"Just banged up a bit, but she's a tough one honey," Geneva said. "We'll get her home soon. By the way, have you talked to Terry again? The kids okay?"

"Oh yeah, he done called again, but I told him we were still waiting. He said the kids were having a blast outside with Sherry, and haven't brought their mama up one time yet," Elijah said. "I'm sure it's not because they don't miss her. I figure Sherry is spoiling those kids like crazy."

"Good," Geneva said, nodding her head. "They need to be spoiled."

"I haven't gotten a chance to meet them yet," Stacey jumped in. "I just heard about them."

"Oh, my gracious, honey. Them are the most precious little'uns I think I've ever seen, next to my Ella that is. And boy they're like little sponges, absorbing up everything anyone says when they're around, especially that Joshua," Geneva smiled. "He's a little heart breaker that one is, but he sure does miss his daddy."

"Yeah," Stacey grinned. "Terry told me about how their faces lit up when they got all those new clothes and shoes and things. I'll tell you one thing about Terry. He'd give the shirt off his back to anyone who needed it and wouldn't give it a second thought."

"That's for sure," Elijah said, joining the conversation. "Been that way long as I've known him."

Geneva noticed the doctor coming in their direction once again, his pleasant disposition standing out. "I've examined Emily and feel like she needs to stay with us one night for observation, but pretty sure I can release her tomorrow. She's a very lucky girl. Most people who get hit straight on like that, well, the scenario is much different."

"God was watchin' over her doc," Geneva said, glancing up like she was looking to the Heavens. "God was definitely watchin'."

"Ma'am," the doctor grinned. "I truly believe that. I do think she'll be okay with some time to heal and rest. She'll have headaches for a good while, but that's completely normal. At the end of the day, she needs rest. We're moving her to a room for the night. If anyone wants to stay with her, you are welcome to, but I promise she'll be fine."

"Thank you, doctor," Geneva said. "I'll leave my phone number if you need to get in touch with me."

After the doctor left, Geneva went to the lady at the first desk from the door. She gave her all their contact information. Elijah and Stacey were waiting at the exit in the emergency room, for her. They started to leave and were making small talk heading outside when Stacey looked toward the steps in between the bushes on the other side of the emergency driveway and immediately stopped.

CHAPTER SEVENTEEN

"It's him," Stacey whispered to Geneva, then pointed in his direction. "I think that's Chris."

The man was sitting on the short steps coming from the driveway behind him where employees parked with his head lowered. His hands were fidgeting, and he glanced up a few times in their opposite direction.

"You sure?" Geneva muttered back softly.

"I am Geneva. He's got on the same clothes; same cap and I would give anything he's got on that black and silver ring. I'd bet all I've got it's him," Stacey answered. "He looks like he's in a bad way. I think he really loved Emily, or he wouldn't be out here waiting at the hospital. Don't you think?"

"I suppose," Geneva said.

"I'm going to talk to him," Stacey said.

Elijah patiently waited and heard their conversation, filling in the blanks, understanding exactly what was going on. He didn't get involved. He just stood there. It was obvious he knew Geneva would do what needed to be done and he just stayed out of it.

"I'll come with you," she told Stacey, then turned to Elijah. "We'll be right back honey."

Traffic on the cross street behind the hospital was heavy and the noise from that and the ambulance they heard not far away, made it hard to hear much. A few steps in, he still didn't look up, but about the time they reached him, he did. His eyes were bloodshot, and had noticeably, been crying. He wiped his face with his left hand and low and behold, there was the ring Stacey had described. The shabby appearance he depicted, showed he needed help, but when Stacey started to say something, he stood quickly and began to walk away.

"Wait," Geneva hollered out. "Are you Chris?"

He stopped in his tracks. Instead of responding verbally, he started crying uncontrollably, muttering words here and there, none of which were understandable. The only thing they could make out was, *I'm so sorry.*

"Oh, honey," Geneva said, her tears welling up in her heart and making their way out the same as his. "It's gonna be okay. I promise."

"I am Chris," he said, his voice cracking as he spoke. "I'm not a good person. I don't deserve to live."

"Why you say that honey? Everybody deserves to live. And can I tell you somethin' you got to live for?" Geneva said, slowly going around where she could look him in the eye. "Emily loves you and your little'uns do too, especially that Joshua. Joshua misses his daddy so much. I heard him say just that."

"My sweet Josh," Chris said, floods of tears starting all over again. "And Katy…my beautiful Katy."

"Don't you think they're somethin' to live for honey?" Geneva continued, reaching out for his left hand. "And this here ring you're a wearin', that's a symbol. God joined you two and don't want nothin' to come between ya."

"God doesn't want anything to do with me," Chris responded emotionally. "After all I've done."

"Chris, you ain't done nothin' too bad where Emily won't forgive you. She loves you. Just like with God. When he forgives you, it's like you never did anything wrong. Like it says in the bible, when he forgives us, our sins are erased," Geneva said, with almost an angelic way about her.

"What's your name?" he asked. "I don't even know your name."

"Oh, good gracious honey," Geneva said. "I done gone and left my manners at home. I'm Geneva and that man over there is my husband, Elijah. Of course, you met Stacey. In fact, you helped her."

"You rescued my family, Geneva. You saved them," he said, squeezing her hand and nodding his head. "Thank you so much."

"I didn't save nobody son," Geneva responded humbly. "I just did what I was told to do. B'sides bein' with Emily and them young'uns was a blessing. Our home's been empty for some time and havin' them there, gave me somebody to care for other than just Elijah."

Geneva studied his face as she talked, scruffy and worn, and his green eyes had a weary look about them. Deep down, she knew she had to help him the same as his family but wasn't sure exactly how to do it.

Stacey wiggled her way into the conversation because it was obvious she had something to say. "You saved Emily today. I saw the passion you had to put her first when you saw she was hurt. That says a lot, Chris. You can't hide that kind of love."

Chris looked a little off-center and began to sway left, then right, so he went and sat back down where he was when they first saw him. "I just did what came natural," he said. "I do love her. I just couldn't make her live with the bad decisions I was making and I didn't want my kids to suffer either. I left because I figured they were better off without me."

Geneva whispered to Stacey and told her to call Terry and fill him in on what was going on. She knew if anyone had any way to help Chris, it would be Terry, and if it would help those precious kids, there was no doubt.

Stacey walked off toward Elijah, and called Terry while Geneva took a seat on the concrete step next to Chris. With his hands covering his face and low murmuring, in a way it looked like he was praying, but Geneva knew better than that. In the state of mind he was in, his confusion had distorted any sense of reality where he could find real answers. Constantly feeling like a failure, kept Chris on the run, doing his best not to face his problems head on.

"If you don't mind me askin'," Geneva started again. "How long's it been since you…"

He answered her question before she could finish it, "It's been a few days and I'm feeling really bad Geneva. I ran out of money, and I feel like I'm losing my mind. I need something…something to make me feel better."

"You need somethin' alright, but it's not what you think honey," Geneva said, squeezing his hand. "And I think I know somebody who can get you that kinda help."

"I'm not worth all the trouble miss Geneva…I'm really not," he replied woefully.

Geneva sat there and her mind started turning, trying to figure out what to say to talk him in to agreeing to let someone step in supporting his recovery. She knew doing it alone was almost impossible to do.

"Can I tell you a story?" she said, showing energy in her voice.

"I guess so."

"Like it says in the bible, when you're a trying to pull a heavy load, when you got more than one person pulling the weight, it takes half the energy honey. It says in Matthew, *Take my yoke upon you.*"

"What does that mean?" Chris asked, hanging on her words, knowing it was something he needed to hear.

"Well, honey," she said. "When you try to take care of your own problems pullin' with just one yoke, on your own, you can't get much done. But when you take up the yoke of Jesus, you can accomplish twice as much with half the effort. Why would you do anything else?"

Chris started smiling, peering at Geneva like he couldn't believe anyone would take so much time on him.

"I bet Emily loves you," he said. "The kids too."

"Oh, my gracious honey, I feel like I've known them forever. And we been doin' our best to take care a them. I could tell she was in a bad place the first time I saw her and when I was told to step in and help, I did," Geneva said.

"Who told you?" he asked.

"I'll tell ya Chris, sometimes I hear God talk to me and I done learned how to listen. When I saw them over by the center, I couldn't get'em outa my mind."

"I haven't gotten'em out of my mind either Miss Geneva. What do I do next?" he said, finally starting to reach out for help.

Geneva looked back and noticed Terry coming up the sidewalk toward Elijah and Stacey where they were sitting on a bench outside the emergency room. They both got up to greet him. Stacey talked to Terry for a minute or two, then he walked over to Geneva and Chris. He was sporting the welcoming smile he was known for and extended his hand.

"I'm Terry," he said. "I'd like to help you if you'll let me."

Chris looked at Geneva first, staring into those blue eyes who had already gained his trust, then back to Terry. He didn't respond right away but looked into the distance like he was trying to find the right answer. So many questions ran through his mind as well as thoughts of his wife and kids that had been haunting him since he left them.

"I did something," Chris said. "I didn't mean to. I never would have…"

"It's okay Chris," Terry said. "You can tell me anything. I promise I'll do all I can to help you. And I'm not one to break my promises."

Geneva broke in, "You can betcha he's a good fella Chris."

Chris stood and sluggishly walked a good fifteen or twenty feet away, looking down the entire time. His hands were shaking, and he kept trying to make them stop. When he turned and started back, step after step, if thoughts could've been seen, there would've been a million floating all around him. More than likely, his regrets were eating him alive, and it had come to a point where he had to do the right thing.

When he was face to face with Terry once more, "It was me," Chris said, sitting down by Geneva.

"What are you talking about son?" Terry asked, resting his hand on Chris's shoulder, providing support best he knew how.

"Earlier today, I was having some terrible withdrawals and I was walking. I saw that ole truck sitting in a driveway. This old man had gone into his house and I snuck over. I noticed he left the keys in the ignition, so, I helped myself to it," Chris said. "I was so tired of walking."

"What truck Chris?" Terry asked.

Chris got upset once more with a surging of genuine emotion pouring out of him. Between the state of mind he was in physically, combined with the feelings he was completely wrapped in, it created a tornado of problems he couldn't find a solution for. Then, he looked up and locked eyes with Terry, wiping his tears.

"I'm the one who hit Stacey and Emily. I'm the one who hurt my own wife," Chris said, shaking his head, almost in disbelief of what he just spurted out. "I don't know how to live with that."

"I don't know what to say," Terry replied, shocked at his admission of guilt. "But you did save her. Her pulled her out."

"Yes sir I did, but…but then ran away scared," he said. "I should've owned up to it right then and there."

Geneva and Terry peered at one another, both looking more confused than ever. It was a situation that was going to be tough to deal with, especially with everything and everyone involved. Before another minute could pass, Terry took it upon himself to find an answer to so many difficult questions.

"Can you trust me enough to come with me right now," Terry asked.

"Right now?" Chris asked. "I'll be honest…I'm scared."

"Everybody's scared sometimes Chris," Terry replied. "I'll be with you the entire time. I promise."

"Why are you doing this? You don't even know me," Chris said.

"I know that woman in there, the one who loves you and who you love. I know those two adorable kids of yours who shouldn't have to go on without their daddy. And I know what God is telling me to do," Terry said.

"What's that?"

"To get you on the right track and get you back with your family. And I always do what I'm told," Terry answered, patting him on the back.

"I'll go," he told Terry, standing slowly, then looking at Geneva. "It's like you're an angel."

"Honey, I ain't no angel. Elijah over there would tell ya that, but I do want to help. It'd do my heart good to see your family together," Geneva countered right away. "B'sides, I think you're a good egg. You just need somebody to believe in ya. You gotta believe in yourself too honey."

"Maybe that's the problem," Chris said. "Anyway, I want to thank you. Will you tell Emily something for me?"

"Nope," Geneva said. "When you're better, you can tell her yourself."

"Deal," he said, then walked off with Terry.

Geneva joined Elijah and Stacey by the hospital door, but none of them had anything to say. The overwhelming facts of everything that happened that day, was unbelievable to say the least. The sun must've been tired too, because it had already dipped down where there was little light left. Elijah stood and grasped onto Geneva's hand and went toward the van. Stacey followed close behind as the slight breeze was gentle on her skin.

They climbed in Geneva's van and buckled themselves in, still no words being uttered, at least not aloud. Elijah fiddled with the radio until it landed on his favorite old time country favorites station, some gospel songs, and some singers like Hank Williams. Anytime they got in the vehicle, it was almost a given what they would listen to. Elijah swayed his head left to right, then would bob it up and down if the tune got a little peppier. Geneva did the same. They were just a few blocks from Emily and Keith's house when Geneva turned around.

"You sure you're a feelin' okay honey?" Geneva asked. "You sure are welcome to come stay with us."

"I think my sweet husband likes waiting on me sometimes and I think today I'll let him," Stacey said about the time Elijah brought the van to a stop. "I do appreciate the offer though. You're a good soul and so is Terry. Like what you did for Chris."

"Honey, I didn't do anything for Chris. All I did was listen and give a few comfortin' words. Anybody could do that," Geneva answered sweetly.

"Not like you, Geneva. Not like you," Stacey said, getting out, then waving goodbye.

Elijah turned back on the main road, then slowed down, "You have to be hungry sugar," Elijah said. "And I know you don't feel like cooking tonight. To be honest, I wouldn't want you to. Why don't you let me buy you some supper?"

"I suppose," Geneva quickly answered. "I really don't feel like a cookin'. Where we goin'?"

"How about you just ride and let me surprise you?" Elijah said, letting out the rascally grin she loved.

"Surprise me then honey."

He drove to a place down the road called Pop's Place. For the first time in, what seemed like forever, they had time alone. Although Geneva kept bringing up Emily, the kids, Chris, and Stacey, they found other things to talk about, finding themselves laughing and enjoying the special time they were given. Sherry called while they were there and said she told the kids they were staying the night with her, and they didn't have a complaint one. For one night they would have the place to themselves.

When they were almost finished with dinner, they got one more phone call and it was from Terry.

"Hello," Elijah answered.

CHAPTER EIGHTEEN

"Elijah," Terry said. "I got Chris in a detox facility."

"How long does that take?" Elijah said, then putting the call on speaker so Geneva could hear."

"The detox is only three to five days, but then he has a long road ahead of him to stay clean," Terry replied.

Geneva's caring eyes said many things in the short silence after what Terry said, then, "Well, he won't be a goin' it alone. I can tell you that Terry."

"Why did I know you were gonna say that Geneva?" Terry laughed.

"Probably 'cause you know we wanna get this here family back together and get them there kid's daddy back," Geneva answered quickly.

"That we do," Terry said. "But what do we tell Emily?"

"I figure we don't tell'er nothin' right now. Get that boy's system cleaned out and we'll go from there. And when she does see Chris, it won't be a bad thing."

"Yes ma'am," Terry said. "We'll talk soon."

After a nice supper, just Elijah and Geneva, they went home. They both looked like they were dead tired. It was hard to believe how one day could seem like it was a week-long, but so much happened at one time, that's exactly how they felt. The moon had already found its place in the stunning sky above, and on the drive back, the light it put off was beaming. When they pulled up at home, that same moon looked almost big enough to reach out and touch. Geneva got out and couldn't help but stare at it.

"Man," she said.

"What Geneva?" Elijah asked, stopping, and waiting for her.

She stood there slowly shaking her head and lacing her fingers, all the while never taking her eyes off such a sight. "He sure is an artist, honey. It's like he created that there sky to be his eternal canvas and every day, he paints us a new picture."

"It does seem that way dear," Elijah said, going and wrapping both arms around her. "It is a sight."

"You know, I bet lots a folks don't even take one minute in the day to notice stuff like this. They take it for granted doggonit," Geneva said. "Every day's a miracle, Elijah."

"What's on your mind Geneva? I've known you long enough to know this isn't just about the moon or the sky," Elijah said, taking her hand and leading her to the swing she loved so much.

When they sat down, her fingers automatically began to caress the carefully carved cross on the swing. Like a habit, she did it every time without fail. There was something about every curve etched in the beautifully stained wood Elijah took the time to build just for her. Even though he didn't care much for it at the time, that very cross became etched into his heart after a while.

"I was just thinkin' how blessed we are honey and how I always try to make everything okay for everybody. I know I can't do that. And I make lots a promises to folks, like to Emily, the kids and even to Chris," Geneva said.

"What are you talking about?"

"I was thinkin' what it says in the bible 'bout makin' promises you can't keep," Geneva continued.

"What promises did you make Geneva?" Elijah kept on, trying to figure out the jumbled-up thoughts coming from her lips.

She didn't answer immediately, but instead, rested her head gently on his shoulder, looking into the yard. The crickets chanted their tunes as every night before and the fireflies lit up the front yard.

"When we found Emily and the kids, before I even knew what she was a goin' through, I promised her everything would be okay," Geneva said. "And the same with the kids even after I knew. I'm not God Elijah. I can't predict the future. I can't save the world. And I don't wanna give somebody hope when maybe there ain't none."

Elijah made her turn to look him in the eye. Obvious he couldn't believe those words came from her. "Is your name Geneva James?" Elijah questioned. "Because my Geneva would never give up hope."

"It says somewhere in Ecclesiastes not to make rash promises or be hasty. It says to bring matters before God and let your words be few," Geneva muttered, her emotions taking hold of every word she spoke. "And I been tellin' them it was all okay. I don't know if it's gonna be okay Elijah. I been tryin' to do God's job."

"Honey," Elijah said, holding her tightly to him. "You mean well and just want to make them feel better."

"But what if..."

"No what-ifs, "Elijah interrupted. "It also says in the good book, to pray when you feel anxious...right? And what does it say in Psalm forty-six?"

Geneva let out a big sigh, "God is our refuge and strength, and ever-present help in trouble," she said. "You tryin' to quiz me honey?"

"No, I'm trying to tell you God put you in their life for a reason, and those promises you're making them, I think God told you to, so he can make'em come true. That's what I think dear," Elijah said, sweetly giving her a peck on the forehead.

Geneva let out a short cackling laugh, "Boy oh boy, if your old self could see you now, he'd be makin' fun a you Elijah. I used to be teachin' you and now, well, you're a teachin' me. I needed that honey. I really did."

"How about we go call the hospital to check on Emily then hit the hay?" Elijah said, standing and reaching his hand for hers. "I'm tired and I know you are."

She took his hand and nodded to him, giving that unique Geneva grin God gave only to her. They went inside and Geneva took the phone in the living room, sitting on the couch. When the phone rang a couple of times, the switchboard answered and transferred her to the emergency room where one of the nurses she had talked to earlier, answered.

"This is Geneva James," she said. "You remember me?"

"How could I forget you miss Geneva? And I know what you're going to ask. Emily is resting well. We gave her some more medicine to sleep and it's doing the trick," the nurse said. "No reason to worry. The doctor said we can discharge her sometime around mid-morning tomorrow if she's still stable. As far as I can see, I believe she will be."

"Thank you so much. I worry," Geneva said.

"Get some rest and you'll be coming to get her tomorrow Mrs. James."

She hung up the phone and trotted into the kitchen for a snack. Earlier in the day before everything started, she had made a big batch of homemade chocolate chip cookies to greet Emily and the kids home. She didn't know they wouldn't be there to enjoy them. Elijah poured two glasses of milk and they indulged in her homemade confections. Geneva kept looking around every time she dipped a cookie in the milk and take a bite.

"What?" Elijah asked.

"It's so blame quiet in here," she said. "I used to think I liked quiet, but…"

Elijah chuckled, "I was thinking the exact same thing. I keep thinking Joshua's gonna run down those stairs and jump in my lap for a story."

"Yeppers," Geneva said. "And Katy wanting me to brush her hair."

"It's strange isn't it," Elijah muttered with a faint smile.

"What honey?"

"I feel like they've been in our family forever," Elijah answered.

They both dipped their last cookie and finished off what they set aside as their nightly snack, put everything away and headed upstairs.

After finding the most perfect and comfortable spot in bed, the kind you fall into and drift off, both Geneva and Elijah did exactly that. The day's events took its toll on their elder bodies and minds for that matter, leaving them longing for rest. It didn't take but a few minutes after their heads hit the pillow to close their eyes and travel in time carrying them to the next day. No dreams of any kind wiggled into their thoughts, only a solemnness only God could give.

When the morning sun woke for the day, sharing its light through the bedroom window, Elijah and Geneva rose from the gift of a peaceful sleep. The tired bodies they had the day before, were replaced with energy and pep. Of course, Geneva always had energy and pep, but somehow, Elijah followed his wife's lead and hopped out of bed.

CHAPTER NINETEEN

From across the field, they heard some banging and hammering. It appeared to be on that piece of property to the left when you turn on their road and it sat off just a little. There used to be a house in that spot, but it burned years ago. Neither Elijah nor Geneva ever knew who owned that land, but never really gave it much thought. All they knew, was, they heard a commotion coming from there.

"Makin' so much noise so early in the blame mornin'," Geneva said, pouring their first cup of coffee for the day. "They coulda started later on, shoot."

"It's their job I suppose Geneva," Elijah said. "We'll go by there on the way out to see what's going on. Would that make you feel better?"

Geneva sipped her coffee and the steam started to fog up her glasses, "Yessir it would. And I suppose we need to shake our tail feathers honey so we can go get Emily and pick up the kids too."

"You cooking breakfast?" Elijah aggravated, knowing it was always part of her morning routine.

"Does a bear live in the woods?"

Elijah finished his cup of coffee, gave her a sweet kiss on the cheek, "I'll get a quick shower while you're whipping up your all famous…"

"Flattery'll get ya everywhere honey," Geneva laughed. "Now git up them there stairs and git cleaned up."

"Yes ma'am," he said, like he was taking orders from a drill sergeant, then went on his way.

The noise coming from down the way started echoing and getting louder. Always being in love with the solitude out there and the peace around her, such a noise wasn't welcomed in the least. When she was finished cooking and set the plates on the table along with another cup of coffee, Elijah's timing was perfect. He slid into his chair like he was sliding at homeplate in a baseball game, and with the first bite, that grin showed a home run.

"Ooooweee," Elijah moaned. "I didn't marry you for your cookin' but it sure is a plus."

Just about to throw some words back at that husband of hers, the phone rang. Elijah wiped his mouth and ran to answer.

"Hey Terry," Elijah said. "How are the kids? Yep, uh-huh, okay, I'll let you know."

"Well, that was a short conversation honey," Geneva said. "What'd he have to say?"

"He said the kids were good. They don't know about what happened with the wreck and wants us to call them when we bring Emily back home," he answered. "That was about it."

"Okay then," Geneva said, taking the last bite of eggs and sopping her biscuit in the runny part, practically cleaning it spotless. "I won't be long."

She scampered up the stairs and Elijah could still hear the hammers beating and electric tools doing their job. He went outside and walked to the driveway, trying to see who was doing the work. It was a little too far to see anything, so he went back inside and cleaned up the little Geneva had dirtied cooking breakfast. By the time she came back down, the kitchen was spotless clean.

"Well, looky here," she said, her entertaining attitude floating around. She rested a fist on each hip, lowered her head, and raised her eyebrows. "You do know how to do dishes Elijah. I was beginnin' to wonder honey."

"You're a comedian Geneva," Elijah answered. "You might a just messed up your chances of me doing them again."

She rushed up to him and gave him a quick smack right on the lips, "You never could take a joke Elijah. I sure appreciate you a cleanin' up my mess. You're welcome to do it anytime you like."

Elijah looked up and noticed it was going on ten o'clock. "We best get going," he said. "We don't want Emily to wait on us. I'm sure she's shaken up enough as it is. Besides, I know she's ready to see them two precious kids."

"You're right," Geneva said, snatched her purse off the table in the entryway and opened the front door.

Elijah was dragging a little, but when Geneva got in her red van, he hurried to get in before she ran off and left him. When they had just about made it to the highway, Geneva looked over and saw a frame of a house going up. The slab had already been poured even though she didn't know when, and the workers were running around like crazy. A few were sitting on the tailgate onsite, and she decided to pull up and see who was moving in.

Geneva rolled down her window, "Howdy fellas," she said. "We live just down this road here and heard all the ruckus goin' on."

"Yes ma'am," the young guy said respectfully. "Sorry about that, but we were told to get this done. My boss said he was getting paid a lot extra to have it done by a certain date, so we'll be starting early every day."

"If you don't mind me askin', who's movin' into this here place? Looks like ya'll are buildin' a log house," she kept prodding.

"Ma'am, I don't know who's going to live here. All I know is that I'm making money building it. I wish I had more answers," he said, tipping his work hat to her and getting back to his job at hand.

Elijah began to laugh at Geneva. The expression on her face showed curiosity multiplied times a hundred. One thing she couldn't stand, was not being able to figure out a mystery. And at the moment, whoever was building that house, was a mystery. The entire way driving, she kept muttering below her breath, but not a single word could be made out. It's like she was talking to herself and answering herself at the same time. Elijah didn't dare interrupt the internal conversation she was having, for fear of the evil look she was notorious for shooting at him.

When they reached the hospital, she parked as close as she could get to the door. Just about every park was taken, but there was one lonely spot left forgotten closer than the rest. She whipped in quick as she could before someone tried to steal it. They got out and made their way inside.

Most of the faces were different, but the doctor taking care of Emily the day before was walking down the hallway toward one of the entrances to the emergency rooms.

"Doc," Geneva hollered out.

Since her voice was unmistakable and unforgettable at the same time, he stopped suddenly and turned around just before going through the double doors.

"Mrs. James," the doctor said. "Follow me. I think we can get her papers ready to discharge her. She did very well through the night. She will be extremely sore for a while, but that's to be expected in any kind of wreck like this. Her arms is just sprained and should be okay sooner than I thought, I'll say what I said yesterday. She's lucky to be alive."

"Oh doc," Geneva grinned. "Luck ain't got nothin' to do with it. God took care a her, I can promise you that."

The minute she said the word *promise*, she glanced at Elijah and laughed, remembering their conversation the night before. For some reason, she was sure God told her to say that because it was true. To her, there was no doubt about his presence when that truck hit Emily.

When they reached Emily's room, the doctor opened the door and went inside. Emily was sitting up in bed with a tray in front of her. She was picking through something that looked like scrambled eggs, a few pieces of toast, and a slice or two of bacon. To drink, there were two small cartons of milk, one white and one chocolate, and a glass of orange juice. The way she stared at the food in front of her told the entire story. After a bite or two, she was done. She did drink her milk and juice, but that was it.

"Looks good Emily," Elijah said, aggravating still. "Geneva's breakfast looked almost that good this morning."

Geneva didn't waste a minute, whopping him on the arm, muttering her words once more, then found a seat next to Emily's bed, scooting close as she could get. Emily was still attempting to eat what they brought her, but it was a lost cause.

"Geneva, this is not like what you cook," she smiled, pushing the rolling tray away from her.

"I tell ya what honey," Geneva said. "When we git back to the house, I'm gonna whip you up anything you want. You just name it."

"Are the kids okay?" Emily asked, concern showing in her eyes.

Geneva patted her hand and smiled, "Honey, they're just fine. I betcha that there Sherry is spoilin' them two somethin' awful. Anyway, they're bringin'em over when we get home."

After a few minutes, the nurse came in and brought a few things for Emily to sign so they could leave. She did what he asked, but then stopped her before she left. "I don't know how I'm going to pay for this," Emily said sincerely. "I don't have any money."

"Oh, I meant to tell you," the nurse smiled. "The bill's been taken care of."

Emily, Geneva, and Elijah stared at the nurse after hearing her say such a thing. "Who paid for it doc?" Geneva asked, knowing it wasn't her.

"It was anonymous," she answered. "That's all I know."

"I don't understand," Emily said. "Who would…"

"Honey," Geneva stopped her. "If somebody wants to bless you, let'em bless you. And it looks to me like this was a big ole' blessing sugar."

"Can we go home?" Emily asked, her eyes shining bright, ready to get out of that place.

"You betcha we can," Geneva replied, getting the few things she had with her and putting her in a wheelchair.

Considering she was in a sling for her arm, they were very careful with her. Geneva went and pulled the van in front of the doors and Elijah helped her in. From the black and blue bruises on her face and arm, it looked like she had been in a bar fight. It probably looked worse than it actually was, but when the kids got home, they would see it differently. Geneva drove home carefully, then turned down their road. Geneva threw a cloud of dust in the direction of the guys working on that house and they all looked her way.

She pulled up and there sat Terry, Sherry and the kids waiting on the front porch. The kids ran like crazy to the van, bouncing up and down like Mexican jumping beans, then went to the side where Emily was.

"I called Terry," Elijah said. "I figured we might need help getting her inside. You know we ain't spring chickens no more."

All Geneva did was poke out her lips and give him a familiar look, then got out and went to get Emily. "Hey young'uns," Geneva said. "It's so good to see ya'll."

"Is mama okay?" Katy asked, wrapping her arms around Geneva sweetly. "Miss Sherry said she got hurt."

Geneva kneeled, "Honey, your mama's gonna be just fine. You hear me. I promise. Now, let's get her in the house so she can rest, and you can help us take care of her. You think you could do that?"

"I can," Joshua chimed in as usual.

When they saw her with the sling on her arm and bruises on her face and neck, their eyes grew bigger. Before they could get upset, Emily calmed them. "I'm okay," she said. "It doesn't hurt. It's like somebody took some colors to my face. It'll go away."

"What about your arm mama?" Katy asked, holding her hand as they walked toward the house.

"Well sweetie," Emily muttered softly. "That'll take a little bit longer, so I'll need ya'lls help with some things. Can you help me for a while?"

Both kids nodded as to say *yes*, all the while peering at the shades of black, blue and some purple, across her lovely face. When they got inside, the kids led Emily to the couch in the living room and sat her down like she wasn't capable of sitting on her own. Joshua sat on one side and Katy took the other, both scooting close to her.

"I'll tell you what," Geneva said, standing at the edge of the couch. "If that ain't a perty sight. You young'uns sure love your mama. How 'bout I fix up a mess a breakfast."

"Sounds like Heaven," Emily said, flashing a delightful smile. "I'm starved."

"Yeppers," Geneva laughed. "That there hospital food will keep you alive, but that's about it."

"I second that," Emily replied immediately.

"Well, honey, you just sit there and find ya somethin' to watch on that there television and I'll have somethin' ready before you know it," Geneva said, practically hurrying off to do what she did best, take care of people.

Sherry came inside after talking to Elijah outside for a bit, then sat with Emily for a minute. The kids loved all over Sherry as well as Emily, and the happiness they showed, glowed all around them.

"I'll go see if Geneva needs any help," Sherry said. "I hope she's making her famous home-made biscuits. If she don't, Terry won't let her forget it."

The kids started flipping through channel after channel until they landed on one of their favorite cartoons. To look at Emily, you could tell it didn't matter what they watched. Her eyes were growing heavy, but she kept herself as alert as she could for the kids.

It wasn't twenty minutes and Geneva hollered out, "Breakfast is ready…again," she said. "Emily, you stay where you're at. I'm a bringin' it to ya."

Terry and Elijah walked in when they heard Geneva bellowing about food and they trotted directly into the kitchen. The first step in, Geneva held out a hot out of the oven, buttered biscuit on a saucer, to Terry.

"Ain't you the sweetest thing," Terry said, stuffing his mouth full.

"Good gracious, Terry" Geneva said. "You remind me of Caleb."

"Never could resist your biscuits," he responded, buttering up one more before they were all gone.

"Leave some a them there biscuits Terry. I promised Emily I'd fix her up a big ole breakfast," Geneva said, fixing Emily's plate and serving her in the living room.

"She can't eat'em all," Terry yelled out as she left the kitchen.

After making sure Emily had what she needed, Geneva went to clean what mess she just made, and Sherry stepped in to help. Terry was sitting at the table with Elijah talking about this and that, when that noise down the road started up once more.

"That blame construction folks are 'bout to get on my nerves. You'd a thought whoever was buildin' that place would let the neighbors know," Geneva said, glancing out the kitchen window in the direction of the racket.

"Geneva," Sherry started, but Terry interrupted.

"How does Emily seem?" he asked. "Sherry had to tell the kids something but didn't make it sound like she was hurt too bad. We figured we'd let them see her, so they'd know she was okay."

"Yep," Geneva said, joining them at the kitchen table. "She seems okay, but a little distant."

"They've been through a lot," Sherry added. "But I had a wonderful time with those two kids. Almost made me feel like I was young again."

It wasn't long, and Katy sauntered in carrying her mama's plate, smiling from ear to ear. She dropped it in the sink, clapped her hands together like she was getting dirt off them, then ran over and climbed in Sherry's lap. She found a sweet cuddling position and rested her head on Sherry's shoulder.

"Your mama okay?" Sherry asked, hugging Katy sweetly

"Yeah," she answered. "She's asleep on the couch."

"I guess I best get her up to her room so she can rest proper like," Geneva said, getting up.

"I'll help," Elijah said, knowing the stairs would be an obstacle in the state her body was in at the time.

Before they could even get out of the kitchen, Emily let out a scream.

CHAPTER TWENTY

Still asleep, but obviously having a nightmare, Emily was screaming out "Chris…Chris."

Tears were streaming down her face and she was reaching out like someone was there. Geneva woke her carefully until Emily's eyes popped open. Her breaths were intense and appeared more like panting than anything else. After a moment or two, she began to calm down, seeing everyone surrounding her.

"Where's Chris?" she asked. "I heard Chris. I swear I did Geneva."

"Honey," Geneva started to answer until Terry stepped in.

"Sherry, why don't you take the kids outside to play? You know how they love to play in the yard," he said, not really wanting them to hear what he was about to say. Then, he went over and sat next to Emily. "You did hear Chris."

Emily closed her eyes and took in a breath at the same time, "I knew it. I think I was unconscious, but still heard what was going on around me. He was calling my name and telling me to open my eyes."

"You didn't dream it Emily. He pulled you out of the car before the paramedics got there, but then…" Terry stopped.

"He ran away," Emily whispered, lowered her head, and glanced away from everyone. "He always runs away."

"But Emily, he has a…"

"I don't care what he has or hasn't got," she said, cutting Terry off abruptly. "If he cared, he'd be here now. He'd be right beside me. He'd be here for our babies. But he's not.

He's probably strung out somewhere just trying to get more so he can get high again."

"What I'm trying to tell you…"

"Miss Geneva," Emily said, interrupting Terry once more. "Can I go to my room? I'm so tired. Do you mind watching the kids while I rest?"

"Sure honey," Geneva said, glancing at Terry and giving him a very confused look. "Come on."

Elijah got on the other side of her and made sure she didn't tumble down the stairs. Step by step, she made it to her room and Geneva got her comfortable and tucked in. Emily turned on her good side, resting the one in a sling. She was facing the window and Geneva went and closed the curtains to block out as much light as possible, then left the room.

Something told Geneva Emily wasn't really tired, but tired of talking about Chris instead. After hearing so many stories from her, the good and the bad, her emotions were in full on overload and without a doubt, couldn't take much more. Geneva and Elijah went back down, and Terry was sitting there with a heart wrenching look, then rested his face in his hands. Words weren't needed to know he was playing tug-of-war with his obligations and promises made. On one hand, he told Chris he would get him help, but on the other, Emily was hurting along with the kids.

"What do we do?" Terry asked. "I have to get this boy straight, and not just for himself, but for that family."

"I agree," Geneva replied with a hefty nod.

"I have to do whatever it takes to show him what he's missin' out on," Terry kept on. "Right?"

"Yessir," Geneva answered again.

"I have to say," Terry continued. "This sure does seem like a one-sided conversation Geneva. You normally have a lot to say."

"Well, dad burnit," she replied. "You're a sayin' it all. If Emily don't want to talk about Chris, she don't have to, but that ain't gonna keep you from gettin' him help. Right?"

Terry glanced at Elijah, "You got a heck of a woman here Eli. There's something about the way she explained it, that makes it sound like it's all gonna be okay."

"She's always right Terry," Elijah smiled. "At least that's what she tells me."

Suddenly, it sounded like a tornado coming through the front door. Sherry was chasing after Katy and Joshua and their laughter echoed. When they finally came to a halt, they were all catching their breath, especially Sherry. It was obvious she was trying to keep up with those two, but the winners were clear. She plopped down on the couch next to Terry and immediately tilted into him, resting her head on his shoulder.

"I think they could go another round dear," Terry laughed.

Sherry slightly lifted her head and cut her eyes to him, "They might, but…"

"Like I tell Geneva all the time," Elijah cut in. "We ain't no spring chickens anymore."

The kids must've been tired too because they found a spot on the rug in front of the fireplace. Joshua had already fell backwards with his hand on his stomach as it went up and down over and over. Katy, on the other hand, was more concerned about her hair. She had her ponytail holder in her hand and quickly pulled her beautiful strawberry blonde hair up. It looked like a long, thick main on a heavenly horse with a few curls mixed in. Her girly girl attitude, always wanting to look just so, came across all too well, and her brilliant green eyes had already melted all their hearts.

"Where's mama?" Katy asked, finding a place next to Joshua.

"Oh honey," Geneva said, darting to them and scooting between the two. "She's a restin'. You know the more rest she gets, the quicker she'll get well."

Joshua, in the most timid and sweet manner, looked up at Geneva, "I guess we better let'er sleep then, huh Mama G? I want mama to feel better."

"You betcha," Geneva answered, putting an arm around each one and bear hugging them like never before.

There was something about the innocence oozing from those kids, drawing in everyone they met. The caring nature they displayed showed one thing...Emily and Chris had taught them something important, to love others. The way Katy took care of Joshua, was like a miniature grown up, doing her duty. And since their daddy left, she probably thought her mama needed the help. It was sad to see but inspiring at the same time. People always say that everything happens for a reason, and maybe, just maybe, the reason was for her to see the importance of loving each other no matter what.

"Hey," Sherry said, kneeling in front of them. "How about me and Terry take you two to town for a while so your mama can sleep? What do ya say?"

As usual, they both belted out a robust "*Yes,*" and acted like they had ants in their pants from the excitement of going somewhere else. It was more than obvious they had been deprived of lots of things, and just the smallest gesture painted smiles on their faces.

Terry pulled Elijah to the side while Sherry gathered the kid's things, "You know Eli, they'll be releasing Chris this weekend unless I find a place for him to transition into like that one in Camden Arkansas," Terry said. "They have a great thirty-day program that's been pretty successful."

"Five days isn't enough Terry," Elijah said. "He'll go right back to the same ole ways. Don't ya think?"

"I've seen it a thousand times," Terry agreed. "I have to make sure his mind is set on turning his life around before I help reinsert him in Emily and the kids' lives. I can't, in good conscience, put them through it all over again."

"Call that Camden place and see if they will have a bed by the weekend and we all need to pray it sticks," Elijah said.

"Amen to that brother," Terry replied. "For everyone's sake."

"You coming uncle Terry?" Joshua said, looking up at Terry.

Elijah laughed, "Uncle Terry?"

"What else are they gonna call me Eli? Besides, I kinda like it," Terry said, grabbing Joshua's hand.

"Well, dog fire, I like it too…uncle Terry," Geneva said. "We'll holler when she gets up and around."

They left with the kids and the place was quiet once more. Geneva did a little cleaning up and found herself sitting in the wingback chair by the window in the living room, staring out to the field she loved. Somehow, it always gave her a sense of peace and gratitude for God and the nature he so perfectly created. On days when she found herself anxious, that scene in the distance did its job, by calming her.

"How about we take a little walk down the road," Elijah suggested. "It's not hot as it has been honey."

"Shoot, why not? I don't like just sittin' around anyway. I'm sure Emily'll be out for a bit. Then we can come back, and I'll fix up a late lunch," Geneva said, pushing herself up with the arms of the chair. "I'm sure we'll all be hungry by then."

Casually walking around outside, the little breeze blowing was enough to make it a pleasant experience. The shade of blue the sky was painted at that time, was perfect with God's strokes carefully made on such a canvass. Few clouds drifted about, but the ones that did, made Geneva imagine what they were shaped like. It was something she always loved to do from the time she was a kid. Most kids probably did, but she always saw the most farfetched things in them. It's like her imagination took over the minute her eyes peered toward Heaven.

They stopped at the top of the small hill just on the other side of the road from the house. From the first time they stood in that spot years earlier, they fell in love with the view. It was a spot Geneva felt close to God. Before Elijah ever found his spiritual side, she would go and plant herself in that perfect place and pray. The musical sounds of the birds singing their harmonies, filled such a huge space completely.

"Oh boy," Geneva said. "If this ain't a perfect life, I can't tell ya what is."

Elijah chuckled, then "I remember when we first pulled up to this house and you were taken in dear. I was being my usual hateful and aggravating self and I made you mad about somethin' or another."

"If I could remember what it was, I'd probably get mad all over again," Geneva laughed. "We did good here honey."

"That we did," he said.

The songs the birds were singing were quickly smothered out by sounds of hammering, banging and saws down the way, as the guys started back working on that house after their lunch. It sounded like half the town was working on that one little house, but Geneva pushed her aggravation aside and focused once more on the beauty in front of her.

"It's gettin' a touch warm honey," Geneva said, noticing the breeze cooling them at first, had gone away, leaving way for the sun to pound down.

"I'm starting to get a little hungry anyway," Elijah said, holding out his hand for her to grab a hold of. "How about we go cook up somethin' Mrs. James."

"It'd be my pleasure Mr. James," Geneva laughed, accepting his sweet gesture, and taking it in. "What do you suppose would be good to whip up?"

Elijah got that thinking look, one where he couldn't come up with an answer, really. "We really don't have nothin' thawed out to cook Geneva. But I can run real quick to the store and pick up whatever you want to."

"Dag nabbit, we don't do we honey?" Geneva said. "Well, I'll put my thinkin' cap on and make a list when we get inside. With everything happenin', I forgot to plan on lunch or supper. You know that ain't like me."

"I sure don't go hungry Geneva. That's for sure," Elijah said, nudging her as they walked.

Elijah opened the door, and they went in, being very careful not to wake Emily. Geneva did an inventory of what she had and what she needed and sat down at the table making a list. She knew Elijah wasn't one to like grocery shopping, but in such a situation, he needed to be the one for such a chore. It seemed like the more she looked around, the longer the list became, and Elijah stood over her, probably hoping she would stop soon.

"There ya go honey," Geneva announced. "That oughta keep us for a while."

"It sure should," Elijah replied, his eyes skimming each and every item she wrote down. "I'll be home in a few hours."

She couldn't help but haul off and hit him on the arm hard as she could, shooting a look Elijah knew all too well. "Just git and hurry it up. You're not the only one whose stomach's a complainin'."

He folded the page and put it in his wallet, grabbed his keys and went out the door. The dogs started barking more every time they heard hammering and she hoped it didn't wake Emily. It immediately felt different in the house. It wasn't often she was there like that without a host of folks roaming around her. It wasn't but a few days since Ella and Caleb went home, but she always missed them. Although she did call and tell them what happened to Emily and the situation with Chris, it wasn't the same.

Geneva did the one thing she loved most when she would find herself alone, read the bible. To her, getting in God's word, was one thing she couldn't get enough of. As she opened her old bible, she couldn't decide what book to go to, so she flipped the pages and it stopped on something fitting. Strangely enough, it stopped in 1 Corinthians chapter ten. She began to read where it was talking about temptation and what God promises when the adversary attacks. His promises appeared to jump clean off the page, hitting her right in her heart. As much as she'd been talking about promises and if she was wrong, ironically, he led her to a scripture that talked about promises.

In such silence, she closed her eyes, clutched her bible and pulled it close, then started to pray.

Oh, dear Heavenly Father, so much is happenin' Lord. And I know you know it all, but I've been tryin' to fix everything and everybody and God I don't think I can. I been promisin ' them kid's things would be okay and their mama too. Lord, I even told the same to their daddy who's in a really bad way. Am I doin' somethin' wrong God? Am I lyin' to these folks or is it that you're helpin' me make it come true. Lord, Chris is so messed up and in turn, this family is messed up. I want good for'em all. Please help me to keep my promises, to follow your lead, and to do what you say. I don't have the answers Lord, but I'm prayin' right now, you send'em my way. Thank you so much for dyin' on the cross for me and payin' the price for my sins. I love you Lord, in Jesus name…AMEN

Looking up after an intimate moment with God, *I'm gonna go check on her,* Geneva whispered out loud to herself, getting up, then tip toeing up the stairs. *Am I talkin' to myself again.*

She got herself tickled from her own silliness, but when she got to Emily's door, she opened it very carefully, so the old hinges wouldn't creak like always. When she was inside, Emily was still in the same spot facing the window as slow and steady breaths showed she found some relaxation amidst the craziness surrounding her.

There were a few pieces of clothing strewn around, so she decided to pick up a few things while she was in there, tidy up. As she picked up the last thing, a lightweight robe that appeared to have fallen off the hook on the closet door, she saw something under it.

CHAPTER TWENTY-ONE

Never one to be nosy, something told her to look at what was inside. The flaps of the box were half open already, so, after glancing to make sure Emily was still asleep, Geneva sat on the floor, legs half crossed, and put the box in her lap.

Lord, what am I doin'? I know this ain't none a my business, she said to herself, but something coaxed her to continue on.

She opened the box. Inside were quite a few folded pieces of notebook paper which looked like writings of some sort. Geneva hesitated to go any further, but yet again, she couldn't stop herself. It's like a mystery was placed in front of her and it was one her curiosity wouldn't let her leave alone.

The first piece of paper she pulled out, looked like it may have been written right after Chris walked out on Emily and the kids. Geneva's eyes rolled over each word, each sentence, then found herself sitting on the floor bawling, feeling the hurt it took to write such words. Clutching the page in her hands, the emotional ache that went into the letter, transferred to her, feeling Emily's pain just the same. Then, after wiping the tears away, she re-read the letter, trying to figure out how to get through to Emily. She wanted to find the core of her emotions and address that best she could.

My Love Chris,

I don't really know why I'm writing this letter. You'll never see it, but somehow, I have to get my feelings out. I have to find a way to feel better, not feel so alone. As much love as we found in each other, it hurts to know you love the drinking and drugs more than you love us. As much as it took to find sober living together after a long road of bad mistakes, you left me to chase it again. I don't know what I'll tell the kids. They love you so much, especially Josh. He thinks you hung the moon and stars, but now I have to be the one to tell them you're not coming back. If I was a religious person, I'd ask God to help, but then again, if there is a God, why would he let this happen. It makes me wonder if he even exists sometimes. I just want to scream to the top of my lungs and get it all out, but I can't. There's too much hurt. I hope you are okay. I hope you find your way back to us one day, but not like this. I love you so much and I will always love you. I'll be here…

LOVE,
EMILY

Geneva folded up the paper neatly and placed it where she knew it was one she'd already read. She pushed herself up from the floor and started to leave, but when the door's hinges showed their age, making the usual sound, Emily turned her head.

"Miss Geneva?" Emily muttered in a groggy voice. "What time is it? Where are the kids?"

"Shhh," Geneva whispered. "Go back to sleep honey. I'll wake ya up when I get something whipped up to eat."

"The kids?" she asked once more.

"Oh, Terry and Sherry took'em to town. They sure do like dotin' on them two. Anyway, get a little more rest. It's good for ya and I'll come back when the food is ready, okay?"

"Miss Geneva," Emily said, rolling on her back where she could see better. "Did you see Chris?"

Geneva took in a slow breath and released it as she went toward Emily, then sat next to her. "Yeah baby, I did."

"Where'd you see him?" she asked, so many questions visible in her eyes.

"At the hospital. He was a sittin' outside the doors when we started to go home."

"Was he…"

"Honey, I think you need to rest some more, and we'll talk afterwhile," Geneva said, not really knowing what to say.

"I need to know Miss Geneva," she pushed forward. "Was he…was he…"

"He wasn't in a good place Emily," Geneva answered before she could even finish the question. "I talked to him."

"I know I'm guilty of doing some bad things Miss Geneva. I've never denied it, but after the kids were born, it's like they were my drug, my life…ya know?" Emily said. "How can somebody choose something like that over their family?"

"I don't know honey," Geneva said. "I'll tell ya one thing though. Folks can change. I know that for a fact. So, don't count him out just yet."

Emily gave a short, half-humored chuckle, "I think I already have."

Geneva got a look on her face like when she was about to say something profound and memorable. She scooted closer to Emily, then started, "You ever heard the story about Saul in the bible?"

"No ma'am," Emily answered, knowing she was about to hear it.

"Well, ya see honey, Saul was an ornery sort. He did what he could to destroy the church and went door to door in Jerusalem. When he found people who was followin' Jesus, he'd have'em thrown in prison. He didn't stop there," Geneva continued. "He wanted to track down all the Christians those folks sent mail to."

"What happened then?" Emily asked, showing her interest in the story Geneva carefully told.

"So, when he set out to find them other Christians, he ran into Jesus, after he'd done rose from the grave," Geneva said.

"What did he do Geneva?"

"I suppose what he wrote in 1 Timothy says it all honey," Geneva answered. "Bad as that fella was, condonin' murder and huntin' down Christians, one visit with Jesus changed his life honey."

"What did he write?" Emily replied curiously.

Geneva hopped up and went into her and Elijah's room and came right back. She was holding a smaller bible she kept in her nightstand. Her fingers began flipping through the thin pages, and it was obvious she knew exactly what she was looking for.

"Sorry honey, my mind slips here and there, and I can't remember exactly what it says, and I wouldn't want to misquote the word, ya know," Geneva blurted out with a half laugh weaved in. "Yep, here we go. It says, *Christ Jesus came into the world to save sinners – of whom I am the worst. But for that very reason I was shown mercy so that in me, the worst of sinners, Christ Jesus might display his immense patience as an example for those who would believe in him and receive eternal life.*"

Emily's focus stayed on every word Geneva spoke. The look in her eyes showed she was absorbing it all, every sentence, and the meaning it portrayed.

"After that, God changed his name to Paul and he wrote most of the new testament books in the bible," Geneva continued.

"So, what am I supposed to get out of that Geneva?"

"Oh honey, it just means, when you put your trust in Christ, even if you been an awful person like Saul, he can transform you. It don't matter what you did, what you thought about doin' or even if you're ashamed of yourself. When you ask him to save you, everything before that there moment is gone. The way the bible says it, they're wiped away."

"It's hard to believe he could change after what he's done," Emily replied with a skeptical tongue.

"Did you hear what I said girl? Anybody. Me...you... and even Chris." Geneva said, trying harder to get her point across.

"I don't really care anyway," she said. "I have to take care of the kids. That's my main priority right now," Emily said. "And repaying all of you for your kindness."

From downstairs, the sound of the front door opening, and closing rang clearly. Elijah had made it home from the grocery store and probably needed help getting things inside. Geneva thought for a second on what Emily had just said, knowing she still cared about Chris.

"I tell you what," Geneva said. "You think on that a while, and I'm gonna go down and help Elijah get them there groceries in, and cook. We'll talk later."

With tired eyes, Emily nodded, "Okay Miss Geneva... and thank you for always taking the time to talk. It's kinda nice."

"You betcha," Geneva said, leaning and giving her a tender kiss on the forehead. "It shouldn't be long, and we'll get you down to eat."

Emily grabbed Geneva's hand before she could get too far away, "Geneva, to be honest, you're kind of like a mama to me. I haven't had one in a long time and I almost forgot what it feels like."

"Oh sugar, I'd be honored to be your mama. And I know they are smilin' down on you, proud," Geneva said, smiling inside and out, and it showed. "We didn't find each other by accident."

Not missing an opportunity to show how special Emily's words were, Geneva gave her a cuddling hug, careful not to hurt her arm in the process. The bond they had started growing the minute they met and continued to grow with each day that passed. Geneva told Elijah several times, God put them at that very spot at that exact moment to find Emily and the kids, and without a doubt she truly believed it.

"Comin' honey," Geneva called out, going downstairs.

"It's about time woman," Elijah said, then burst laughing, knowing if he didn't, her bad side would come out.

"You better watch it," Geneva muttered. "Just set them there sacks on the table and I'll put'em up."

Just like she said she would, she came up with a meal fit for a king. Emily got up and around while Elijah called Terry. He said they would bring the kids back by the time supper was ready, which meant he would get there in time to eat. He always told Elijah, he never could resist Geneva's cooking.

The next few days flew by. The dark bruises began to fade and there was no doubt she enjoyed every minute with the kids. She even took off her sling as the pain in her arm started to subside. Stacey came by both days and visited with Emily. Mostly, they sat on the front porch and talked. Geneva could hear them from the kitchen, laughing every little bit and it was a delightful sound to her ears. The kids were constantly running and playing. Every little bit, they'd stop and ask their mama if she needed anything, then they would scamper away once again.

For some reason, Emily didn't bring Chris's name up. It's like she was afraid to utter his name for fear there would be a flood of emotions come in and drown her. But she was healing physically. Her emotional state of mind was questionable, but one thing was for sure, there were plenty of people who cared.

"Want some sweet tea?" Geneva called out to Stacey and Emily.

They were in their spot swinging and Stacey was the first to answer, "Yes ma'am."

"Don't call me ma'am," Geneva hollered back. "Makes me feel old."

Emily and Stacey couldn't help but laugh at her. It didn't matter who was around or what she was doing, she was the same person, never wavering from the nature she exuded. Her comical ways were genuine and true, just the way God made her, and those ways were contagious. You couldn't help but smile around her.

"Here we go," she said, coming outside with a tray of glasses filled with her special sweet tea.

She sat it on the table between the two wicker chairs against the house and gave them out one by one. When the kids came running up, she had smaller glasses of lemonade for them. They snatched them up and took off again.

"Boy, oh boy," Geneva said. "I'd give anything for that kinda energy. I'd get a lot done."

Stacey got a shocked look, "You are that way. You're not five or six, but you got that kind of energy. Me and Emily were talking one day and we don't know how you do all you do. You're like superwoman."

"Oh, shoot fire," Geneva laughed. "You girls done lost your ever-lovin' minds. I do what I can."

"You bushhog, bail hay, fix anything and everything, take care of everybody, volunteer…" Emily started.

"Well, now those things need gettin' done, so I done 'em," Geneva replied quickly. "Like Popeye would say, I yam what I yam."

All the sudden, paying attention to the scenery around them, took over. It looked like the kids ran a hundred miles before they ever stopped, and the birds gracing their Prescence that day, were the most beautiful they'd seen. From vibrant red birds to blue birds and everything in between, Geneva's eyes focused on each one as it came into view. Some perched on the porch railing, some in pairs. When they did, no one moved a muscle, for fear it would scare them away, but when the kids came running by, the birds found a new place to rest their wings.

"It's so peaceful out here," Stacey said, taking in all God made for their eyes to see.

"It is most of the time," Geneva said. "But that blame sawin' and a hammerin' down that there road just gets on my last nerve. I wish they'd get that blame house finished."

"Geneva," Stacey started, but was stopped by the sound of a vehicle coming down the road. It was Terry.

When he pulled up and parked, Geneva wasn't the only one with a surprised look, Emily's expression changed immediately. It was something they didn't expect, not then anyway.

CHAPTER TWENTY-TWO

Terry got out, but the passenger he was carrying wasn't Sherry. Emily carefully stood, holding onto the arm of the swing with one hand for balance, and took a few steps forward. The laughter from moments earlier, turned to something else, a mixture of emotions unexplainable.

From the other side of the truck, the door opened, and they could see him more clearly. Chris was standing there, his hands in his pockets and half-way hanging his head. To say it was an awkward moment, would be an understatement. No one knew what to say. It's like everyone was waiting for Chris and Emily to start the conversation, but that wasn't the case either.

Terry motioned to Chris, "Come on son. Go talk to your wife before we have to go. We have to be there in a few hours."

Emily was paying close attention to what Terry said to Chris, and her silence was immediately broken, "Go where?"

"Emily, he's been in a facility to dry him out the past few days, and now I'm takin' him to a place in Camden Arkansas for a thirty-day program to keep him straight," Terry said. "I tried to tell you the other day, but…"

"I wouldn't let you," Emily interrupted.

Chris still wasn't moving a muscle, but when he lifted his head, his eyes were focused on Emily. It was hard to tell if he was smiling or starting to cry. About then, the kids came running from the hillside like two lightning bolts. When they got close enough and realized it wasn't just Terry, they both started screaming for their daddy, especially Joshua.

They ran to him fast as they could, and he kneeled just before they reached him.

"Daddy…daddy," they both screeched, covering him with so much love, hugs and kisses, everyone witnessing such a sight, had tears rolling, even Emily.

The joy in Chris's face was unmistakable, holding his two kids so tight like he never planned on letting them go. "I'm so sorry," he kept saying to them. "I love you both so much."

Emily took a few more slow steps closer, unable to take her eyes off her kids and Chris. It was almost like she was watching a movie, the kind that pulls on your heart strings, her body language showing such feeling and emotion. Then Chris stood up and their eyes finally connected. The kids were still holding onto his hands, but he started walking toward the porch. Geneva was getting antsy, unsure of what to do.

"Hey kids," Geneva said. "Why don't we go inside and let your mama and daddy talk?"

"But mama G…" they replied, still clinging to Chris.

"I got some fresh home-make chocolate chip cookies," she added. "And I betcha I got some good cold milk to go along with'em."

That's all she needed to say. Those two jetted in quick as they could, following everyone inside. Emily and Chris were still standing in the same spot, staring each other down like they were in the old west. After a moment or two, Chris made the first move, going to Emily. He kept looking at her and the bruises on her face. Something inside him burst open, an array of emotions he had been holding in for too long. He still couldn't find any words and he sat on the swing and started crying. Cradling his face in his hands, softly muttering the words *I'm sorry* over and over, Emily turned facing him.

One step, then two, and she sat next to him on the swing, her left hand gracing the cross etched into the armrest. Somehow it gave her peace just like Geneva said when Elijah first made it for her. In that moment, she needed such peace. Her mind was filled with hurt, anger, confusion, but at the same time, it was still filled with love. Although the love part, was one she didn't want to address considering her anger was still overriding it, she looked over at him. In the same instance, he did the same, looking to his left. Their tear-filled eyes focused on each other and the air around them was thick as molasses. Words in the moment were like trying to find a needle in a haystack. It was more than obvious they both had so much to say, but nothing was being muttered. The only sound was the birds singing for them.

Finally, "It's really great out here," Chris said, his voice shaking.

Something about that being the first time she had heard his voice in months, the flood gates of her feelings broke free. So many dreams of him, but he was sitting there with her, and she was speechless.

"I know I'm sorry isn't enough Emily," Chris said, doing all he could to hold back from completely losing it. "So, I want to give you more than that."

"You left us Chris," Emily whispered. "You left your family."

"I didn't want to ruin your lives with my problem. I didn't want to be that kind of influence on the kids. I knew you'd be okay. You've always been the stronger one Em."

She wiped her tears, "We got kicked out of the loft. We had to sleep where we could and get food when we could. Do you call that strong?"

Chris thought it best to try and change the mood, "I met Miss Geneva. She's a pill."

Half smiling, "She is that. The kids love her and so do I. I don't know where we'd be right now if not for her and everyone else."

"I thanked her for taking care of you," Chris said.

"When?"

"At the hospital. I had to thank her for saving you," he answered.

"There's something about her," Emily said. "It's like she glows love and…"

"Faith," Chris finished her sentence.

"Yes, how did you know?"

"She glowed to me too. She gave me a little bible story," he smiled.

That remark brought a smile to Emily's face, recalling the story Geneva told her just a few days earlier. "She has a way of making you see the bright side somehow Chris. I need that right now."

"Well, I'll be gone for a month. That's why I wanted to come tell you in person. Terry wasn't sure it would be a good idea for us to just show up like this, but I told him I had to see you and the kids. I needed something to hold onto Em," Chris said, raising his arm and resting it on the back of the bench. "I need you to know, I can beat this. I did before. We did before, and I don't know how I could let someone talk me into doing it again."

They heard the front door open, and Terry walked out. It looked like he had something important to say and their focus turned to him. Chris figured it was time to go, so he started to stand.

"Sit back down son," Terry said. "Miss Geneva had a suggestion, and I called the Camden facility and asked them if we could wait until tomorrow evening to get you down there."

"What kind of suggestion?" Emily asked.

"Well, you know, tomorrow is Sunday, and she wants to take you to church. In fact, I'm gonna go too. I suppose you have no other choice since I'm responsible for ya. B'sides, it's almost impossible to say no to Geneva. You'll figure that out the longer you know'er." Terry finished.

Chris turned to Emily, "Is that okay?"

"You heard Terry. If she's going to church so am I. So, it looks like we'll be there together," Emily said.

"Oh, good gracious," Geneva said, shooting out the front door after eaves dropping on the conversation. "It's gonna be a great Sunday young'uns."

"You'll stay at our house tonight," Terry said to Chris. "In the meantime, we gotta run to town and get the things they said you need in Camden. We can come back later if you want to, but right now, let's get that taken care of."

Chris stood and faced Emily. He put his hand over her hand that was covering the cross and it immediately sent chills through her. It had been so long since she had touched him, it was like electricity was being transported through her entire body.

"Is it okay if I come back later?" Chris asked respectfully.

Emily paused, took in and let out a breath slowly, "Well, I guess it couldn't hurt anything."

"Good golly," Geneva belted out. "I guess I need to figure out what to cook. Oh, boy it'll be a great supper too."

"She's a little energetic, isn't she," Chris said to Emily.

"You don't know the half of it Chris," Emily stated, letting the grin he always loved, come out.

The kids came running out and met their daddy on the steps of the porch, hugging him like they would never see him again. Joshua hung on ever tighter. His little arms clung around Chris's neck like they were locked, and when they released, Emily heard Chris say, "I'll see you this evening son. Daddy loves you. Katy, I love you too princess."

The kids joined Emily on the swing cuddling close to her. She hadn't seen that much joy on their faces since before Chris left. It's like seeing him, rejuvenated something in them, they'd forgotten about. That infectious grin on Joshua, showing his adorable dimples shined like the sun, and, in turn, brightened Emily's perspective on things.

As they were leaving Geneva called out to Terry, "Hey would ya tell them fellas down at that there house to stop bein' so blame loud and get finished already so I can get my quiet place back."

"I'll tell'em Geneva," Terry grinned, shaking his head at her unique personality, always being straight forward, no matter what.

"Don't you forget," she repeated.

They got in the truck and went down the drive, Chris staring back the entire time until they were out of sight. Emily's gaze never veered from his direction and when he was gone, she looked down. Geneva knew she probably had a million questions running through her mind and her emotions had taken over. With her kids nestled close, for the moment, things started looking better.

For the remainder of the day, until supper, Emily found time to rest and to watch the kids and their rambunctious activity, laughing and running. They found a new energy unlike before. Their smiles showed brighter and laughter more buoyant. Although Emily didn't want to admit it, the space inside her that had been empty for some time felt a little fuller. Even though she only saw Chris once and she didn't know what would happen next, Geneva had taught her to think positive.

Time flew by and Geneva was in the kitchen whipping up, what looked like, everything she had. That room looked like a tornado had struck it and Geneva was happy as a lark, dancing around in her apron frying this and chopping that. She had fried pork chops going, fried potatoes, boiled okra, sweet corn and, of course homemade gravy and biscuits, in the works.

"My goodness Miss Geneva," Emily said, stepping in the kitchen. "You think you have enough food?"

"Honey," Geneva answered, her head popping up and eyes big and bright. "You think I need to make more?"

"I was kidding," Emily laughed. "Looks like more than enough to me. Looks like you could feed an army to be honest."

"Leave her alone," Elijah said, entering the kitchen. "She loves cookin' for lots of people. She likes to play hostess. Let'er enjoy it Emily."

"Yes sir," Emily replied kindly.

"Oh, Terry called, and they'll be here shortly," Elijah said. "I told him you was about done with supper."

"It won't be long," Geneva said. "Just waitin' on these here biscuits to brown."

Elijah went into the living room, turned on the television, and got out the TV trays for those who wanted to sit in there while they ate. Emily went upstairs to get the kids ready for supper while Geneva pulled out plates, silverware, and glasses. Although it was unexpected, it kind of felt like a special occasion. There was something in the air that spoke change, hopefully for the better. Something kept whispering to Geneva to not veer from her course. She knew it was God talking to her, so she did just that, focused on how she could help that family even more.

It wasn't long and Geneva heard Emily coming down with the kids. Those little ones were gabbing all the way down, the excitement obvious in their voice.

"Is daddy coming back mama?" Joshua asked with a gleam in his eyes.

"Is he mama?" Katy added.

When they reached the bottom of the stairs and joined Elijah, "He is," she answered. "He's having supper with us kids."

Joshua started bouncing up and down like he had springs in his feet and the smile Katy wore, was indescribable. The atmosphere in the room was different than before. Somehow, hope was floating around, filling the space where doubts used to be, and Emily sat there struggling with what to believe. A part of her was afraid to think things would be okay, but another part was saying to have faith.

They heard Terry's truck coming down the drive and before Emily knew it, the kids took off running to meet the man they had missed for a while. Emily, on the other hand, just sat there and waited. Nerves were having their way with her, shaking a little, facing her fears head on. All the talks her and Geneva had, kept coming back to her. Every inspiring word or story from that amusing lady, played back like a recording.

Emily could hear Geneva banging things around, probably trying to hurry and get things done. She was a stickler on getting everything ready at the same time and didn't really like folks in her way when she was doing so. Regardless, Emily went to help. She already had everything laid out, displaying a spread like she'd never seen before. It was perfect, and Geneva wiped her hands and untied the apron she had on, folded and hung it on the hook.

"Hungry Emily?" Geneva said, her character shining through.

"Yes ma'am," Emily said, glancing out and noticing Chris carrying both kids.

"You still love him, I know," Geneva said, giving Emily a little nudge.

"Geneva...I..."

The front door opened and in walked Terry and Sherry. Then, right behind them, was Chris with Joshua and Katy holding onto him tightly. If it's possible, it felt like no one was there but her and Chris the minute their eyes locked once more.

CHAPTER TWENTY-THREE

That single glance was filled with love, fear, and confusion all rolled into one. All the kids knew, was that Chris was there and, as the gift from innocence, they didn't worry about tomorrow. It's funny, when folks grow up, they lose that. People find themselves worrying about what happened yesterday, what's going on right now, and what next month has to hold. As kids, it was just about the *now*. It's a shame we can't go back to that frame of mind and enjoy every day like we should.

Emily couldn't stop staring at Chris. Terry must've bought him new clothes because he had on a red colored collared, starched shirt, tucked into a pair of stylish faded jeans. It looked like he had shaved, leaving just the right amount of scruff just as Emily liked. Lastly, his gorgeous green eyes appeared to be looking clean through her. She remembered how that's the first thing she noticed about him, those eyes that drew her in. Then, suddenly, she was snapped out of her momentary trans.

"Mama," Joshua said. "Daddy's goin' on a trip tomorrow, but he said he'd be back…he promised."

Instantly, the fear part of her took over, afraid the kids would get hurt all over again as well as herself. "That's great baby," Emily said, going and picking Joshua up. "That's really great."

"I thought you'd be happy mama," Joshua continued.

Emily kissed him on the cheek then the tip of his nose, "I am happy Josh."

"Alrighty," Geneva called out. "Any a you folks that's hungry, go ahead and dig in."

Funny enough, Terry was the first to grab a plate. He filled it clean to the brim, grabbed a glass of tea and headed into the living room.

"Make yourself at home," Elijah told Terry.

"I always do Eli. I always do," he laughed back.

Everyone got their plates. Chris fixed his and Josh's, while Emily fixed hers and Katy's. From the outside looking in, someone who didn't know any better, would think they had the most perfect little family, but the truth was far different. No one would guess there were secrets, lots of regret, and terrible mistakes they had yet to work through. But, for the moment, it was nice to pretend.

"Emily," Geneva said. "Why don't you, Chris and these here young'uns sit in the kitchen and the rest of us'll eat in yunder. How's that sound?"

"Thank you, Miss Geneva," Chris said politely, taking his spot at the table and sitting Josh next to him.

Emily sat down and did the same for Katy, but about the time Chris was about to take a bite, Joshua interrupted.

"Wait daddy," he hollered out. "Mama G says we always have to say grace before we eat. Right mama?"

"That's right honey," Emily answered with a nod.

"Well son, I'm not real sure I know how to say grace too good Josh," Chris replied, almost embarrassed to admit such a thing.

"I been listening to Mama G," Katy said. "I can do it, but we have to hold hands."

Chris and Emily glanced at one another from across the table and the kids on each side of them held out their hands. Forming a circle, "Now bow your head," Katy said. "*God thank you for this food and thank you for my mama and daddy. Thank you for bringing my daddy back home...AMEN.*"

When Katy was finished with her prayer, her and Joshua immediately started tearing into what delicious meal Geneva had prepared. In such a short time, she had spoiled them all, enjoying playing mother hen. While the kids were stuffing their faces Chris couldn't take his eyes off the woman in front of him. Anyone could tell his mind was going in a hundred different directions, hopes and regrets running into each other and starting an internal war he'd been fighting since he left.

"Eat," Emily said. "As Miss Geneva would say, she don't take kindly to folks who don't appreciate good cookin'. There's too many starvin' people out there."

Chris raised one side of his mouth, half-grinning, revealing that one lone dimple, "Sounds like her Em."

Emily didn't really know how to start the conversation, especially with the kids there, but her focus staying on him said a lot. They both gobbled up everything on their plates and when they were finished, cleaned theirs and the kid's plates and put them away.

"Can we go talk to Uncle Terry and Aunt Sherry?" the kids asked, showing their attachment to them already.

They watched the kids go into the living room where everyone else was and there was a momentary silence where neither Chris nor Emily knew what to say. Many words were lingering all around them, things they both wanted to say, but something was keeping them from it.

"C...can we go take a walk?" Emily asked, apprehension showing in the crackling of her voice.

Chris didn't answer, but instead, took a step closer to her and extended his hand to hers. It was his silent way of saying *yes*. A part of her wanted to take his hand and another was scared that the minute she did, she'd be sucked in once again and all of the healing she had been through would be for nothing. Her fears of him hurting them again, was forefront in her mind, and with good reason, but ultimately, the heart won. Slowly raising her hand until it reached his, the smile Chris wore said it all. It was the encouragement he needed to keep on in his recovery. It was what he needed to know she still loved him and that the kids still loved their daddy.

They went to the front door and Chris opened it and shut it behind them. Emily was sure everyone saw what was going on, but in the moment, all she cared about, was what future, if any, they had left.

They traveled off the porch and to that spot Geneva said was a place her and Elijah loved, atop the hillside across from the house. There were a few large rocks and big logs to sit on, think, and even talk to God. That's what Geneva did. When they reached that spot and the stillness of the night surrounded them with fireflies lighting up the entire area around them, they took it all in.

"Wow," Chris said. "No wonder you love it here Em. It's about the most peaceful place I think I've ever seen."

"I do, and so do the kids," Emily said, finding a seat. "Can I ask you something?

"Shoot," Chris answered, making himself comfortable on an old log in front of her. "I'm an open book, at least now I am."

Emily glanced away at the night sky then back to Chris, "Did you think about us after you left? Did you wonder where we were and how we were doing?"

"Oh Em, I thought of you every day and most of the time I knew where you were. There were times, I was watching when you didn't even know it," Chris said. "I couldn't show my face."

"But you're here now," Emily said, peering at him with expectations. "What now?"

"I'm doing what Terry said. He offered to cover my recovery program in that place in Arkansas, then…"

"Then you're coming back to us?" Emily asked frankly, needing an answer.

With tear filled eyes, "I want to. I want you to want me to come back. I need to know you love me and forgive me."

"I've always loved you," Emily said. "I'm not sure I know how to forgive. I guess me and God haven't had many conversations lately…not much ever, to be honest."

"Of course, being around that Geneva, it's hard not to think about it," Chris laughed.

"I know what you mean," Emily replied. "But you know what…she sees good in everybody. It's like she sees a diamond in the rough and finds the diamond inside. Not many like her, that's for sure, and I think you'll like her church. It's different. It's country."

"I know where it is," Chris lowered his head and muttered. "I was there."

"You were there when?" Emily asked, caught off guard from what he said.

"I have a confession to make," he said. "I was keeping an eye on you. I saw when you went home with Miss Geneva and followed you to church that Sunday. I thought you saw me when you were leaving, but I ducked away until you drove off."

"I felt someone watching me," Emily whispered to herself. "I told Miss Geneva."

"I wanted to talk to you, but I was ashamed. After the service started, I stayed in the entry and sort of listened to the sermon but was more focused on you.'

Emily's curiosity was peeked, "How did you get there Chris?

Chris turned his head and looked away from her, unsure how to admit to something so terrible, then realized he had to start being honest at some point. "I…uh, took a truck."

"You took a truck? From who?" Emily inquired, but still trying to be understanding at the same time.

"I'm not proud of it, but I need you to trust what I say. I need you to believe me. No matter what terrible things I've done, I need to be open with you from now on," Chris said.

"We better get back," Emily said. "The kids are probably looking for you and I know you want to spend time with them before you leave tomorrow."

She turned and took a few steps and Chris grabbed a hold of her hand. "Please don't give up on me."

When Emily looked back at him, she didn't say anything, but he could tell, deep down she hadn't given up. She was just so hurt by what he'd done. The stare between the two of them spoke grand conversations being surrounded by an unbelievable masterpiece of beauty.

"Go play with your kids Chris," Emily said. "They deserve it. They need it."

Chris nodded and they left that perfect spot and went back to the house where the kids and everyone else, were clearly heard outside. Geneva's voice stood out, yelling at Elijah to stop his aggravating.

About to go inside, Chris stopped, "I need to hug you. I've dreamed of it a thousand times, missing you so much… please."

For the first time, Emily gave in to the feelings she had pushed deep inside of herself since he left. She dug up the buried feelings longing for the very same. She wanted to put her arms around him far before this moment, but she didn't allow herself to feel. Then, carefully, and respectfully, Chris put his arms around his wife, the one he abandoned. Emily reciprocated, and they remained locked in a moment, one neither wanted to pass. They held each other like they never wanted to let go, but both knew they had to.

After a long, enduring embrace, they finally released one another gradually. The front door swung open. Katy and Joshua were standing there, looking back at Terry who was chasing after them. They took off like a jet, shooting across the yard, then coming back to sit on the porch steps to rest, huffing and puffing.

"Go on," Emily said. "Talk to'em."

Emily went inside and joined everyone while Chris stole some, much needed quality time with the kids. She sat in one of the wingback chairs next to the window. She wasn't necessarily trying to spy, but her curiosity of how the kids were taking to Chris after him not being around, got the best of her. She could hear them talking and laughing although she couldn't make out exactly what was being said. Emily looked to her left and glanced across the room noticing Geneva peering at her with that unique kind of grin.

Soon as their eyes met, Geneva got up and joined her in the other chair adjacent to Emily. "They're happy to see'im," Geneva said. "He seems pretty tickled to see them too."

"Yeah, I know," Emily responded quietly, still keeping her focus out the window. "It's so strange Geneva."

"What's strange honey?" she asked. "He's your husband and their daddy. He has a problem and is gonna get some help. It's not your everyday kinda thing, but it's life Emily."

"I just thought I hated him, but…"

"But when you saw him, it wasn't hate at all, was it sugar?" Geneva interrupted.

"It was love," Emily muttered in the lowest tone, her eyes tearing up as she spoke those three little words.

"Well," Geneva said in a spunky tone. "There ain't nothin' wrong with that honey. You keep a hangin' onto that love. It's what'll get you through."

The front door flung open, and the resonances of children's laughter consumed the place. Chris, wearing the biggest smile, followed after them. He grabbed each one up and gave them the most gigantic hug. It was obvious how much he loved them. There was no acting involved. He was sincere and it showed. Emily sat there watching on, listening to the joy in Katy and Joshua's voices, and showcased a sweet half-grin.

"I have to sit down kids," Chris said, huffing and puffing. "You got daddy tired."

Chris noticed the rug by the fireplace and plopped down on the floor, trying to catch his breath. Both kids looked like they did a cannon ball on top of him, covering him completely, then resting their heads on his arm on each side.

"Now ain't that picture perfect?" Geneva said.

"That it is," Emily agreed. "I'm gonna remember this moment and hold on to it Geneva, until he comes back."

"You betcha honey," Geneva replied quickly. "And he'll be back. Besides, we still have church tomorrow. You have a little more time Emily. Use it wisely honey."

"Yes ma'am."

The clock ticked away, minutes flew, and it started getting late. Terry and Sherry stood and nodded at Chris, a sign it was time to get home. Everyone had enjoyed their time together, but it was over until the next day. Sadness displayed evidently across Chris's face when he knew he had to go, but he also knew it was for the best.

"Supper was incredible as always," Terry said to Geneva, then turning to Elijah. "And Eli, we always have a good time reminiscing, don't we old friend?"

"See you in the morning," Geneva said, looking directly at Chris.

"We'll be there," Sherry squeezed into the conversation. "We'll all be there. Right boys?"

Terry and Chris both nodded, knowing they better and then headed outside. Chris was slow walking, hoping to get one last minute with Emily. She followed close behind him and stopped at the top of the steps. He had one kid wrapped around each leg and a hand on both of them.

"I'll see you in the mornin' Em," Chris smiled, leaning over and kissing her sweetly on the cheek, hoping she didn't mind. "That's a promise."

Emily didn't find any words, but the communication was clear. The positivity floating in their midst was beginning to overshadow the negative thoughts and feelings from before. The kids gave their daddy one last hug for the night, although they didn't understand why he wasn't staying, and he left.

The crickets were out by the droves, louder than ever, putting on a magnificent performance. The sounds were coming from every direction. Geneva offered the kids some cookies and milk before bed and, as usual, there was no turning that down. Emily stayed on the porch and watched as Terry's taillights disappeared down the dusty road. Still listening to the sounds around her, she began to pace back and forth on the porch, then stopped, leaning against the corner post. The kids were quiet. There were no more stories being passed around inside, and she was standing there, just her and God. Her eyes fixated on the stars lighting up the darkness of the sky like tiny diamonds illuminating their sparkle for all to see.

God, Emily spoke aloud. *It's me Emily. God, a part of me is so happy, but another part is still scared. I really don't know what to do. Seeing Chris brought back so many good memories, but then, somehow, I let the bad ones get in there too. I need something to hold onto…something to believe in…something to trust. I know I need to trust in you Lord. Geneva tells me that all the time. She showed me all the promises you've made to us and I want to believe it. Please God help me to believe. Oh, and God, please help Chris get better. Please help him fight his demons as Miss Geneva would say. Because I know he has plenty of 'em. And help me to be strong for my kids. They need me. Thank you for listening…AMEN*

Emily pushed out all the undesirable thoughts and replaced them with good memories the evening carried, then went to join the kids. When she walked in, they were dunking their cookies and gobbling them down quick as you please, and that included Geneva. With crumbs here and there, Emily couldn't help but shake her head at the vision of those three having their nightly snack.

"Where's Elijah?" Emily asked, knowing he wouldn't miss out on Geneva's homemade cookies.

"Ahhh," Geneva said. "He said he was tired, so I told him me and these here young'uns was gonna finish up these chocolate chip cookies. No sense in a wastin'em."

"You kids ready for bed?" Emily asked, cleaning up the crumbs from around where they were sitting, and putting their plates away.

"Mama," Katy said, looking with those green eyes that would melt any heart. "We'll see daddy tomorrow?"

"You will sweetie," Emily answered, kneeling, and pulling her close. "He's going to church with us."

"Oh boy," Joshua announced. "I get to make stuff. That's what the other kids said."

Geneva and Emily immediately belted out laughing at Joshua's quick wit and enthusiasm about going to Circle J. His first impression of the church was a good one and he made that very clear. He hopped down from the chair and made his way up the stairs in a hurry. Katy was right behind him but wasn't in as big a hurry. Emily gave Geneva a hug and turned to go upstairs.

"Hey Emily," Geneva said softly.

"Yes Miss Geneva," Emily replied.

"You know, what's already happened can't be changed, don't ya?" Geneva asked.

"Yes ma'am."

"When you lay down tonight think about somethin'," Geneva continued. "We talked about this before, but somethin' tells me I need to say it again. Folks make mistakes Emily. And when we keep them mistakes in our heads, and don't let'em go, you can't move on. Just like it talks about in Psalm. It talks about far as the east is from the west, that's about how far God removed our mistakes from us when we ask forgiveness."

"I don't think Chris asked for forgiveness Geneva," Emily said.

"You don't know that. I don't know that. Shoot, the only one who does know is the almighty God," Geneva said. "So, don't be so fast to judge. Let it go."

"You're one in a million Miss Geneva," Emily said, hugging her once more.

"I sure hope so," Geneva laughed. "If there's another me runnin''round, we're all in trouble."

Amused by that unpredictable lady, Emily went upstairs to check on the kids. They were already in the bed looking nice and snug and she sat down.

"I love you both. You know that right?" Emily said, kissing each of them on the forehead.

"You love daddy too right mama?" Joshua asked.

"I do sweetie, but…"

"We'll be together again," Katy said. "Night mama. I'm awful tired."

Not going into what was really going on, Emily let the kids have good thoughts, the kind she wanted to have herself. She wanted them to embrace the happiness they were feeling at the moment, something she didn't want to steel away from them.

"Goodnight," Emily whispered, leaving their room as they found fast slumber.

After shutting their door, she made her way to her room, closing the door and getting ready for bed…so many thoughts looming.

CHAPTER TWENTY-FOUR

Emily's wandering thoughts left her lying in bed wide awake fixing her eyes on the spotlight from the moon through her window. Events of the day, moments etched in her mind and thoughts of the future, swirled around together creating a tornado of mixed emotions, leaving her pondering what will happen next. She thought about the difference in Chris since the day he left and the promises he was making. Before things got bad, she never would've questioned him, but circumstance seemed to change that for her. Thought after thought, created such a burden in her mind, and was too tired to think any longer and found peace briefly by way of perfect slumber.

The next morning, Emily woke to the pitter patter of little footsteps going up and down the stairs and then the hallway, as well as Geneva's unique voice ringing out about breakfast. One thing Emily wasn't used to, was getting up early, but Geneva was curing her of that real quick. *Mama,* she heard the kids holler out, forcing her to climb out of the comfy bed her body was melted into. She also remembered hearing Geneva on the phone to Ella the day before, telling her they may surprise them and drive in early to go to church. Coming from just this side of the Dallas area, it was a little piece, but they didn't seem to mind. Besides, Emily figured Caleb was missing the kids. They had gotten pretty close in the short time they spent together.

She stood and reached her arms far above her head, stretching every muscle she could, making that awkward morning groan at the same time. It probably sounded like a grizzly bear had come into her room from the other side of the door. Funny as it sounds, Elijah was walking by about that very time.

"You okay in there?" he lightly knocked.

Emily couldn't help but laugh, "Yes sir, I'll be down in a minute."

"You better. These young'uns are runnin' Geneva all over this place," Elijah replied in a witty manner.

"She's got more energy than those two put together," Emily called out, meaning every bit of what she said.

After such comical words, she heard a small chuckle from him and then he went downstairs. It was still early, so there was plenty of time to eat and get ready for church, but she also knew if she didn't come on down, Geneva would be up to fetch her any minute.

Emily threw on a pair of comfy pajama pants and shirt, along with a pair of extra soft socks, and went to join the others. By the time she made it to the kitchen, both kids had their mouths so full of waffles and sausage, they couldn't say a word. Geneva and Elijah looked on and got tickled at the sight of those two crazy kids.

"What'll you have honey?" Geneva asked. "You want me to fry you up a few eggs?"

"No ma'am," Emily replied, going, and pouring a glass of orange juice, then sitting next to Katy. "I'll just have what they're having."

In a jiffy, Geneva had her a hefty plate piled up and sat in front of her. It's like she lived to take care of others. One thing was for sure, she had it down pat. She always told Elijah, she just liked makin' people smile.

"Honey, we're goin' to get ready for church. If you want any more, there's plenty on the stove," Geneva said, smiling, patting her on the shoulder, then marching off like she was going to war.

Joshua was a little fella, but you wouldn't have been able to tell it by how much he ate. Emily wasn't sure how much was on his plate when he started, but when he was finished, there was nothing left. He picked up the last piece of sausage and ran it all over his plate in a pattern like a racecar, sopping up the last bit of syrup left. It took a few minutes for Emily to finish hers, but when she was done, they all went and got themselves ready.

Emily was anxious in a way, her nerves doing somersaults at just the thought of seeing Chris, and she did her best to keep good thoughts. The time kept ticking on until she looked up and it was about a quarter til ten. Church started at ten thirty, but Geneva said she always liked getting there early so she could wander around and visit with everybody.

"Emily…kids," Geneva called out. "We don't wanna be late."

Katy and Joshua got new energy and took off downstairs, minding what Mama G told them. Emily followed right after and found the others waiting at the door, bibles in hand. Somehow, her mind took a snapshot of that very moment, an image she wanted to keep with her from then on. The kids were smiling and looked more content than ever and, they were headed to church. Something about the whole thing, felt right, felt perfect. It's like she was meant to be right there in that moment.

Geneva jumped into the driver's seat of the van and everyone else found their place. Quickly, she was on her way. As before, they put it on a local Christian station that played old country gospel, right down Geneva's alley. She knew most of the words, and sang right along, amusing the kids the entire time. They had fallen in love with her, and she kept them laughing.

Not far from the exit to the church, Geneva glanced back "You okay Emily?"

"I'm fine Miss Geneva," Emily said.

"Alrighty then," Geneva replied, turning back around, taking the right turn, then immediate left between the two iron gates entering the church.

Something about that place gave Emily the feeling she was being embraced by something utterly spiritual, keeping her at peace. Considering her nerves were trying to get the best of her, she needed that. When Geneva pulled up to her usual spot, in front of them, standing next to one of those tall wooden spool tables, was Terry, Sherry, and Chris. Emily's mind wandered briefly, remembering the very first time she saw Chris. There was something about him that drew her in. She wasn't sure if it was those eyes, green as glistening emeralds, or just his beautiful smile he wore so flawlessly. None-the-less, they were like two magnets, drawn together through fate or whatever you want to call it.

"Mama," Katy said. "We getting out? There's daddy."

Emily snapped back to the present and got out, helping Katy and Joshua after. Chris was still standing there looking their direction. Since they were at a cowboy church, it looked like he was truly playing the part. He had on a pair of jeans, cowboy boots, and western print shirt. The only thing he was missing was the hat. He had one foot crossed over the other, the tip of his boot resting on the concrete porch. Emily took extra time picking out something to wear that day, subconsciously trying to impress that man who she really didn't have to impress at all.

"Don't you look pretty Em?" Chris said, walking to Emily and lifting both her hands up so he could get a better look. "Pretty as a picture."

"Daddy," the kids rang out in unison, running to him.

They lavished him in hugs and kisses and the glow it produced on Chris's face, was unmistakable. He absorbed every last bit of love they were throwing at him and he returned it just the same. Geneva and Elijah found a place around that wood table and were talking to Sherry and Terry. They watched as people started pulling down the drive, filling the parking lot. Chris and Emily made small talk, trying their best to act normal, when a white vehicle pulled up at the corner and parked.

A slim, brown-headed, middle-aged lady got out and went to the back and opened the door. You could tell she was struggling with something, then she pulled out a sort of small wheelchair. Next, she leaned in and lifted out a little blonde haired, beautiful young man, no more than four years old. She buckled him tight so he wouldn't fall out. Chris, Emily, and the kids watched them, outwardly showing the questions floating in all their minds as to what happened to the boy. Geneva could tell that's what was happening, and she scooted closer to them.

"That there is Christy Works and her nephew Cam," She explained. "Back over a year ago or maybe longer than that, there was a fire, and he lost his mom. Them doctors said he wouldn't make it either."

"Where's his dad?" Emily asked.

"Oh, he'll be here. His name's Todd and he's a great daddy to that little boy and their lucky to have each other," Geneva said. "Anyway, them there doctors said he wouldn't survive, and if he did, he'd never walk and talk."

"He's talking mama G," Katy said in a hurry.

"You betcha he is," Geneva said, followed by that laugh she gave when she felt inspired by something from above. "See kids, them doctors ain't God. What they said didn't matter. What God said, did."

"Hey Miss Geneva," Christy said, rolling Cam by. "Say hi to Miss Geneva Cam."

That handsome fella raised his hand and gave a robust *AMEN,* surprising everyone. His stunning blue eyes were like looking into a pool of perfection. Add that to the smile he put out so sincerely, he was definitely a miracle.

"Wow," Chris said, standing there, unable to take his eyes off that little boy as she pushed him to the front door.

"Wow is right," Geneva said squeezing Chris's hand. "That boy inspires everybody here, I'll tell ya. He's walkin' and talkin' now because God wasn't done with him yet Chris."

"Geneva," Chris muttered, looking down. "You think he's done with me?"

"Oh baby, if he was done with you, you wouldn't be here. I got a feelin' he's saved you more times than you realize," Geneva replied in the most comforting manner. "So, you best figure out what you're still here for."

With those words spoken from a very wise lady, Chris turned and looked at Emily and the kids. "I think I know why I'm still here."

"We better git so don't nobody take our seats," Geneva said, her gitty up and go, taking off.

Everyone followed her lead, stepping toward the front door, someone stopping Geneva constantly for a hug or handshake. She used to be the greeter there and it looked like she still was. When they made it inside, they could see the band going up on stage and getting in a circle. Emily took the kids to their classrooms after they snatched a donut each, then went to the usual seat.

Chris, like everyone else who walked into that building, kept his eyes on the gigantic cross hanging on the wooden wall behind the pull pit. Even though he was there briefly once, it didn't get his attention like it did then and there. Somehow, it was his focus, studying it, and trying to figure out what it was saying to him. The simplicity of his surroundings, everything covered in wood and tin, gave a feeling that he belonged.

After the band prayed, the singer stepped up to the microphone and his voice rang out in a powerful way, reaching every crevasse of that place. A passion for what he was singing floated in the air around them. It wasn't only in the words, but a spirit intertwining in the midst of it all. And after three or four songs, a few old hymns turned country and a few newer songs, the service was turned over to the preacher. He walked up the steps on the right side of the stage in his country attire and goatee, smiling. Then he began.

"Have you ever lost somethin' that is really important to ya?" the preacher said, immediately grabbing Chris's attention. "When you lose somethin', it can be devastating."

There was no doubt Chris thought about what he lost that he was trying to get back, but he continued to listen to that country preacher. "So, Jesus, he talks about a story, the parable of a lost coin…so turn to Luke, chapter fifteen, verse eight. Find that in your bible, this is a great place to mark. *Or suppose a woman has ten silver coins and loses one. Won't she light a lamp and sweep the entire house and search carefully until she finds it? AND when she finds it, she will call in her friends and neighbors and say 'Rejoice with me because I have found my lost coin.'* This is Jesus's point here, keep reading. *In the same way, there is joy in the presence of God's angels when even one sinner repents.*

Immediately after the reading of the word, the preacher said, "*Lord, I come to ya with a heavy heart. I pray Lord as we read your word, that you open the eyes of everyone here in this place, everyone watching online. Snatch the blinders off. I'll say like Jesus did, he that has an ear, let him hear. I pray this in Jesus' name…AMEN!*

In front of Chris stood a man he'd never met, but one who was talking directly to him. Deep down, he knew he was very lost, but had no direction. The only thing he knew he needed, was his Emily and the kids. As he continued to listen, never taking his eyes off the man delivering the message, something special happened. Emily slowly rested her hand on his and gave him a look that silently said *I forgive you*. Just that simple touch from a woman who had no reason to ever talk to him again, was still there with him, giving him another chance.

The preacher continued, "You see everybody…we are the precious coin to God. Jesus is carefully searching for you. He wants to find you, so you'll have eternal life with him in Heaven. The scripture does not say every coin will be found. But it is his will that everyone come to know the Lord and it's his will that none shall perish but have eternal life. But in Luke chapter thirteen verse twenty-three, *Lord will those who are saved, be few? And he answered them, strive to enter through the narrow door for many I tell you will seek and enter and will not be able.*"

During the sermon, Emily turned to see Caleb and Ella finding a seat in the row behind them, walking in a sneaking up on somebody, kind of way, not to disturb anyone. Geneva noticed them and shined a big grin, then turned back to give her attention to the message being given.

Chris, still trying to understand what he was hearing, one thing said, concerned him. The preacher said that not everyone will be found. That got him thinking and touched on the core of who he was becoming, someone who never wanted to go back to the life he was living, someone who wanted more. Immediately, the strong manly man he had always been, turned into a bundle of uncontrolled emotions, welling out of him, whispering to himself, *I want to be found, I want to be found.*

Only Emily heard Chris, but when she did, their hands laced together, squeezing tightly, on the same page for the first time in a long time. Still, letting every word brother

Todd said weave in and out of their minds, taking in all they could, Chris and Emily were communicating in a way they never had. Something was speaking to both of them, something began to climb into the deepest part of their hearts to make a change.

"I do too," Emily whispered to Chris. "I don't want to be lost."

They looked at one another, trying to figure out exactly what was going on, but then brother Todd made a statement that made lots of sense. He said *A lost coin has value, but only when it's found. In other words, you may have great value, but you're not valuable until you are found by the Lord Jesus Christ.*

Chris struggled internally with so many things since he chose to walk out on his family, and he found himself, in that place, at a crossroads. When he was younger, he remembered his parents told him that everyone has two choices to make, the right choice and the wrong choice. And it was up to him to figure out which was which. Like every minute, hour, day, and month of his life was flashing in front of him, the only thing that mattered, was the moment he was sitting in.

At the end of the service, the powerful preacher, reached out to him through prayer, he said, *"Bow your heads before God. I don't know if this is you or not, but if you want to be found, ask God to please remove the blinders. Say God, Satan has blinded me. I'm lost and I'm in darkness, but Jesus would you pull the blinders off... would you give me one more chance, would you let me hear your voice one more time God. Right now, I haven't heard your voice, I haven't had the desire to be saved. I'm the lost coin. In the name of Jesus, pull the blinders off that Satan put on me and speak to me and call me one more time. Lord, today I give you my life. I've sinned against you and I ask you to forgive me...AMEN*

When Chris and Emily raised their heads after the final prayer, they both looked at one another with tear filled eyes...connecting in a way that was new to them both.

CHAPTER TWENTY-FIVE

"What do we do now Em?" Chris asked, confused, but clear headed at the same time.

"I'm not sure," Emily replied, wiping the residue of the tears on her face. "Something weird just happened to me."

"Me to Em," Chris said. "I feel different. I feel..."

Before he could finish his sentence, Emily gave him an emotional embrace, telling him she knew exactly what he was talking about. The others looked on, wondering what was happening, but smiling at the view of them reconnecting.

The band played one more time and after they passed around the offering bucket, row by row, folks started making their way around, visiting, then toward the entrance way. Everyone was wearing contagious smiles, laughing, and hugging one another like it was a big family reunion or something. Chris watched everybody, absorbing the friendly feel of the place. Before, he was hiding in the shadows just watching Emily, but this time, he was a part of it, amid good Christian people who cared about each other. That was obvious.

Caleb and Ella introduced themselves to Chris, making him feel accepted and welcomed. After all he had done, it was unbelievable to him that folks who knew who he was, could be so kind. They talked for a few minutes, Caleb giving him some words of encouragement, knowing where Chris was about to go. They ended with a firm handshake and eye contact that spoke volumes between the two.

Terry looked at his watch and went over to Chris, "We've got to go son," he said. "We have to be there by two thirty or they can't guarantee a bed. Me and Sherry will be in the truck."

Terry patted him on the back and walked off leaving him standing there with Emily by his side. Her expression faded from joy to an immediate look of melancholy, her smile being covered by the anxiety of being without him once more.

"Let's get the kids from their class so I can tell them bye for now" Chris said, taking Emily by the hand.

Geneva stopped them, "Chris," she said. "Keep lookin' up if ya know what I mean. He'll get you through this, I promise."

"I know he will Miss Geneva. I know he will," Chris replied, smiling genuinely, then giving her a hug and Elijah a strong handshake.

They picked up the kids from their classroom and both Katy and Joshua were talking ninety to nothing about everything they did, talked about and more. The excitement they put out, bounced on everyone around and it took a minute to bring them back down to earth. Chris had to find a way to tell the kids goodbye.

"Kids…kids," Chris said, kneeling in front of them as they reached the wrap around porch outside the church. "Listen, daddy has something to tell you."

"What daddy?" Katy asked, as Joshua scooted closer to him.

"Well," he said, kissing both on the forehead. "Daddy's gotta go away for just a little while, but I'll be back."

"Promise?" Joshua said sadly, like he didn't believe what Chris was saying.

"Look at me son," he said, turning Joshua's face to his. "I will be back. And when I do, things will be different, better. Please believe me. I love you both."

"Come on kids," Geneva said, realizing Chris needed a moment with Emily alone, and she let them say their final goodbye. "Caleb said you can ride with him and Ella back to the house."

"Alright," Joshua said enthusiastically, giving Chris a quick hug and kiss, then running to Caleb.

Katy did the same and followed close behind her brother leaving Emily standing there with mixed emotions fighting inside of her, unsure of how to feel. Chris stood and their eyes connected in a new way.

"You better get going," Emily said. "Terry's waiting.

"Walk with me," he muttered thoughtfully, grasping her hand, and taking slow steps toward the truck. "I'm sorry Em."

"How 'bout we just look ahead Chris?" Emily responded surprisingly. "I know you're tryin' to change."

"I want to so badly Em. And after hearing that sermon, I don't know, it did something to me…it struck a chord, ya know?" he said sincerely.

"I kind of had the same feeling," Emily continued, almost reaching Terry's truck. "He makes you think about your life, but more importantly, your life after all this is over."

With a short chuckle, "That's it," Chris said. "Made me think of more."

"Chris," Terry called out, looking at his watch as he spoke.

"Coming Terry," Chris answered, then turned his attentions back to Emily. "Em, will you write me? I know it's only thirty days, but…"

"I wrote you lots a letters Chris after you left, saying everything I felt," she replied quickly.

"I'd like to read them Em, if you'll let me," Chris said, squeezing both of Emily's hands and never ceased to look her in the eye.

"Chris," Terry said, raising his tone.

"Here's where you write," Chris said, digging in his pocket, lifting out a piece of paper and placing it in Emily's hand, then a short tender kiss, "I love you."

Before Emily could say a word, Chris had climbed in the truck, and they were leaving. Chris held his arm out the window in a wave and Emily raised her hand high just the same. By that time, most of the parking lot was empty and the last few folks were getting in their cars to leave. It left Emily standing in the same spot for a few moments remembering a tender moment she desperately wanted to hold dear until she saw him again.

"Emily," Geneva said, walking up and putting her arms around her. "You okay honey?"

Wiping her emotions from her face, "As you would say Miss Geneva, I suppose I'm a gonna have to be."

They had a short laugh, trying to make the best of the situation and went home. By the time they made it, Caleb and the kids were already out in the front yard running around. They got out and all found a place to sit on the porch.

"I swear Caleb turns into a kid when he's around those two. He's been talking about them ever since we left," Ella said. "And when mama mentioned us coming down for the day, he didn't even hesitate."

"I appreciate that," Emily said, watching Katy and Joshua. "They talked about him too. I really don't know where we'd be without all of you. And then Chris…"

"You want to take a walk?" Ella asked, extending her hand to Emily.

"Why not," Emily said.

They walked past Caleb and the kids as they ran circles in the yard along with the dogs and went toward the path they took when they went fishing. For a few moments, they just listened to the sounds of summer playing all around them, along with enjoying every small breeze easing the July heat on their skin. Ella noticed a few cut off stumps that made perfect seats to stop and talk. They took a seat, still able to hear the kids faintly.

"Chris seems very nice," Ella started. "Not bad lookin' either."

"I guess he's okay," Emily replied, blushing. "I can't lie…I think I fell in love with him the minute I laid eyes on him. I never really thought love at first sight existed until then."

"How are you handling all this Emily? I know you're in your head a lot. I can tell. And I figured talking away from Geneva and the rest would be good for you."

Emily turned her head, admiring the picture of summer painted all around her. "I want to believe him Ella. I really do, but…"

"What is your heart tellin' you?" Ella interrupted. "And haven't you thought about him since the minute he left?"

"Yes, but…"

"To be honest Emily, we can all tell what you want, but you have to have a little faith," Ella added.

"Oh, my goodness," Emily laughed. "You've been around Geneva way too long."

"Luckily since God gave her to me as my mama, but I'd tell you that anyway," Emily replied. "I saw how you were in church this morning. I know you believe."

Silence filled the air momentarily, then, "This morning something, well, unusual happened. When brother Todd was preaching, it's like he was talking to me. I felt…"

"Convicted," Ella said, finishing her sentence.

"Convicted?" Emily questioned, unsure of exactly what she was saying.

"Listen," Ella explained. "When you let yourself completely open up to God, truly hear what the word says, that's when the holy spirit talks to you. That's when you realize you can't go on without God in your life. That's what the prayer is about. But it's not just a prayer, its life changing."

"I think Chris felt the same," Emily said. "I felt it."

"That's great Emily. It could be a new start for you two and those sweet kids," Ella smiled. "And if you ever need a break, just give us a call. I think you know by now, Caleb makes a great babysitter."

"Thank you, Ella. You're a good friend. I almost forgot what it was like to have a true friend. Thanks for reminding me," Emily smiled. "I guess we better get back before Joshua runs Caleb ragged."

They joined the others, then helped Geneva whip up a late lunch while Elijah and Caleb kept the kids busy outside. Ella and Emily chipped in on making homemade cookies. Other than learning new things from Geneva, Emily tried to keep her mind busy, so it didn't wander to thoughts of Chris and how long it felt like until he came back.

After eating, Caleb and Ella stayed a few hours, but had no choice but to go back home that night. Caleb was working on finishing his children's book and working with a publisher on illustrations. He told everyone about it and the excitement in his voice was unmistakable. He even brought his story and read it to the kids, adlibbing the ending. As much as the kids, especially Joshua enjoyed his company, it was short-lived.

"Come here little man," Caleb called out to Joshua. "Give uncle Caleb a hug."

"Why do you have to leave?" Joshua said. "My daddy left too."

All conversation going on, stopped with his comment and Caleb handled it like a pro, he responded quickly. "He did Josh, but he's coming back just like I am. I'm not far away. Just hang onto good thoughts and remember all the fun we had, and I'll be back before you know it."

"My daddy too?" he asked, his voice echoing the sadness he felt inside.

"Your daddy too little man," Caleb said, finishing with a comforting hug, then tickling him to make him laugh.

Geneva showed her sadness of such a short visit, but at the same time, she was happy to see them, if even for a little while. The sun was beginning to bed down for the night when they left. Geneva and Elijah joined Emily in the living room. She was sitting in her favorite chair by the window, that looked out into the yard.

"You workin' tomorrow aren't you, Emily?" Elijah asked, making small talk to veer her mind from other things.

"Oh, yes sir. And I look forward to it. It'll be good for me to stay busy," Emily replied. "Besides, there's lots of people to help over there. I think it really helps folks like me."

"I bet them blame builders will be busy tomorrow too with their bangin' and a sawin'. I'll be glad when they get done," Geneva complained.

"Woman, why don't you stop jabbin' about that house. They'll get done when they get done," Elijah said, aggravating and making a point at the same time.

"Elijah James," Geneva snapped at him, fists firmly on her hips, like she did when her attitude would rear its ugly head.

"You two crack me up," Emily said. "And right now, laughter is a good thing."

"Well, I'll tell you what honey," Geneva said, sitting next to Elijah on the couch. "One month is gonna fly by in a jiffy, then we'll figure it out from there."

"I hope you're right Miss Geneva," Emily smiled.

That was the first night of a month-long waiting period, where anxiousness made Emily pull out a calendar to start crossing the days off as they went by. After the kids went to bed, Emily found herself in her room with the door closed, nursing her thoughts of the day and what might happen in the future. Footsteps came her direction.

Emily heard a light knock at her door, "You still awake?" Geneva asked, not wanting to bother her if she was already asleep.

"Yes ma'am," Emily answered respectfully.

Geneva opened the door and scurried over and sat down on the bed. Emily was finishing her nightly routine of taking off the little make up she wore, and combing her long, thick, beautiful, strawberry blonde hair. Emily went over and climbed into bed, pulling the thin sheet and bedspread over her legs. It was too hot for anything else.

"We haven't had much time to talk today," Geneva started. "I know your minds a goin' in a hundred different directions and I can't blame ya."

"He asked me to write him Miss Geneva," Emily said, pointing to the piece of paper laid on the nightstand with the address to where Chris was going.

"Well honey, it's not like you ain't had no practice. You got a mess a notes in that there closet," Geneva chuckled. "I think you should."

"I told him about those letters," Emily added.

"What'd he say?"

"He wants me to send them to him. I told him I wrote 'em after he left," Emily said.

"To be honest honey, I think it'd be good for him to read them there letters you got. You wrote 'em from the heart and right now, that's what he needs. He needs a reason to keep walkin' the straight and narrow," Geneva said. "Don't ya think?"

"Maybe, but…"

"Ahhh," Geneva sounded off. "You're afraid if he reads these here words you wrote, he won't come back."

"Some of 'em are harsh Miss Geneva," Emily said, struggling with what to do.

"And some a them letters you pour your heart out honey. He needs every part of you. He needs to know how he made you feel and what he needs to do to make things better," Geneva kept on. "See honey, he's gotta see the part he brought out in you, he don't want to see again…your hurt."

"I may, but…"

"How 'bout we both get some rest? You gotta work tomorrow and I'll run the kids over to Sherry's. I talked to her earlier and she misses them two already. By the way, they said Chris is doing okay so far. Terry got him settled in and checked on him a bit ago. The folks at that there Camden unit told Terry, he was bein' cooporative."

"That's good Geneva, but what happens when he comes back and runs into those same people, doing those same things he was doing? What then?" Emily said, overthinking every little thing that crossed her mind.

"Do you hear yourself Emily? I'll tell you just like I told my ole stubborn husband after my little mishap a while back. You can't go worry'in 'bout what's gonna happen. Just like it says in the good book…you have to live for today. Tomorrow's got troubles of its own," Geneva said, trying to reassure Emily best she could that things would be okay.

"How is it you know exactly what to say Miss Geneva? How do you know what I need to hear?"

"Hee hee," Geneva cackled slightly. "Some folks say I'm just plain ole crazy, but I know one thing honey. Sometimes words just come to me at the right time. I suppose thats God makin' sure I don't say somethin' stupid. Well, goodnight. I'll call you for breakfast in the mornin'."

The following day and days after that, Emily had the same routine. She got up, ate breakfast Geneva loved to prepare, and told the kids good-bye for the day. Sherry became like a permanent fixture in Katy and Joshua's life, spending days with her while Geneva and Elijah continued fixing this and that around the house. Geneva had a list and said she was determined to get it all done whether Elijah objected or not.

It was like things had always been that way. Stacey and Ella had become Emily's best friends and she got to where she could tell them anything. Since Ella lived further off, they talked a lot and Stacey always had an ear to lend as they worked each day, helping people in need. That was the part she loved the most, helping others. Sometimes she could see a reflection of herself in a few who stumbled into the center. With a smile and a caring heart, she gave all she had in her, to them.

About a week and a half or so after Terry took Chris to the rehab unit, Emily came home after work one day and on the table in the entryway, was an envelope addressed to her. Geneva was in the kitchen like clockwork, cooking something that left the entire house smelling incredible, and Sherry had just pulled up in front of the house to drop the kids off.

"Geneva," Emily called out. "When did this letter come?"

"Today honey," Geneva answered. "I figured if I didn't put it there, I'd plumb forget to give it to ya. I'm pretty sure it's from Chris. It says Camden on it."

"Thank you," Emily replied, picking up the envelope, running her fingers across it, then flipping it over and doing the same.

Emily heard footsteps behind her, "You gonna rub on it or read it honey?" Geneva laughed. "I'll take care a the young'uns while you go upstairs and see what he's got to say. I know you are itchin' to rip it open."

Without responding verbally, Emily's uncertainty turned to a smile and she ran upstairs, letter in hand, went into her room, and shut the door behind her.

CHAPTER TWENTY-SIX

Like a kid, Emily ran and plopped down on her bed, anxious to open the small envelope she was clutching in her hands. A million thoughts twisted and turned in her head, but after a minute of anticipating what it said, her fingers ripped it open and pulled out the letter. She could hear the kids and Sherry coming in the front door downstairs, but her focus was in front of her. Carefully, she unfolded the page, hand-written by the man who stole her heart the first time they met. Emily took a deep breath, and her eyes began to run across every word, every sentence.

Dear Em,

I don't really know where to begin. What I do know is that I love you and the kids with all my heart. I always have, but I let the drugs and drinking, take me away from you. I couldn't think clearly and put something before you, Katy, and Joshua. Please forgive me for that. When they brought me up here, Terry gave me a present, a loaner really. He gave me a bible to read while I'm here. After my classes I have to go to every day, I have lots of time to read. He told me that's the best thing he could think of for me. You may believe this or not, but I have been. I still remember that day at the cowboy church. I can't forget it. I begged God to take my addiction away. I begged for help. You know I've never been a spiritual person, but that day, something came over me, I couldn't deny. I'm still not sure what it was, but I know I feel different Em.

I sit here every day and wonder if you still want me in your life, if you can ever trust me again. I want you to. I want to be that kind of man again for you and the kids. Please send me the letters you told me about. I need to read them. I have class so I need to run, but please tell the kids I love them. It won't be long although it feels like a lifetime. It'll all be worth it.

All My Love,
Chris

Emily fell back on the bed, her head landing in the middle of the pillow. She thought of every single word he wrote. It made her smile knowing he took time to write it in the first place, and parts of what he wrote, were somewhat poetic to her. Somehow, it all sounded genuine and from the heart, or at least that's what she wanted to believe. She held the pages close, pressing them against her chest as if she were holding Chris. That's when she heard a clap of thunder outside the window. With such a sound, the kid's footsteps could be heard almost as loud as the thunder itself. They burst through her bedroom door and piled on top of her, clinging on tightly. They had always been scared of storms and always wanted to be close to her when they were scared. Joshua climbed under the covers next to her and covered his head as if it would make the sounds go away. Katy snuggled tight as she could, her arms wrapped clean around Emily.

Sherry came up to visit for a minute before she had to leave and couldn't help but laugh at the two scaredy cats hiding. There was something about Sherry that always left a calming feeling for Emily. It's like no matter what was going on, kind of like Geneva, she didn't let much shake her. As they talked, Emily couldn't help but think how she wanted to be just like them.

"See you kids tomorrow," Sherry said, peeking under the covers to kiss Joshua and giving Katy a sweet peck on the forehead.

Still, lying there with her two most precious gifts, the words Chris wrote to her kept coming back. They were somewhat poetic, yet from the heart at the same time. That's what meant the most to her.

"I'll have supper ready shortly," Geneva said, walking in, untying the back of her apron and laying it across her arm. "Will you look at ya'll? Lordy mercy, ain't ya'll a sight."

"I don't like that noise Mama G," Joshua muttered, poking his head out from under the covers just enough to see his eyes. "It scares me."

"Me too," Katy said, still clinging to her Emily.

"Well, why in the world would you be scared?" Geneva said, standing boldly in front of them. "God's just movin' his furniture around young'uns. Sometimes he does that."

Emily looked at Geneva and couldn't help but smile, seeing how, once more she came up with something witty to diffuse the situation. Joshua immediately popped up from under the covers and Katy sat back and stopped holding on so tight.

"Really?" Joshua asked, a questioning look across his innocent face.

"Why sure honey," Geneva continued. "Sometimes he wants to rearrange things, so I suppose he picked tonight to do it."

Without another question asked, the kids jumped up and took off downstairs. It was like they were never scared in the first place. It was more than amazing how Geneva was able to pull off what would normally seem impossible.

Geneva sat down on the bed, "Not to be nosy honey, but I suppose I am a bit nosy…how was the letter?"

"Sweet, apologetic…"

"That's good ain't it?" Geneva continued. "You wouldn't want it to be mean would ya?"

"No, but…I, well, I'm scared he won't change for good," Emily said.

"Can I tell you a story honey?" Geneva countered.

"Do I have a choice?" Emily answered, grinning.

"See, Jesus was in Capernaum teachin' a big bunch a folks and he got interrupted by four strongminded fellas who brought their friend to be healed."

"What was wrong with their friend?" Emily asked.

"He was paralyzed honey. Anyway, what happened next was somethin'. See, it was so durn crowded, they couldn't get to Jesus, so they took their friend, and they made an opening in the roof right above Jesus and lowered the mat their friend was layin' on."

"Wow," Emily said. "That's amazing."

"I hadn't got to the best part honey," Geneva said. "It says in the scripture that when Jesus saw their faith, he said to the paralyzed man, *Son, your sins are forgiven.* Then he told him to get up, take his mat and go home."

"But he was paralyzed," Emily remarked.

"*Was* paralyzed," Geneva said. "That man got up, got his mat and walked outta that place where everybody could see."

"That's a great story Geneva, but why are you telling me this?" Emily said, a little confused.

"Honey," Geneva said, resting her hand on top of Emily's. "He healed that man because of the faith his friends had. Just like Chris. You gotta have faith enough for two. If you want it, talk to God about it. Don't let him forget about Chris. Don't let up. Lift him up every chance you get honey.

If that paralyzed man's friends hadn't been so determined, he never woulda been healed in the first place."

"Yes ma'am. I understand," Emily said. "Can I help you with supper?"

"Sure can, but why don't you put them there letters in an envelope and I'll get'im mailed for ya tomorrow," Geneva said, trying to be sneaky. "You was sendin'im right?"

"Yes ma'am," Emily said, getting up and gathering the letters she had kept.

"Alrighty then," Geneva answered, hopping up and went to set the table. "See ya shortly. I bet them young'uns are already sittin' there with fork and spoon in hand waitin' for the viddles."

Emily laughed at her as Geneva went on her way, and she placed the letters in a larger envelope, big enough to fit them all. She figured Chris would have a lot to read once those reached him. She didn't want to take away from him reading the bible, but those letters came from the heart.

She went down and placed the envelope on the table in the entryway and told Geneva where it was. As usual, supper was fantastic. Each day that passed, she seemed to spoil Emily and the kids more and more. Of course, she loved doing it, but they all knew, at some point they would have to find their wings and fly on their own.

Geneva mailed the letters Emily had written Chris and a little over a week passed. The following day was Sunday, and everyone knew what that meant. It was the norm for Sundays to be filled with worship, family, and lots of food. They started off with worship and the rest fell into place.

That particular Sunday, after church, Emily got to thinking. It was only one more week until Chris was going to be coming home. She played so many different scenarios in her mind, from good to the worst, and it would start all over again, replaying in her psyche. Somehow, she couldn't push it away.

"I'm glad they finally stopped that blame poundin' down the road," Geneva said, sitting at the table with Elijah, Emily, and the kids. "It was about to get on my nerves."

"I think I heard you say that once or twice Geneva," Elijah commented sarcastically. "Maybe."

"It looks like they're about done," Emily replied. "But they sure had lots of guys working on it. I never saw a house go up so fast."

"It's a good thing," Geneva said. "Now I can get my peace and quiet back. God intended us to live in peace, not all that clammorin'."

Joshua always paid close attention to Geneva when she talked. Her entertaining, unique, country slang, kept him smiling. It's like he was trying to memorize every word so he would never forget them. He was always one to pay attention to things most kids didn't. Chris used to say how smart the kids were, constantly bragging. That's one memory that never left Emily's thoughts.

Monday rolled around, a start to another work week. Emily was getting used to being there, meeting new people, and helping everyone who walked in the door. She told Stacey a number of times, how it kind of gave her a sense of purpose. Until then, she never did much for anyone, but somehow it fit.

"I can't believe it's almost been a month," Stacey said, organizing things as she talked. "It's like it flew by."

"For you maybe," Emily replied giving a raise of her eyebrows. "It's been a lifetime for me."

They put away the last few boxes of food to finish stocking up the kitchen and freezer and found a comfy chair in the great room. There were only a few people there who needed a place to rest. Other than that, it was quiet. Most days it was busier, more people realizing the place was open. The only noise was the faint sound of the radio playing in the corner.

"Are you nervous?" Stacey asked, knowing the answer all too well. "That's a stupid question. I know you're nervous."

In an unusually calm manner, Emily tilted her head, slightly grinned, and answered, "A little, but…"

"But…" Stacey said, trying to make her finish.

"But I've been praying for him Stacey," Emily said. "Just like the four friends who brought the paralyzed man to Jesus, I've been asking God to heal his addiction. I ask him all day, every day. I figure if God can heal someone through the faith of a friend, I've finally grabbed a hold of my faith, and I'm not lettin' go."

"I see it in you Emily. I do," Stacey commented sweetly. "I see a difference in you."

"You do?" Emily asked, glowing inside from such a comment. "I want to be better. Not just for me, but for my kids… for Chris. I want to be like…well…Geneva."

"That's a tall order," Stacey laughed. "Well, you know what I mean."

"You know what?" Emily said. "Since the day I met her, she's been promising me everything would be okay."

"That's Geneva."

"But what I wasn't realizing, is where those promises were coming from," Emily muttered.

"What do you mean?"

"I know God made our paths cross. I know it. I have no doubt…so I think he was speaking through her," Emily said. "Now I'm sounding crazy, I know."

"It makes sense," Stacey agreed. "She is an angel, and we all know where angels come from."

A loud noise came from outside and, in walked Terry and a few new helpers he had employed the week before.

They toted in some more boxes of frozen goods to be put in the freezer. It was almost filled to the brim as it was, but they could always find a little more space.

"Got more chicken?" Terry hollered out. "We got room?"

"We'll make room," Stacey answered promptly, then her and Emily followed him into the kitchen.

One of the guys who wasn't carrying anything, called out, "Hey Terry, we goin' to the…"

"Yeah," Terry said, interrupting before he could finish his sentence.

"I was just wondering because you said…"

"I know," Terry said abruptly. "We're goin'."

Emily and Stacey laughed at such an odd conversation, then Emily spoke up, "You talkin' some kind of pig Latin Terry? I didn't understand anything you guys were saying."

"I just have to keep these guys busy, that's all," Terry replied swiftly. "Keep'em on their toes, ya know Emily. Can't let'em get lazy."

"I'll tell you like I tell Geneva. You're somethin' else," Emily replied.

"That's what Sherry says," Terry said. "By the way, I'm supposed to pick Chris up Saturday. They said he's doin' great."

"I know," Emily said. "He sent me a few letters."

Terry walked up and looked Emily in the eye, placing a hand on each shoulder, "Give him a chance Emily. We all make mistakes, and we all deserve a chance. I've had my share of screw ups and Sherry never left my side. I don't deserve her, but she still believes in me although I never understood why."

"I believe in him Terry. I do," Emily smiled. "Now I'm going on faith. If I've learned anything from Miss Geneva, it's that."

Terry gave Emily a sweet fatherly hug, then was on his way, motioning for the guys to follow. Although she hadn't seen Terry much, his genuine smile always made her day when she did. Something about the way he carried himself and how he treated people, that gave her the want to be better every day.

"Terry acted a little strange, didn't he?" Emily said to Stacey. "Did you think so?"

"Well, he is a bit strange sometimes, but you can't find a nicer guy. He'd give the shirt off his back," Stacey replied. "I guess we better get to puttin' this stuff up they just brought in. I don't know how he gets so many folks to give."

Emily smiled gigantically, "There's nice folks. I guess I never realized it until I met all of you. I used to think I was alone, but something showed me I never was."

Sherry came by the center with the kids on their way to town. She thoroughly enjoyed spoiling Katy and Joshua to the point, she overdid it sometimes, but it was okay with Emily. The happiness the kids displayed from such attention was worth it all. Besides, Sherry had become like a grandparent they never had, something they needed.

"Mama," Joshua hollered out, running to her and jumping in her arms. "Sherry's taking us to a bounce place. I like to jump."

"It's Ijump," Sherry said. "The place is filled with trampolines and I figured it would run off some of their energy and they'll be tired by the time they're ready for bed."

"Maybe Sherry, but you know these two can run circles around most," Emily laughed.

"What's our surprise?" Joshua asked Sherry completely out of the blue.

"What in the world are you talking about?" Sherry asked, squeezing his cheeks.

"Terry said he had a surprise for us," Joshua continued.

"Yeah," Katy added. "We may be little, but we hear things."

"Kids," Sherry started to say.

"I heard you and Terry talking and…"

"Let's go or we'll be late," Sherry said, rushing them along.

"Late?" Stacey chimed in. "That place is open all day, Sherry."

"Yep, well…I have errands to run too." Sherry said, waving and taking the kids by the hand. "See you when you get off later."

When they left, Emily and Stacey were left standing there in a daze, trying to make sense of the conversation. They looked at one another with the utmost confused look across their faces.

"Something weird is going on," Stacey remarked, then joked. "Maybe it's gonna be a full moon tonight."

"I agree. It's like they have a secret," Emily said. "If they do, they better not tell Joshua. He can't keep a secret if his life depended on it."

When they had finished putting up the rest of what the guys had brought in, they heard someone come in the front door.

CHAPTER TWENTY-SEVEN

Emily stepped out of the kitchen and into the great room, where there stood an old man with a white misshaped beard. It was obvious he was a street person by his ragged attire, but there was a kindness in his eyes that was unmistakable.

"How are you sir? I'm Emily? Is there anything I can get you? Something to eat or a place to lie down," she said, letting him know they were there to help.

The man hobbled to the closest couch against the wall and found a seat, letting out a big sigh when he did. He placed the backpack he was carrying, on the floor in front of him, then smiled an infectious smile. Somehow, he was communicating in the silence around them, in an indescribably powerful way. The fact that he was homeless didn't define him, instead, the many question marks as to why he was homeless, filled the air.

"Are you thirsty sir?" Emily asked.

"Yes child. Anything you have would be a blessing," he answered.

Stacey overheard and went to get something for the man to drink and a few snacks as well, while Emily stayed with him. She joined him on the couch, sat back and got comfortable, studying everything about the man in front of her. Emily wondered how someone in his stage of life, could be left alone to live in such a way.

"Here you go sir," Stacey said, handing the man a drink and a few snacks in case he was hungry.

"Name's Emmett," he replied, immediately taking a drink. "Thank you, kindly ma'am."

"Stacey," she smiled, nodded, and went back to the kitchen.

Emily continued sitting with him as he took a few bites of what he was given, chasing each bite with a drink. He glanced to Emily a few times, his salt and pepper shaggy eyebrows showing prevalent. She was sure the lines in his face were like roadmaps to where he'd been, some roads harder than others, and she waited until he wanted to talk.

"Saw this place a couple a days ago. A few folks told me ya'll take care of people here," he said, downing the last few peanut butter crackers in his hand. "I'm not one to ask for a handout though young lady."

"You from around here?" Emily asked, trying to find out more about him.

"Born and raised," he chuckled. "I bet I seen every change this town's had for over seventy years now. And boy has it changed."

Emily said. "Where's you're family?"

"All dead and gone young'un," he responded sadly, wiping a few crumbs lingering on his beard. "Had a brother and sister, but they've been gone for years now."

"Kids?" she continued.

"Never had any," he answered, looking away briefly. "My wife Bess couldn't have any, so we just had to deal with it. Things were okay though, until she got sick. I lost her a couple a years back and lost everything."

"What happened?"

"Dr. bills…utility bills…you know the drill. I couldn't work no more 'cause a my health and…here I am," he said, opening up to Emily like he'd known her forever.

"I'm so very sorry," Emily sympathized. "I fell on some hard times too and well, me and my kids didn't have anywhere to go for a while, but…"

"But God intervened," Emmett smiled. "He does that, ya know."

"Yes sir, I know," Emily said. "Would you like to take one of our rooms to rest your head? We'll fix you up a nice supper too after while."

He answered with an agreeing nod, then followed Emily to one of the rooms with several beds in it, centered in the middle. It had all the comforts of home, even a television in the corner of the room. Emily pulled the covers back and fluffed the pillow, then placing it back down.

"Can I get you anything else before you lie down?" Emily asked, extending such grace to the man she just met.

He shook his head, then went closer to Emily. He looked up then back into her eyes, "Let us then with confidence draw near to the throne of grace, that we may receive mercy and find grace to help in time of need. No thank you child. You have been a blessing to me."

Emily was sure he had just quoted a scripture from the bible and more than likely from being thankful for the help, but somehow, she got a strange feeling. From the top of her head to the tips of her toes, a warm, loving, sensation overcame her. His words ran out like melted butter, smoothly and confidently, landing directly into Emily's heart.

"I'll be out here if you need me Emmett," she said, slowly shutting the door behind her.

Stacey was sitting on the couch by the door and Emily joined her, glancing back a time or two as she walked. She had never had such an odd feeling in her life. As she approached Stacey, she must've had a bizarre look about her.

"You okay?" Stacey asked.

"Fine…" Emily replied, still looking peculiar, as thoughts of the man roamed in her head. "There's something about him."

"What do you mean?" Stacey asked, both of them constantly looking at the door to where he was resting.

"I can't put my finger on it, Stacey," Emily said. "It's like I knew him, but I didn't."

Stacey didn't know what to say. What Emily was saying, did sound a little unusual. She went to start a meal for the few folks who were staying there and needed help. Emily straightened and organized in the front room, putting chairs in place, and doing a little sweeping to clean up. After a short while, she could smell the food Stacey was carefully preparing in the kitchen and she started her direction. Before she went too far, the front door opened. In walked Geneva and Elijah. They usually tried to swing by every day, even if, for a few minutes and they found their usual spot to sit. Geneva sat down a few sacks next to her.

"Kinda quiet today honey," Geneva said, her country twang sounding a little extra country that day. "We been out shoppin' and thought we'd swing by."

"She's been shopping," Elijah said, correcting Geneva's comment. "And she wanted to see what you kids wanted for supper tonight. You know she's got to do it up right every night."

"Miss Geneva, you need to stop going through so much trouble for us. Let me cook one night," Emily replied sweetly.

"Honey, by the time you get off and get home, all you need to be a doin' is spendin' time with them there kids a yours. This old lady ain't got nothin' better to do than take care a ya'll," Geneva shot back.

"Yes ma'am," Emily answered.

"You got many folks here?" Geneva questioned.

"There's a few," Emily said, glancing to the door going to Emmett's room. "And there's this one…well, I got a strange feeling…"

"He a scary one?" Geneva said, standing up like she was ready to fight somebody.

"No…no, nothing like that. Like I told Stacey, I can't put my finger on it. It was just a feeling like I never had before," Emily continued. "Anyway, Stacey's fixin' to bring out supper for those here and you can meet him. His name's Emmett."

"You betcha," Geneva said, taking off toward the kitchen. "I'll help'er get it all out."

Elijah and Emily laughed at the energy Geneva always exhibited no matter what was going on. And a few minutes later, Stacey and Geneva brought out the main dish, several side dishes, rolls and glasses of tea, placing them on the round, community dinner table in the middle of the room. That table was designed so that everyone who was there, could sit, talk, and get to know each other, simulating eating as a family. That's how Terry put it anyway.

"I'll let everyone know supper's ready," Stacey said, going to the few rooms they had guests.

"I'll let Emmett know," Emily said, going to his door and knocking. "Emmett, we have supper ready."

There was no answer, and she didn't want to just barge in, so she knocked once more, "Emmett?"

Geneva came over, "You think he's okay honey?"

"I don't know Miss Geneva," Emily answered. "He seemed fine when I left him."

"Maybe you should go in and make sure," Geneva replied quickly, getting antsy, thinking something could be wrong.

With one more knock, Emily called out again. Once more, there was no answer, and she began to turn the door handle slowly, hoping she wasn't disturbing him. When she opened it completely, she couldn't believe her eyes. The room was empty. Emmett was nowhere to be seen. His backpack wasn't there, and the bed was still made neatly as it was before she turned the covers down for him.

"Good gracious honey," Geneva said. "You look like you done seen a ghost."

"Maybe I did," Emily muttered softly.

"Is Emmett coming?" Stacey called out, then walked over. "Where is he?"

"He couldn't have left the room," Emily said. "I've been out here the entire time Stacey."

Curiously, Geneva joined in. "What'd he say to you Emily?"

"He quoted me a scripture," Emily said, still staring into the room she left him in, then telling Geneva exactly what he said.

"That's in the book of Hebrews honey," Geneva replied quickly. "Talks about bein' giving to others and helping people. Shoot Emily, you mighta just met an angel. God mighta been testin' you."

"Testing me?" Emily questioned. "Why?"

"I don't know sugar," Geneva continued. "Talk to God. Heck, it mighta been God."

Emily went over and sat down at the table, thinking about everything the man had said and how she felt when he was there. It was strange from the minute go, but not scary strange, comforting strange. Then, out of nowhere, a smile was suddenly painted across her face. The kindness she saw in his eyes, was like the same kindness he wanted in return.

I was nice to him, Emily said to herself. *Maybe it was a test. God were you testing me?*

Somehow, she didn't bother to dwell on it another minute. Something deep down, told her everything would be okay. A unique feeling of peace began to ooze into every bit of her as she sat there in deep thought of what had just happened. In a way, she figured she'd been tested times before, but for the first time, felt it.

The few folks who were in need that day, were seated around the table filling their plates when Stacey stopped and said grace. Afterward, not much was left, thankfulness of such a meal was evident. The days residence, went in the corner sitting area and turned on the community television, sat back and relaxed.

"Terry's doin' something great here Emily," Geneva said. "You're doin' great."

"Thank you, Miss Geneva. I feel like I need to pass on what you did for me and the kids. I'll be forever grateful," Emily replied sweetly.

Before they left, Geneva turned back around, "Oh, and Emily. If it was God, I know he was pleased with you. You can't ever go wrong doin' for folks. See ya in a bit."

Emily finished up the day, and the night crew came in to sit with and help those who might wander in. Something about that, was filling to the soul. Some folks only worry about how they can fill their own plate, but the minute you start thinking about how to fill someone else's, it's another story. At that point, you start putting others before yourself and those are the people who change the world one life at a time.

When the workday was over, although it didn't really feel like work, Stacey and Emily both headed home. Stacey mentioned wanting to spend some quality time with her husband Keith and her kids. That sounded good to Emily too, making her miss Chris even more.

"See you tomorrow," Stacey waved as she got in her car and drove off.

Responding with a friendly wave in return, Emily started home as well. It turned out to be a beautiful day and the sun was shining bright with a few small clouds here and there. As she turned on the dirt road from the highway, she noticed a big crew of workers at that house on the corner. It was unique to say the very least. It had a log cabin feel to it. There was a small wrap around porch, kind of like Geneva's but not quite as big. There wasn't a swing, but Emily imagined one would be perfect.

The guys noticed her staring and each one waved as she slowly rolled by. She smiled and waved back, trying not to appear too incredibly nosy, then went on her way home. When she pulled up, she noticed the kids running around the porch. She figured they ran Sherry ragged and she brought them home a little early. It was understandable. Their energy surpassed most, except for Geneva. Sometimes Geneva out ran them and it was a sight to see.

Emily went inside and, once again, Geneva was standing in the kitchen with her apron on, cooking away. She was humming and singing like she was in her happy place and it gave that place a peace nothing else could possibly match.

"You ever find that fella?" Geneva asked.

"No ma'am. I can't explain it," Emily said, fixing a glass of tea and sitting at the kitchen table.

"Well," Geneva added. "Sometimes you ain't supposed to explain things. Sometimes, you just gotta go on faith."

"But he was there," Emily stated firmly.

"Then he wasn't," Geneva said.

"You know you talk in riddles sometimes Miss Geneva," Emily laughed.

Geneva laughed, "That's what Elijah tells me too. I don't know what either of you are talkin' 'bout."

"Terry's going to pick Chris up Saturday," Emily muttered softly, sipping her tea.

"That's what I heard. I bet you're ready to see 'im," Geneva said, putting a pan of biscuits in the oven, then sitting with her at the table.

Emily was unable to hold back the smile she felt coming from the inside out. The love and trust she had fought for, was beginning to hold together for the first time in a long time. Something gave her the strength to keep going after what she wanted, her marriage and her family. She wasn't sure if it had to do with what Emmett said to her or just her completely different view on life since being around Geneva and everyone else. The truth was something inside Emily changed.

That night was no different than any other. From a wonderful meal, great conversation, and the best company to be around, being there was like being with family.

"Young'uns you best git in bed," Geneva said. "Good gracious, it's almost ten o'clock."

"We don't have school Mama G," Joshua said.

"You might not have school, but you see, if you don't get good rest, your brain won't grow," Geneva said.

"My brain won't grow?" Katy asked.

"Oh no," Geneva said. "That's why God wants little boys and girls to get in bed early. He wants'im to be smart. You wanna be smart don't ya?"

Comically, Katy and Joshua took up the stairs fast as you please, tickling all everyone's funny bones in the process. Geneva gave her little *he he* laugh and followed behind them. There was something about tucking them in, that did Geneva good. Sometimes she'd tell them stories, mostly from the bible and before she was done, they'd be fast asleep.

Emily was tired from the day and decided to go ahead and turn in, but Elijah stopped her before she walked away.

"I meant to give this to you earlier. I got the mail today and there was a letter for you," Elijah said, pulling the letter from the drawer in front of him and handing it to her. "Night Emily."

CHAPTER TWENTY-EIGHT

With the wind slightly whistling outside her window, Emily got in her comfortable spot on the bed and opened the letter. Chris's handwriting was easy to recognize, not the neatest, but more legible than most guys. As she unfolded the one page in front of her, the only thing she felt was the beating of her own heart.

Hey Em,

It's me again. This time everything is even more clear to me. My time here is almost over and I've learned a lot. They've helped rid my body of all of the things that took me away from you in the first place and, in turn, making me see my future is only with you and the kids. I've been reading the bible Terry loaned me and, the more I read, the more I think I hear God talking to me. I don't know if you ever feel that way, but I know it's what I've needed all along. I can't say I'm sorry anymore because words don't mean much. I want to show you how much I love you and the kids for the rest of my life. Terry's picking me up next Saturday and I am counting the hours and minutes until I see your beautiful face again. He said he would put me to work and help us get back on our feet. The day you met Geneva, you met an angel, one to take care of you until I was able. I know I'm able now.

I have to go, but the next time we talk, we will be face to face. I can't wait until that day. Tell the kids their daddy loves them so much and I can't wait to get home.

ALL MY LOVE,
Chris

Emily wiped the happy tears trailing down her face, wearing a smile as she did so. Something told her, he was being sincere, and her doubts no longer existed. That's when she dug into the depths of her heart and talked to God.

"Lord, as Chris said, it's me again. It's been a long road God. Sometimes I didn't think I'd make it and other times I didn't want to, but then you sent Geneva. I don't know if she's an angel, but she is to me. You used her to show me that my life wasn't over. And God, I don't know who that old man was today, but if he was one of yours, thank you. The scripture he quoted, reminded me how important it is to be kind to everyone. At one time, I lived a selfish life, but somehow all that has changed. I've changed. I still don't know what's going on, but I know it's because of you. I know I don't have the right to ask for anything, but please give me the strength I need to get through. Thank you for this family you placed me in and the friends I'm surrounded by now. In Jesus name...AMEN"

Like a thousand-pound weight had been lifted, Emily sat there with nothing but positive thoughts for the future dancing around in her head. Finding peaceful sleep wasn't hard and the next few days flew by. Before she knew it, Saturday morning had approached. It was the day she had been waiting for since Chris left for his treatment. She felt like a schoolgirl nervous and giddy about seeing him. Of course, the kids didn't realize he would be home so soon, and she wanted to make it a surprise for them.

"Breakfast," Geneva called out from downstairs.

Emily hurried getting dressed and, with energy seeping out of her, she ran down the steps like she was in a marathon. Both Elijah and Geneva noticed the difference in her that morning, but they also knew why. The kids were already inhaling the homemade biscuits they had gotten accustomed to every morning, along with the delicious sausage gravy on top.

When Emily sat down with a enjoyable plate in front of her, she bowed her head momentarily, and gave thanks. The smiles shining on Geneva and Elijah's faces, showed they were proud of her without a word spoken. Emily didn't waste any time putting away the homemade confections Geneva prepared so perfectly. Since it was Saturday, Emily was off work and had all day to spend with the kids.

"Gonna be a long day," Emily commented, anxious.

"He said he can't get'im until later this evenin'…you know with all the paperwork and things he's got to fill out." Geneva said. "You've waited this long honey."

"Kids why don't you go outside and play and I'll be out in a minute," Emily said, giving each of them a kiss as they left the table.

"You got two angels there Emily," Geneva said. "I knew it the minute I saw you three. I knew I was supposed to do somethin' to help. I know I made you a bunch a promises, and…"

"And you kept them all Geneva," Emily cut in. "In a lifetime, I could never repay you and everyone else for all you've done. What did I do to deserve it all?"

"Oh honey, none of us deserve anything, but he gives us Grace, kinda a like you did that old man yesterday," Geneva said. "You kept it goin'."

"I guess I better get outside before they terrorize those dogs too much," Emily said, giving Geneva a sincere hug.

For hours, Emily and the kids played and romped in the yard and even went down by the pond where they had gone fishing. They didn't fish, but Emily drug out memories of when she was a child and tried to teach the kids how to skip rocks. She wasn't very good at it, but it didn't matter. Time with the kids is what mattered most. After a while, all three were smooth worn out and made their way back to the house. Geneva was sitting on the front porch with a fresh pitcher of cold lemonade and glasses to the side.

"I betcha you all want some lemonade," Geneva called out as they walked up, pouring each one a glass before anyone could answer. "This'll hit the spot."

"Thank you," Emily gasped, taking her drink, and sitting in the wicker chair against the house. "I swear. I'm tuckered out."

"You sound like me now," Geneva laughed.

"I'm around you enough," Emily said, still catching her breath.

"Elijah's fixin' up some sandwiches for lunch. He figured ya'll would be hungry pretty soon," Geneva said.

"Isn't that sweet of him," Emily replied.

"You know what honey," Geneva said, looking into the distance then back. "He was a mean ole codger at one time, but God changed him. I never woulda thought he'd be like this."

"I guess people can change," Emily smiled.

"You betcha they can. And don't you forget it honey," Geneva said. "Now, let's go eat somethin'."

The kids followed Geneva and Emily inside and they all had a simple lunch, but soon after it's like everyone felt like napping. Elijah and Geneva fell asleep in their chairs watching television, and the kids laid down on the rug in the floor and were out like a light. Emily's eyes were heavy as well.

All that running and playing took its toll and she laid on the couch. Almost immediately, she was out.

Two or three hours had passed like a flash and everyone was still in slumberland until the phone rang. Elijah jumped up the minute he heard it and stumbled over to answer.

"Hello," he said in a groggy voice. "Yep…yep, okay…I'll tell 'er."

The kids started moving around, stretching, and groaning as did Geneva and Emily as Elijah made his way back into the living room.

"That was Terry," Elijah mumbled, still trying to wake up. "He's pulling into Camden, but they said it might take longer to get him processed out than they thought, so it'll be late when they make it back."

"How late?" Emily asked.

"Daddy?" Joshua hollered out.

"He didn't say, but said we'd see them at church tomorrow morning," Elijah answered. "Yes, little man…your daddy."

Katy and Joshua jumped up and started dancing around like they had ants in their pants and Emily couldn't help but laugh at their amusing behavior. It was odd to see Geneva sitting for too long at a time, but figured her body had to give out once in a while.

"Look how late it is already," Geneva said, glancing at the clock. "It's after four o'clock. Land sakes, how did we sleep so long? I got things to do."

"What things?" Elijah asked, knowing it was just something Geneva always said.

"I'll whoop you," Geneva replied, swatting at him, and aggravating right back.

The kids found it entertaining to listen to Geneva and Elijah go at it, not really fighting, just picking at one another. In fact, it had somewhat rubbed off and they were starting to do the same thing, especially when Caleb was around.

"Good golly," Geneva said, hopping up. "I didn't even lay out no meat for supper."

"You don't have to cook every meal Geneva," Emily said, stopping her. "We can fix up more sandwiches. That's fine with us."

"Well," Geneva said, looking frustrated. "Doggonit."

It took a little talking, but Geneva finally gave up on a big meal. Her stubborn nature was hard to overcome, but it all came from the heart. There was something about her, always wanting to do for other people, that was the influence Emily and the kids needed at that time in their life. She was the influence that made everything seem okay.

In a way, Emily was glad it would be morning before she saw Chris. There were still some things she had to work out in her mind and heart for that matter. The questions that kept rearing their ugly heads, needed to be squashed so they could start fresh with nothing from the past to ruin what the future was holding for their family. So, as they enjoyed a relaxing, lazy Saturday evening, little by little those questions dissipated, leaving only positive feelings.

"Kids, get your bath," Emily said, noticing it was almost nine o'clock. "That way you can just get up and get dressed in the morning for church."

"Yes ma'am," they both responded, going upstairs to do as they were told.

"Yep…good kids," Geneva muttered, sitting in one of the wingback chairs by the window working on a quilt. "They're excited to see their dad, just like you."

"I know Miss Geneva," Emily said. "And you know what…no more bad thoughts. If I think it'll be okay, it will be."

"That's my girl," Geneva said, taking in an letting out a long breath. "Honey, I'm 'bout tired. I don't know why. We slept half the day, but I suppose my body's talkin' to me. I'll see you in the mornin'."

Geneva gave Emily a motherly peck on the forehead and went to join Elijah who had gone to bed not long before that, leaving her downstairs by herself. Emily always admired the stars from there, so she went outside and sat on the steps going to the porch. Her eyes were fixed on the tiny sparkles placed ever so perfectly in the sky above her and the flickering mesmerized her. She sat there for a little while, but when she was getting up, she caught a glimpse of a shooting star. For some reason, it took her breath away and she immediately closed her eyes and made a wish. When she re-opened them, she smiled and went in to go to bed.

As the nights before, sleep found her well, resting every ounce of her body and mind to the fullest. And, as every morning, Geneva was calling to everyone to come and eat. All the kids had to do, was get dressed, and Geneva had already put their clothes out and tended to them. Emily took a few extra minutes picking out what she wanted to wear and when she was dressed, Geneva walked in.

"Don't you look spiffy?" Geneva complimented. "Pretty as a picture honey."

"Thank you, Miss Geneva," she answered, looking in the mirror, making sure every hair was in place. "I just want to look…"

"Perfect," Geneva said, finishing her sentence. "You do honey. You do. Now, come eat before your two gobblins eat it all."

"I'm not that hungry," Emily said, nerves taking over.

"Oh no, you gotta eat. Even if it's a few bites. You gotta have your strength," Geneva winked and went on her way.

Emily had no choice, so she went down and sat with the kids. They were sharp as a tack. Joshua had on a handsome outfit and his hair was slicked back just so. Katy was wearing a light and dark pink dress with some shiny shoes Sherry had bought her, along with a perfectly matched bow in her hair.

"You look pretty mama," Katy said, leaning into her.

"Yeah mama…pretty," Joshua said, shoving the last bite in his mouth.

"I tell ya what," Geneva said. "These durn dishes can wait. Let's get to the church early. What ya'll think a that?"

"Yes," the kids hollered out and took off running outside.

"Alrighty then. Elijah, grab them there keys and let's hit the road. This young lady's got a fella to meet," Geneva said energetically, hurrying out the door.

Emily went outside and took a deep breath, then glanced up like she was looking at God, *I need you now,* she whispered. About then, a cool breeze brushed over her, leaving her with such a feeling of peace. It's like he answered her with the most subtle thing, but powerful at the same time.

Since they left early, when they arrived, there were only a handful of cars in the parking lot. The kids jumped out and ran to the little play area to the left of the building. Emily, Elijah, and Geneva found a seat at one of the picnic tables on the porch. One by one, people started showing up, greeting them as they walked by. Then, a few minutes before the service was to start, they went to get the kids to take them to class, when Terry, Sherry and Chris pulled through the big metal gates of the parking lot.

"He's here," Emily murmured to herself.

Geneva went ahead and got the kids situated and came back. They got out of the truck and Chris didn't hesitate to walk straight to Emily and give her a long, tight embrace. Neither said a word, and the others left them alone and went inside to find their seats. Somehow, Emily or Chris didn't know what to say, but when they released one another, Chris took her by the hand and walked inside. The entire feeling surrounding them was felt by all who saw them together. Geneva saved two seats at the end of the aisle and they sat down.

"Oh, looky who's preachin' today? Brother Wallace," Geneva said. "I love to hear him preach. You'll love him Chris."

As they sang three or four songs, the spirit in that place absolutely overwhelmed every person in the room. There was no denying it. And when Brother Wallace took the stage, something else happened. People talk about witnessing a moment that touches you to the core, that man on the stage created such a moment.

"Ya see, I was gettin' gas one day over by where I used to pastor," Brother Wallace started. "This big ole fella pulled up in a huge truck…tires almost tall as me. Anyway, the man was smokin' a cigarette and he hollers out 'I'm gonna blow us all to hell.' I said, no sir, I'm goin' to Heaven."

Chris and Emily were listening to his story, hanging on to every word, as he continued, "The man looked around that pump and said, what do you do? Now at this point, I'm thinkin' do I tell what I do or…well, anyway, I said, I pastor that church right over there…and pointed at the church. He said, alright then preacher, I'm comin' to see you Sunday. You better be there?"

The more he told, the more everyone in the room listened. It's like his story telling was so to where you couldn't pay attention to anything else.

Brother Wallace said, "I thought to myself, Oh, dear God, wait a minute. Yeah, I'll be there, and I tell ya what. I'll meet you at the double doors Sunday morning. The fella left and Sunday morning rolled around, and sure enough, I saw that big ole truck pullin' into the parking lot. I have to be honest. I was thinkin' to myself…Oh my Lord…"

The church was compelled by his story and you could've heard a pin drop as he paced back and forth, talking with his hands, and adding more and more information as he walked.

"Anyway, the man asked where he can sit. The place held fifteen hundred people, but he was a big man I wasn't gonna tell him what to do, so I said you can sit anywhere you like," Brother Wallace continued. "Anyway, somethin' incredible happened. After the message and when I was giving the invitation, asking folks if they wanted to know Jesus, I saw the man get up from his balcony seat and head down. He came down the aisle but didn't go to the prayer team in front of the stage. He came on the stage and walked straight to me. Let me tell you friend. That man walked up to me, and he took me by the hand and said *I want what you got.*"

Instantly Emily was filled with an emotion that was indescribable, welling her eyes with tears. Then she looked at Chris and those same tears were rolling down his face. He was squeezing her hand tightly and crying.

"Let me tell you folks," the preacher said. "The only thing that we got that this world needs, is Jesus. And if we'll just live what he's put in us, there'll be those that say, I want what you got. You know what's happenin' here this morning? Some of you folks came because someone invited you. Can I tell ya this? You are here for no other reason than by the providence of God. God brought you here this morning to hear whatever part you heard, to make a difference in your life for eternity. He'll save ya if you give him that hope. He'll make you what you want to be if by faith you'll trust him. Jesus will change you for the better. One of these days when you die, he's gonna take you to Heaven. If you've never been redeemed, I pray this morning that you will. Let us pray…"

Emily and Chris bowed their heads, holding onto one another like they had never done before in their life. When the service was over, Chris and Emily walked hand in hand to Brother Wallace and everyone witnessed something amazing. Through tears and happiness, not one, not two, but four lives were changed that day. A family was saved that day.

When they had finished praying with the preacher, they met the others on the wrap around porch and the kids were standing by Sherry, then ran to Chris the minute they saw him.

"Why are you crying daddy?" Joshua asked, tightly wrapping his arm around his neck.

"Because I'm happy son," Chris said, putting his arm around Emily.

"Hey," Terry broke in. "What do ya'll say we do some cookin' at your house? I brought the stuff to cook 'cause I didn't think you'd mind."

Chris and Emily wiped the flooding from their eyes, found smiles amidst them and went to Geneva's van. Joshua climbed in Chris's lap and Katy in Emily's. Terry took off ahead of them. When they were fixing to turn on the road to Elijah and Geneva's, Terry whipped into the house on the corner, the one just completed. It had only been a little over a month, but considering they had several dozen people working day in and day out, they got it completed nothing flat. It was an old style, country house with a porch wrapping all the way around. The railing encircling the place, was dark green and the house itself was a medium brown wood with the bottom half made of logs. It wasn't a huge place, but the character it displayed spoke volumes. There was a wooden sign hanging by chains in front that had the words *Welcome Ya'll* etched into it.

"Why are we here?" Geneva said, her fists planted firmly on her hips. "I been tryin' to find out who our new neighbor's gonna be ever since I heard the first hammer hit and won't nobody tell me nothin'."

"Come on," Terry said, motioning for everyone to follow him.

Chris and Emily, with their fingers laced together holding hands with the kids walking by their side, they did as he asked. Sherry scooched Geneva and Elijah along with a smile. On the porch sat two sets of wooden rocking chairs, two full size and two for kids, with a table between them.

"Did you buy this place?" Geneva kept on. "So you can bother me all the time."

Terry took a key and opened the door, revealing an incredible rustic atmosphere of a place like they hadn't seen. It had a second floor that overlooked the living room and as they walked further in, Emily gasped and started to cry.

"Chris…look," she said, pointing to a long table up against the stairway. "It's us. I thought I lost all that stuff."

"Well," Terry said. "I have connections and that place you used to rent, I got the stuff he put back of yours, and put it here.

"But why…" Chris asked, already overtaken by emotion.

Chris and Emily walked over by the handmade table and, sitting on it, were two bibles. One had Chris's name engraved on it and the other, Emily's.

"I figured since you gave my bible back, you needed one of your own," Terry said, then lifted the house keys in the air and placed them in Chris's hand. "Welcome home son."

"You built this place?" Geneva asked, then turned to Sherry. "You knew all along?"

"Terry, we can't accept this. It's too much," Emily said, looking all around like she was in the middle of a dream.

"Kids, your rooms are down the hall," Terry said, motioning for Sherry to show them.

Chris and Emily sat on the couch, leaning on one another. The place was fully furnished, and from what they could tell, stocked with food as well. The wood accents everywhere they looked, somehow gave a feeling of home. There were pictures she thought were gone, placed here and there, framed ever so beautifully and new ones mixed in of the kids. Then, Chris looked up and noticed something. On the wall, in the center of the vaulted ceiling, was a miniature version of the cross like at the church. It even had lights behind it so it constantly glowed.

"Look Em," Chris said, pointing at it. "The cross."

Everyone found a place to sit and couldn't get enough of the happiness showing on the faces of the couple who had gone through so much. Terry, always trying to be a manly man, found a few tears the same as the others.

"How can we thank all of you?" Emily started. "Two months ago, I was homeless doing my best to take care of my two kids, and now…"

"And Terry," Chris added. "You didn't have to get me help. You didn't have to do any of this. But until today, I wouldn't have understood. Today, I want to say, I want what you have. After praying with the preacher, me and Emily do. I can't thank you enough for being our angels. I know we have a long road, but I know we're not alone."

"You sure aren't honey," Geneva said, crying her ugly cry as she would say. "And I'll cook for ya'll every night."

"How about you let us cook for you sometimes?" Emily replied. "I owe you lots of meals."

"You'll still let me spoil the kids, right?" Sherry chimed in, returning the room with a kid on each arm.

Chris looked at Emily, his eyes filled with pure love and joy, "And I'll spoil Em."

"Amen to that," Geneva hollered out. "I told you everything would be okay."

"From the first time we met," Emily smiled. "You promised me that."

"Well," Geneva said. "God made that promise. I was just the messenger."

2 Peter 3:9

The Lord is not slow about his promise, as some count slowness, but is patient toward you, not wishing for any to perish, but for all to come to repentance.

About the Author

With a passion for words since she was a little girl, Tammy D. Thompson started with writing poetry. Her mother would find little writings around the house and put them up for keeps. As the years passed, and she attended college at Southern Arkansas University in Magnolia, AR, her verses changes into fiction, starting with her first book, *Buried, But Not Forgotten.* As it does, things changed once more, and her books turned into Christian Inspirational books, with the hopes to leave a smile on the reader's face and hope in their hearts. After the *Dream Mountain* Series and her last book, *The Beggar,* Mrs. Thompson's goal was to relay a message in every story she wrote. In her most recent title, *Geneva's Cross,* and the Geneva book series to come, the message is very clear. Throughout many changes in her life, the one constant was always God and his love for her. So, in this latest series, each book is meant to lead and direct the reader in the direction of the light and away from any darkness. "At the end of the day, I want to touch hearts and changes lives," Mrs. Thompson said. "There's nothing more rewarding than knowing you made a difference in even one person's life. And that's my goal as a writer, as a person, and as a Christian." One of her favorite scriptures is Mark 11:23 *"Therefore I tell you, whatever you ask for in prayer, believe that you have received it, and it will be yours."* She does everything through her faith and her hope is to convey every ounce of that faith to her readers, praying it is received in the way it is given. Using her gift of words, she wants to change the world, one person at a time. You can keep up with Tammy's books on her website at www.TammyDThompson.com.